Financial District Fantasy

LOVE IN THE BIG APPLE BOOK 3

NICOLE SANCHEZ

First paperback edition January 2024

Edited by Amanda Iles

Proof Reading by Deliciously Dark Editing

Cover Art by Angela Haddon Designs

Vector Image by Vectezy

 Created with Vellum

For all the women out there who have had to deal with sexists in the work place and wanted to tell their boss to fuck off–this one is for you.

One

OF ALL THE fringe benefits available at my company, the gym is probably my favorite. Another Monday and another morning where my feet pound the treadmill, my mental finish line at the end of this project. I've spent hours upon hours trying to get this project done, which means that my routine has been more about one a.m. quesadillas and less about working out.

I need this release. I need to take my frustration out on my body instead of on Tweedle-dee and Tweedle-dum, especially since I'm not getting any other kind of release. My team on this project is small, with just three of us and the managing partner overseeing it. The only female on a team of men with their tiny egos and even smaller–

I punch the speed up, angry all over again. When we were still brainstorming how best to tackle the project, I offered my thoughts on how we could be most efficient. I was plainly ignored, and now we're three months into the project, falling further and further behind. Now, Tweedledum, Darren, is proposing *my* idea for a way to streamline the work processes. Which our boss, Manny, *loves.*

It's cool.

I don't need any sort of recognition for my idea. Just knowing that I'm smarter than the MIT brain trust is all I need. Tweedledum may have gotten the pat on the head, but I'm secure in knowing that if he had to perform again, he wouldn't be up to the challenge.

Said every woman he's been with ever. It's hypocritical of me to employ this double standard, but their bullshit makes me *so mad.*

I drop my speed to a walking rate to try to lower my heart rate. I'm hoping the rush of endorphins helps get me through the day and through the bullshit comments, like how my brain must be stored in my ovaries. At least I was only asked to get the team coffee once this week. You would think I wasn't double Ivy League educated or capable. According to my colleagues, having breasts means I lack intelligence. I never mention that I had to be hired just the same as them for the same job. It's never worth it.

I shower quickly, enjoying the luxury products available. I spend more time at the office than in my apartment, and I'm beginning to wonder if I should ask Elia if I can use her guest room closet for my clothes. I can shower at the gym and maybe save money on rent for a place I haven't seen the inside of in weeks. Cutting corners that way wouldn't be cheap, but it would be economical, and I'm sure someone else could actually use the closet-sized bedroom I currently call home. I'm hoping that maybe I can find a way to sublet my room for half the time.

Anything to save on my horrific New York City rent.

My dread grows as the elevator rockets me up from the gym in the basement to my office floor. I'm not alone by far; so many people choose to get their workouts in at five a.m. I may need to try to work in some yoga to help relieve the tension in my body since getting under someone isn't an option with the hours I work. The people leaving the yoga studio always look so calm, so relaxed. I could use some zen in my life. Zen that doesn't come from the bottom of a bottle.

Tweedledum is crossing the lobby when the elevator opens on my floor. Darren, as I need to remind myself to address him, looks at me, a coffee in his hand.

"If you're going to be late, it should at least be because you put some effort into how you look," he sneers. I love how he's not even done with his morning coffee before bashing me and my looks, as if he's walking through the office ready for a runway in Milan. His short brown hair is longer than usual, making it look unkempt.

I stop short, the doors closing behind me with a dull thud. I glance down at my suit. Sure, the jacket has some wrinkles in it, but it is by no means sloppy. I could have come up with my hair still wet and without makeup, but I didn't. I took the time to give my red locks a blowout, and I'll admit that my eye makeup is less than perfect, but it's there, the mascara, the eyeliner, even lipstick, for fuck's sake.

"Good morning to you too, Darren." I push past him and head to the desk that I left only four hours ago. Of all the options I had when leaving business school, I *had* to choose investment banking.

I made a calculated decision. Dartmouth for undergrad wasn't cheap, even if I hadn't decided to partake in study abroad trips or join a sorority with nearly one thousand dollar a term dues. The decision to go to Columbia for business school felt like a no-brainer, but the student loan statements make me regret every decision.

I sold my soul, and my monthly income is just enough to cover my outrageous student loans and rent. Maybe I should see if there is a cooperative apartment I can get where I only have the bed on Tuesdays, Wednesdays, and Thursdays. I don't have anything valuable that I would leave there; the rest I can send to my parents' house for storage.

I groan, thinking about my parents and the second mortgage they took out to cover all the extras for school, all the little loans they gave me to make sure I got a new laptop when I accidentally spilled beer on my old one, or when they helped me pay for a weekend in Killington for my formal so I could get fucked by my date six ways to Sunday. A second mortgage that they're unable to make payments on after both losing their jobs when their company downsized. A six-figure salary isn't enough to keep all three of us afloat, and now their health insurance is coming out of pocket. It was fun having younger parents until now. Their health insurance is also a decent-sized cut of my salary pie.

I unbutton my suit jacket before settling in at my desk. I don't know why I'm a glutton for punishment, getting to work early when I worked past midnight the night before. I set my laptop out. Fuck Darren and his comments, I need java if I'm going to survive the day. He may get here early to try to kiss ass, but I'm the one actually doing most of the work on this project.

I close my eyes while the coffee machine spits out the mediocre liquid and imagine what life would be like if I just quit and saw if Charlie's new firm was hiring. Making the jump from investment banking to private equity should be easy enough, but it's the pay I worry about.

My loans for school are...suffocating. I have hundreds of thousands of dollars that just accrued compounding interest while I completed my undergrad and got my useless business school degree. Now, my parents are in dire financial straits, and my student loans are only getting worse. I need to hold onto the job I have, even if I'm miserable. Even if it's slowly crushing my soul.

But who needs a soul when you can have money?

I don't bother with sugar or creamer, focusing only on the java in my mug. I turn to leave when I slam right into another person. Immediately, their hands come to my upper arms to steady me after I rock back on my heels, and naturally, one of the heels snaps off from the abrupt change in my weight distribution.

"Are you alright?" a cool voice asks.

This is what I get for trying to actually sleepwalk through my office. Not only did I just lose my cup of coffee, but I also ruined my new white blouse. I kick off my heels.

"Shit," I curse. I look up, and immediately my heart starts to slam in my chest. I finally look at the firm chest, then up into the glorious face of the god I walked into. It takes several seconds for my caffeine-deprived brain to catch up and realize that, of course, it was one of the senior VPs who has been on a forced vacation for the last three weeks. I expect to get a glare in response. After all, it wasn't just my shirt that I've ruined, but his suit, too.

But it's not anger I find in his hazel eyes. It's concern.

"Are you alright?" he repeats, and I realize he's still holding me. I step out of my other heel, glad I have a backup pair at my desk. Lord only knows what shit Darren would throw at me if I had to wear my sneakers all day.

I have to focus on the things I can fix and not the fact that I just spilled cheap coffee on a suit that probably costs more than my monthly salary. I also can't think about how my pussy throbs from the fact that brushing against his built body is the most action I've had in a while. Yeah, that's it, not at all because this man might be the most gorgeous, most off-limits man I've ever seen.

I tend to be on the taller side of women, clocking in at 5'8", and I still have to look up at him. Is it a prerequisite to be a giant when becoming a billionaire? I'll have to ask Charlie – the most understated billionaire I know.

"Just fine. Coffee-less, and now my shirt is partially see-through, but just *fine*." My sarcasm adds a bitter edge to my voice. I'm babbling a little to try to cover just how flustered I am, but I think all it does is show him just how affected I am.

"Sounds like you need that coffee even more now." There is a light lilt to his voice when he says it, so I try to smile because he could be a jerk about this, and he's not.

"After I go change, I'll worry about it then."

The man has hazel eyes that edge closer to green because of the green tie he's wearing. At least, it was green before it was covered in coffee. He has a neatly trimmed beard, which only accentuates the hard line of his jaw. I know him, but only in passing, Joshua Bartlett. He's been making moves through the company, rising faster than most because of his brutal work ethic and willingness to do anything to fight his way to the top. There have been rumors that he's on the fast track to becoming one of the youngest managing directors at the firm.

"We're hardly the same size, but I have fresh dry cleaning in my office. You're welcome to a clean shirt."

I don't think I can possibly imagine a worse solution to this problem. The last thing I need is for Darren or any of the other men I work with to notice that I'm wearing another man's shirt. The alternative, though, is wearing the shirt I wore yesterday, which is black, and while it would match my black skirt and jacket, it would no doubt earn me a stupid nickname like "the undertaker" or worse.

"Josh!" a voice calls, and I look over my shoulder at Manny, the managing director on *my* project. In terms of hierarchy, I'm a lowly associate, while men like Manny reign supreme. He's forty-seven years old, and I don't know what's more expensive, his twenty-three-year-old wife or the nose sugar he likes to do off her ass.

"Manny," Joshua greets with a deferential head nod. We may be on different teams, but the respect is there.

"Oh! Tara, I didn't see you there. We have a client meeting at nine-thirty. I hope you clean yourself up. It's not very professional to wear stained clothes in the office." Manny's eyes linger a little too long where the stain is, and I want to tell him where my eyes are. But reminding Manny that my nipples aren't eyeballs could put *me* at risk for a sexual harassment claim. Make it make sense because I sure as fuck can't.

It's an embarrassment, but it takes me way too long to realize that he means we have a client meeting at nine-thirty *this* morning. Who does that? Who doesn't plan ahead for a meeting, especially when it involves the millions of dollars that we're playing with? Last-minute meetings were something I only heard whispered about in darkened corners of the office like they're the boogeyman. I get it now. They're the literal fucking worst.

"I have to take the blame for that. I wasn't paying attention to where I was going and cost Tara her morning cup of joe." Joshua is trying to be nice and cover for me with my boss, but I cringe.

"My name is actually Taryn," I correct gently, knowing that he's only going off information that Manny has provided. Joshua gives me an apologetic look at the error, and I actually like how the expression softens his face. I don't blame him. I can't. It's Manny who has worked with me for three months on this project, who has been corrected at least once a day, and who should know better.

"Taryn. I'm sorry. I can have my assistant take care of getting your shirt dry-cleaned." I furrow my brow, unsure of why he's being so nice. There has to be some sort of hidden agenda.

"Go get cleaned up. I didn't see a copy of the new files that Darren said you worked on yesterday, so send those over stat." Manny nods at Joshua, the bro nod, so common around these parts, before grabbing his own coffee and leaving. I want to tell Manny that I would have sent them directly to him, but Darren insists on checking my work. *Insists.* So, I sent it to Darren when I finished my part, and then he left for the night without ever looking it over. Since I know the quality of my work product, I barreled forward, eager to get it all handled. This way, when they decide that I did a decent job, we can keep going.

"Please, let me help." Joshua offers again.

"Fine," I relent, grabbing my heels off the floor. My pantyhose are going to get shredded walking around the office, but I don't have a choice. I toss the sad, mostly empty paper cup in the trash, and I follow Joshua to his office.

Even though we're on separate teams, I'm glad we're not also on separate floors. The office is quiet, most people getting in between eight-thirty and nine and not at seven-thirty like me. I could technically do that too, but it's quiet in the mornings. I'm able to think better without the chatter around me or feeling like I'm in the way of the cleaning people.

We turn down a hallway I haven't been to yet and find it's even more deserted over here. Joshua pushes open the door to his office, and I nearly gasp at the sight. We're close to the Freedom Tower. Sometimes, I'll catch a glimpse of it through an open office door, but he has the right angle of it. His office is actually cozy, with one side featuring floor-to-ceiling bookcases stuffed with nicknacks and books. Opposite the bookcases is a long table with some art hanging over the decanter that's placed just under it. Against the wall with the door is a long couch that looks inviting. Beyond the large building is the Hudson River and the Upper Bay.

"Who did you have to kill to get this office?" I ask, stepping inside.

"It was my mentor's office before he retired. He's been helping me move my way up the ranks. He still greases a few hands for me when it comes time for raises and promotions."

Ah, the old boys' club at it again.

He closes the door behind him, and I wonder if I seriously misjudged this situation when his eyes go to my chest, and he starts to unbutton his shirt.

"I'm not fucking you," I blurt out, crossing my arms so he can't stare at my chest anymore. The draped shirt probably only gives him better cleavage, but I'm willing to fight this out.

"What? No." He looks completely bewildered.

I gesture at him and the white t-shirt that is stretched across his muscular chest. "I didn't come back here so you can bend me over your desk. Don't expect me to grease anything of yours just so *I* can get a promotion." I blink back furious tears I can't afford to let fall. This isn't the first time this has happened, and I can only hope that it won't cost me my job...again. The last thing I need is a reputation in this job. I know some women are okay with working on their knees, and I can't fault them for doing what they *believe* they need to, but I refuse. I got one man fired over it, and I'm willing to try again.

His stormy hazel eyes study my face, refusing to dip lower, but I see the moment he realizes what I thought was going to happen. "What are you...? Are you serious right now? That never even crossed my mind. I have my own meetings, so I was going to change too." He pulls at the plastic dry cleaning bags that hold his clean shirts. He's careful as he pulls two of them off the hangers and offers one to me. I snatch the shirt, holding my head high.

"Thank you," I say through gritted teeth, carefully holding the shirt to my chest. He doesn't say anything else to me, turning his back so I can get changed too. I'm quick about it, facing him so he doesn't try any funny business. I pull my shirt over my head and watch him do the same thing. I get an eyeful of his muscled back and a tattoo that peeks out on his side, not enough to see what it is, but enough to know it's there.

The urge to lick all along the ink and investigate it further strikes me, and okay, maybe I would have been okay with *him* bending me over his desk, but I have to stand on that principle.

His button-down is thinner than my shirt, so you can see the outline of my bra through it. I'll need to keep my suit jacket on, but it has the added bonus of not being so tight on me that the buttons aren't straining. Maybe I should start wearing men's shirts.

"You can turn around," I say once I'm safely buttoned up. I take care to tuck my top into my skirt. He does turn, eyes sweeping to make sure I'm comfortable. The sleeves are long and baggy on me, but I'll make due. Joshua walks to me and helps button the cuffs. I'm surprised by the gesture, but I let him while I struggle with the other. Once that's done, I roll them up a touch. He surveys me again, pulling at the shirt around my waist a little.

"What are you doing?" I ask, fighting the urge to actually swat his hand. He is still a senior member of the staff, and while he might not be a Senior Vice President in my department, he is still an SVP, and I can't have him telling other people I'm difficult to work with. It's bad enough Darren has Manny thinking I'm utterly incompetent.

"The shirt was twisted. I have four sisters; I've been trained to be adept at spotting wardrobe imperfections." He steps away from me with a confirming nod. There is something about this sweep that feels less like he's making sure I'm presentable and more like he is trying to sneak a more thorough perusal of me.

His shirt is a little awkward on me, but my strong legs are on display, and I think he just might be looking at the spots where you can see my bra through my shirt. Thankfully, it's a white bra and not a black one, though the part of me that wants to be bent over his desk wishes it was black.

I wonder what things would drive this man, this kind, sweet man, rare for the FiDi fuckboys, to spank my ass as he fucks me on his desk. I sort of want to corrupt him. That dark part of me wonders if I won't have to try all that hard...

"Thanks." My voice is soft. I reach for my shirt, which is over the back of a chair, but he beats me to it.

"I'll have my assistant send this out today."

"Just let me know the bill. I'll pay my fair share."

He shakes his head. "It's my fault. Don't worry about it. Which department are you with? I'll have her bring it to you."

"I'm in Consumer products, but just use the company chat instead, and I'll swing by. Gives me a chance to stretch my legs."

"Will you have shoes then?" he asks with humor in his voice.

I look at my discount store shoes and the snapped heel.

"I have a spare at my desk. Thanks for your concern." Joshua reaches for the door but pauses before opening it. I look up at him, broken heels in hand, and raise an eyebrow. He seems like a good guy, shocked that I thought he would expect something from me. Maybe I was wrong. My heart starts to pound in my chest. It's one thing to fantasize about letting him do wicked things to me with his tongue. It's another entirely to be faced with the pressure of being asked to do them.

"I know we're in different departments, but I want you to come to me if anyone, and I do mean *anyone,* expects something from you that you do not feel comfortable with." Something in his hazel eyes tells me he's serious and seriously ticked off that I thought that would be the case.

"Is that an order?" I wish I could have someone I trusted to go to, to tell them about the comments and the jokes made at my expense, but I don't. I don't trust that anyone will have my back if I make a complaint. I learned that lesson the hard way, twice. Once, when I was younger and naive, I did what was asked of me and was passed over anyway. When it happened again, I complained to HR and was made out to be the jilted, scornful lover trying to ruin her boss's life. I'm lucky I was able to get another job in this industry.

"Yes, Taryn. I have a zero-tolerance policy for bullshit that leaves female associates feeling like they owe men sexual favors for promotions. What was okay in the past isn't anymore." He senses my discomfort and opens the door for me without another word.

It's only when I'm halfway to my desk that I realize he's the first person to get my name right.

Two

THE TWEEDLES ARE ALREADY in the conference room with Manny. I walk in late with my laptop cradled in my arms because they left me a note on my desk telling me the conference room had changed. I shouldn't have trusted the note, but I did. So, I'm off to a great start, and I still haven't had any coffee. I've got these exercise endorphins working overtime.

Okay, and maybe a little bit of pleasure from Joshua knowing who I am. I have to remind myself that I have a strict no office romance policy, even if that's just my own stance instead of the stance of my company.

"Tara," Manny greets without looking up from his laptop. We're doing a run-through before meeting with the client so Manny can supervise how we plan to present. My job is to click the spacebar on our PowerPoint deck while Eric and Darren do the actual presentation. Over half a million dollars in my principal undergrad loan, all to hit a fucking space bar.

I hate it, but I know I'm being punished for turning down Eric's offers to go on a date. In the grand scheme of things, he hasn't been that awful to my face. Instead, he chooses to take credit for my ideas. He lets Darren wear me down emotionally.

I'm opening my laptop and perusing emails when Darren finally gets his laptop connected. His screen is projected to the TV at the end of the conference room, and my blood runs cold. It's set to his background, not the PowerPoint, and it's a picture of me from my friend's wedding. Elia and Charlie chose to get married in Bora Bora, where their love started to heat up. It was a special place to them, so they had close friends and family come for it. His stepfather paid for everyone to attend, including me; otherwise, there was no way I could have afforded the week in a villa over the water. I shared the house with my friends Ainsley and Vivian, both also painfully single, but they also served as a buffer to stop me from falling into bad habits with Charlie's brother, Brad.

The photo shows me sitting beside the infinity pool in my bathing suit. We were goofing off, taking over-dramatized photos of us posing with our backs arched and chests pressed up with our stomachs sucked in. It is a great photo that shows off my banging body, and I don't know how they got it.

"Take it down right now," I grind out, holding back tears of fury.

By the time Manny looks up, it's too late. The picture of me is covered up by our presentation, *my* presentation that the boys insisted on reviewing.

"What's the problem?" Manny asks, glancing at me then Darren.

"No problem, sir," Darren says, smirking. He smooths down his tie with a grin, and I hate him so much. I glance at Eric, who is studiously not looking at me. I know that they were frat brothers, I know that they are thick as thieves, and I know that I made the right call when I told Eric that I have a rule about not dating coworkers.

We go through the whole presentation, and when Darren flubs a part that I know more about, I gladly swoop in with the information.

The praise Manny gives me for having the answer throws

Darren off so much that when we're presenting to the client later in the day, I get to step in even more with the right answers.

It earns me a glare from Darren, but Manny and the client both appreciated how prepared I was, coffee or not. As we exit the conference room, Eric leaves Darren talking to Manny to get the door for me.

"I'm sorry about him," Eric says, trying to smooth over what happened.

"Don't be sorry about him. Make him stop."

"I've tried. He just doesn't like to see me hurt. One date, just one."

I look into Eric's shit-brown eyes and scowl. He's blocking my exit, and it doesn't have the same effect as when Joshua did earlier.

"No."

Eric tilts his head, thinking he's being cute, and maybe if I wasn't almost embarrassed in front of my boss, maybe if his best friend didn't have me in a bikini as his computer background, I would have given in, just a little, but none of those things happened.

Unfortunately, none of what they've done so far has been enough for me to report them to human resources, though. Too much of it has only been witnessed by the other that I know they would have each other's backs even if I dared to make a complaint. No, it's better for me if I just stay silent. In the grand scheme of things, it's not the worst thing I could have to deal with. Not if I want to be taken seriously in this industry.

"Just one," Eric pleads

"Move."

He must hear something in my tone because he finally complies.

I push past him to my desk, where a cup of hot coffee is waiting with a note attached.

Wasn't sure how you liked your coffee.
- Josh

For him to have it still piping hot when I got to my desk meant he had to know when my meeting was going to end. Beside my coffee are sugars and creamers from the kitchen. It's such an unexpectedly sweet gesture that I don't even know how to thank him for it. There's still a chance that he's just trying to get in my pants, but he said he didn't stand for that shit, and I sort of want to believe him, even if that makes him a unicorn surrounded by rhinos. I dump the flavored creamer into the hot liquid and stir. One sip sends my negative mood packing, letting me settle in for a long, long day.

A notification pings in the company messenger. Thankfully, Darren and Eric know better than to send pictures of their junk through it, but they do use it to order me around like they're not sitting four feet away from me.

I open it, and it's from a name I don't recognize: Quincey Martins.

> Quincey Martins: Hi, Taryn? I assume this is the right one since there aren't many Taryn's in the directory. Okay, there aren't any others, but Joshy wanted me to let you know that your shirt is back from the dry cleaners.

I'm surprised that it's already back, but when I look at the clock, I see it's six thirty. Oof. I don't think I've gotten up to so much as pee since getting out of the meeting. I thank Quincey and let her know I'm headed her way.

The interaction with Joshua starts to play over in my head. As far as reputations go, his is pretty spotless. He's known in the office for being very business-minded. There are often big holiday events or outings that always spawn office gossip afterward, like about the one managing director who always uses being drunk at the holiday party as an excuse to kiss female associates or how one of the secretaries saw her married boss on the Sleepless Nights dating app and he asked her out in the office anyway, pushing until she just quit. Joshua Bartlett's name is never mentioned in relation to those shenanigans.

I rise, stretching my tired muscles. I glance at Darren, who is looking at football stats, and Eric, who is actually working. Neither one acknowledges my movement, opting to live in their own little heads.

I remember the walk to Joshua's office and find a cute chestnut-haired woman sitting outside it. Her green eyes lift up to me, looking almost frosty.

"Can I help you with something?" she asks, her tone just as annoyed as she looks. One gatekeeper to another, I get it. When I was a hostess at a brunch spot uptown, I had to deal with the whining, begging, and pleading to be let in. There was an empty table; they saw it!

"Yeah, I'm Taryn. You have my shirt?" I ask.

"Oh! Yes! So sorry. You wouldn't believe the number of female associates who throw themselves at Joshy, hoping he will help advance their careers or, at the very least, have a good f–"

"Taryn," Joshua says, coming to the door of his office and cutting her off.

They share a look that I can't quite pin down. Quincey is fighting a smirk while Joshua glares at her.

"Joshua," I greet, drawing his attention back to me. His eyes rake down the line of me, and I self-consciously smooth the shirt down. I managed to scarf down half a pesto wrap, and now I'm worried I got something on the shirt. When his gaze finally travels back up to my eyes, I see that perhaps he wasn't looking me over to make sure his shirt was returned clean.

"Taryn," he says again, his voice sounding almost interested. He opens his office door wider. "Come in."

"I can just grab my shirt," I offer, but I follow him anyway. I'm surprised, though I shouldn't be, to see the sky painted in vibrant hues of reds, oranges, and pinks as we get closer and closer to sundown.

"Of course. You're working with Manny on that equity issuance proposal, right?"

My shirt is hanging next to the door, and I grab for it.

Joshua seems to be lingering in front of his desk like he wants to talk to me, and I sort of want to talk to him.

But if I stay, I might ask him to scratch that itch between my legs. I haven't actually had an orgasm since Charlie and Elia's wedding, and that was six months ago. Never mind the last time a *man* actually made me come, maybe Elia's bachelorette in Vegas?

My gaze peruses Joshua, my eyes lingering around his crotch, and I wonder what he has lurking behind that zipper.

I give myself a mental slap. Way to promote a double standard, objectifying one of my male colleagues when I get mad about them objectifying me. I lift my gaze to his eyes, and I think there is amusement dancing in them. Does he know I was mentally undressing him? Does he want me to undress him?

It's hard to deny my desire when I'm in his presence. I want to get closer to him and see how he smells, but I wasn't just blowing smoke up Eric's ass; dating in my office is a surefire way to ruin my reputation in what is somehow a large but very small industry. Besides, from what I've heard, this man doesn't fraternize much inside or outside the office.

I also don't know what Joshua is getting at. Is he trying to poach me for his team? "Yeah," I answer. "We're actually pretty deep into it. I should get back. I'll get your shirt back to you tomorrow. Thank you."

"No, of course. I'll see you around, Taryn."

I back out of his office, closing his door behind me.

Quincey looks back at her desk like she wasn't watching and listening to everything we were saying.

"Thanks for this," I say to her, gesturing at my now clean top.

"Anytime. Feel free to find me if you get in a similar bind and it's not even Joshua's fault. I slip my own dry cleaning in there from time to time, and he never notices."

"I heard that," I hear him shout from his desk.

Quincey winks at me before turning back to her work.

When I get back to my desk, Eric glances up at me. "Where did you disappear to?"

"Does it matter?" I shoot back, dropping into my chair.

"Yeah, I need the updated slides for the deck," Darren demands, flinging a paperclip onto my desk with his makeshift slingshot.

"Mature. I was gone for five minutes." I open my computer to see what Darren is asking for. Of course, it's the thing I've been working on all day that I saved before getting up. Because of the size of the file, I knew it would take some time to fully finish saving, so I drop it in our shared folder.

I keep my head down for the rest of the night, listening as the Tweedles bounce ideas off each other about how best to phrase something or how a deck should look. Slowly, the office empties out until Darren and Eric also leave. I take the solitary time to change back into my shirt from the gym that morning. A quick glance around confirms I'm alone, but I'm still lighting-fast, whipping off Joshua's shirt and putting on my own.

I grab a post-it from my desk, one of many that surround me, and scribble a quick *thank you*. With the shirt folded and the note on top, I make the trek to Joshua's office, expecting to find it empty.

The lights are off when I creep in, so I'm not quiet, but when I place the shirt on his desk, a head whips up, and I scream. I'm greeted with a more masculine shriek in response. Joshua's bleary eyes find me, and he turns on his desk lamp.

"Taryn?" he asks, confused.

"I didn't think you were in here. I'm so sorry," I whisper, not sure why. I don't know how I missed his form now. I was so focused that I didn't even realize he was there.

"No, it's fine. I was just taking a catnap before I have a call with Tokyo at 2:30."

"Why would they do that?" I ask, knowing that our hours are brutal. Dealing with foreign markets can make it even worse.

"Because they have been working on their numbers for most of the morning and want me to review them. Is Manny working you this hard that you're still here at two?"

My sex-deprived brain envisions being worked hard by Joshua in a totally different way, and I mentally spank, I mean, slap myself for the horny thought.

"Yeah, but I stayed later. Gives me a chance to get ahead with my team."

"Well, you should get home and get some rest. I was chatting with him again before he left. He mentioned that your team's output has been so great he's talking to the client to add more to the scope of the project."

"You're shitting me, right?" I ask, dropping into the chair across from him. I shouldn't be saying things like this in front of a man who is on the same level as my boss, but I am just so tired. The hope was that I could get ahead and *maybe* eke out a real weekend. One where I wasn't beholden to Eric, Darren, and Manny.

"I wish I was. He mentioned that his team has two killer go-getters." I lift my head and glare at Joshua.

"Of course he did." I stand up, pulling my bag back over my shoulder. "Anyway. Thanks a million for the shirt and the coffee, Joshua."

"Call me Josh." A ghost of a smile pulls the corners of his mouth up. "And it was my pleasure."

My heartbeat stutters at the word and the thought of his mouth against mine, and I know I have to get out of there. It's more than just having caught sight of his trim body and the tattoo that peeked out along his ribs. Office romances are never a good idea, even if it's a man who looks as decadent as this one.

I need to never see this man again if I know what's good for me.

Three

"TARA, can you run this down to Josh Bartlett's office? I'm hoping to get his assistance with a new client." Manny waves a stack of paper at me like I'm a messenger. I mentally file it under Another Way I'm Treated Differently. Not once has Manny asked Eric or Darren to do something that takes them away from their work. I'd be madder if it wasn't so fucking predictable.

I grab the stack from him, actually happy to comply this time, not just because it gets me away from Eric and Darren or because it means it can stretch my legs, but because it also means getting to see Josh again.

It was his face I pictured when I was in the shower at the gym this morning and I was lathering my body. It was his voice I heard whispering filthy words in my ear. The chatter of a group of women getting into the showers stopped me from riding my hand.

I have to keep the skip out of my step as I walk to Quincey's desk. She's sitting there with a cute crown braid keeping the hair out of her face.

"Hello, Miss Robins," Quincey greets. She leans on her forearms to look at me. "You are looking particularly good today."

"Quincey, you are looking particularly meddlesome today. Love the hair."

She pats it while preening. "What can I do for you?"

"Manny wanted me to drop off some paperwork for Josh."

There is a chime on Quincey's computer that draws her attention, and then a smirk spreads her lush lips. Her hands fly across her keyboard before she interlaces her fingers and rests her chin on them.

"Taryn," Josh says, stepping out of his office to where Quincey sits. Her smirk only grows into a full-on evil grin.

"Josh." I turn to face him, and I remember why it was him that I was thinking about in the shower. I remember why he's the one I fall asleep thinking about. It's the perfectly styled hair that I want to reach up to fuck up. It's the cut of the suit that draws my eyes along his lapel to his midline before my eyes naturally drift lower to his crotch again.

Because I bet he has a dick that he knows how to use, unlike those assholes I work with who probably couldn't find a vagina with a guided tour.

There is a tense moment as we stand there, both of us looking at each other, and I wonder if the same filthy thoughts are going through his head. We both take a step toward each other, and I feel like there is a string tied around me, and Josh is the one pulling it. I'm willing to go another step further but halt myself when Quincey speaks up.

"She has papers for you. From Manny," Quincey supplies helpfully.

"Right, yes, paper. Papers from Manny. For Josh. Josh's papers from Manny. Manny's papers."

My babbling draws a twist of Josh's lips. "Why don't you step into my office?" he offers, stepping backward and leading me into his space.

The damn string pulls me with him, and I follow. I think I

would keep following him. I wonder if he's feeling the crackling of electricity between us.

"Are you attending the company retreat next weekend?" I ask, looking for any reason I can to keep talking to him.

"I'm supposed to, but I think I'm going to come into the office instead."

"Mmmmm." I lean against Josh's desk, and somehow, it feels weirdly intimate. I don't know him well enough to be pushing myself into his space like this. But I want to know him better. I want to feel comfortable enough with him to not only lean against his desk, but be spread out on top of it.

"What about you?"

"What about me?" I parrot.

Josh moves closer to me, leaning against the side of his desk so we're facing each other. I wonder if Josh knows about this invisible string between us. Is it pulling on him too, desperate until we're connected in other ways?

I need to stop my crush, even if that's all I'll ever let it be, because I can't give in to this being more. The seriousness in Josh's voice when he thought someone was harassing me makes me think he wouldn't be so keen to have me bouncing on his dick.

He chuckles. "Are you going to the retreat?"

"Probably not. I'm sure we'll have some deliverables due after the weekend." It's the truth, but also, I don't want to be around these ass clowns anymore than I have to be. No, let them go away next weekend. I'll take this weekend easy, knowing they'd ignore me anyway. And while they're at the retreat, I'll move in with cleanup work.

"It's bound to be a great time." His voice has dropped low, and I want to hear that tone while his head is buried in my neck and his dick in my–

I catch myself because I'm leaning toward him, leaning closer to see if I can catch a whiff of his cologne. The shirt he loaned me naturally smelled like dry cleaner, but I want to know how Josh smells for real. I bet he smells like leather and rainwater.

"I'm sure it will be, but I'm going to go to brunch with my friends that weekend." Really, my plan is to sit in my room in just a shirt and try to get off at least once while also trying to bust my ass with work.

"Sounds perfectly basic."

His eyes have definitely dropped to my lips before meeting my gaze.

"Josh, you have Mr. Takomi on the phone following up on your call last week," Quincey's voice breaks through on the phone in his office.

Josh clears his throat. "You had something you wanted to give me?" he asks me.

"Right." I hand him the paper and step away from the desk. And him. I have to remember that Josh is off-limits.

He eyes the distance between us and seems to take the hint, stepping back. Why does that make me feel so cold, and not in a temperature-drop way?

"I'll take this call. Maybe I'll see you this weekend." Josh is circling around to the other side of his desk.

"Sure." I back up and then turn away from him to leave. When I cast a glance over my shoulder at him, he is definitely checking out my ass.

My weekend before the retreat is not as chill as I want it to be after forgetting my laptop charger at my desk. My friend, Elia, canceled brunch this weekend after a bad stomach bug, and as much as I want to see my friends, I'm not mad about it. I want to wander around and take some me-time.

After getting my laptop charger, I head up to Union Square, stopping by a bookstore for something light to read. It's so self-indulgent that my anxiety keeps creeping into my mind, reminding me of all the things I *should* be doing instead. I should be working hard because I need to get a fat bonus this year so I can take care of all the debt that's wrapped itself around my family. I should be pushing myself hard to get a promotion and advance through the company.

It's always hustle harder.

Do more.

Work yourself to the bone.

With a deep breath, I try to push those thoughts from my head. I haven't stopped working myself tirelessly since I graduated college. I can afford an eight-hour break for one day.

Armed with my new book and an ice cream cone, I set myself up on a park bench to enjoy the June day before the hot days of summer set in.

I'm a chapter or two in before I sense someone sit on the other side of the bench. Out of the corner of my eye, I catch a glimpse of slacks that are much too hot for anyone to be wearing, but I turn my attention quickly to my book. It's still early in the love story, and the couple is starting to get closer.

"Must be a good book," a male voice murmurs beside me.

"Mmmhmmm." I'm trying to ignore him actively at this point, and I'm putting out all the best "don't talk to me" vibes I can.

"What's it about?"

I lift the book so he can see the cover and the back without taking my attention off the pages in front of me, but no matter how hard I try, I can't bring my focus back in.

"Must be engrossing if you don't want to talk to me." There's a smile in the voice, and now I'm just mad.

"Respectfully," I start, lowering the book, but when I look up, the angry chastisement dies on my lips. "Josh."

"Taryn," he greets with a shit-eating grin on his face. "Must be an excellent book."

"It was until *someone* decided to interrupt me." I'm somehow not even mad about it. I'm apparently already gone for Joshua Bartlett, so I might as well enjoy this crush until reality ruins it.

"I would apologize, but that would be a lie. I'll admit I'm surprised to see you outside of the office. I thought it was a rule that we chained all new associates to their desks for at least three years before letting them out."

"Since I'm going to be working through the offsite, I'm taking this weekend easy, meaning that I'll enjoy the sun while I can. That included reading my book and having an ice cream in peace." There's a question sitting at the tip of my tongue, and if I had any sort of self-control, maybe I could stop myself from voicing it, but self-control is overrated. "Not spending the day with your partner?"

I make no assumptions about sexuality, but hearing that Josh has a girlfriend or boyfriend might make this whole quitting the feelings between us easier.

"No partner to speak of. My last girlfriend took issue with my unwillingness to introduce her to my sisters. For some reason, she stopped returning my calls after that. Can't imagine why," he says dryly. "Truth is, only the strong survive meeting them."

My stupid heart, and pussy, seem to think that means that this is an all-systems-go alert and that it is time to get *busy*. My brain remains online, thankfully.

"Ah, that's right. You mentioned four of them?" Sisters are a safer topic.

"Five. The last girl I brought home to meet them broke up with me that night. That was high school. If you think the overprotective brother stereotype is scary, you've never had to deal with an overprotective sister."

"You would be correct. I don't have any siblings, and I've thankfully never had to deal with overprotective siblings. My last serious boyfriend is now married to one of my best friends, and even then, I don't think I would have considered us serious. We were freshmen in college, so everything was new."

Why am I telling him all this like this is some sort of cute first date where I can give him little facts about myself to lure him in like a feral cat into a trap?

Obviously, I need to stop thinking about pussies and traps, and Jesus fucking Christ, I need some one-on-one time with my vibrator as soon as possible.

"That's a shame. Having siblings is simultaneously awful and the best. On one hand, they're great, and I love my sisters. They were the best playmates growing up, even if they always wanted to practice doing makeup on me, but on the other hand, they also gave me terrible nicknames and practiced how to apply makeup on me."

"So, I take it you're all close?"

Josh shifts on the seat so he's facing me more directly. He places his hand on the back of the bench, but he never touches me, even if he's so close I think I can feel the heat radiating off him. I wish his fingertips would brush my shoulder and twist in the edges of my hair.

"Very. And saying I wouldn't want it any other way would be a lie. I like being close for them and for my nieces and nephew, but it just creates pressure to see them when I don't have very much time."

"My parents are the same. They live just outside the city, and they want me to come home more often but don't understand why I say I can't."

"Do they still work, or are they retired?"

I know he has no way of knowing it, but his question still smarts all the same. It was so great when a pharmaceutical company moved into the vacant complex in town because it brought new jobs. Until they moved their offices to another part of the country with more favorable taxes, taking all those jobs with them.

"Semi-retired. What brings you to Union Square?" I shift the conversation back to him because talking about my parents is not an area I want to tread.

"I actually just had lunch with some old friends. It's such a nice day I decided to walk a few extra blocks to the subway. We sit so long at work that I take advantage when I can. What about you?"

"You dress like that for lunch with friends?" I eye him up and down, which is a mistake because he's wearing a polo that's stretched across his firm chest. He's not all washboard abs and muscles for days. He's real and firm in a way that I want to snuggle against.

If I was wearing a hair tie, I would have to snap it on my wrist for every horny thought that just crossed my mind.

Josh laughs and then rubs his hand over his mouth. "You caught me. There might have been someone there that I was courting as a client, but he's being very difficult."

"A cocktease of a client?" I ask, and immediately my eyes widen, but I overcompensate and shrink them until I'm basically squinting at the man. He must think I'm having a stroke or something. There is nothing else that could explain my behavior. Josh has already made it clear that he thinks that taking advantage of female associates is reprehensible, so why am I insisting on making it awkward?

But then his eyes flick, for just a second, down to the swell of my breasts created by this amazing camisole that I want to buy in every color under the sun. His eyes keep going, tracking where it's tucked into my shorts that barely cover my ass, not that he can see that. The whole perusal was at most a full second long, but I feel so naked and wish more than anything that I actually *was*.

I glance down, and that's when I see the single drip of chocolate ice cream on my breast that must have melted out of the bottom of my ice cream cone and slid right into my cleavage.

How fucking mortifying.

"Something like that," he says, but my brain is still caught on the ice cream on my boob and how I could possibly clean it now that we both know it's there. I should clean it up, but that's only going to draw more attention to my breasts. The most efficient way would be for Josh to just lick it off me, maybe sucking just hard enough to give me a hickey there, one that I could go into work knowing it's there, but no one else would be the wiser.

How I made it past thirty, I'll never know.

"Something like what?" I ask, having forgotten what we were talking about that doesn't involve having him lick the chocolate off me. Shit.

"This client is something like a cocktease," Josh says. "How about I make up for ruining your afternoon by treating you to another ice cream and a book you can read that's no longer tainted by my memory?"

I finally put a bookmark, okay, it's really just my receipt, in my book before getting to my feet. For a second, he looks disappointed until I offer him my hand to help him up.

"Let's get me some ice cream and save this day you've completely tarnished with your presence."

The way he slides his hand into mine does things to my libido that are too embarrassing to admit. It's clear he didn't need my hand up, because he gets to his feet easily, and he's so close that now I can smell him, and he smells like whiskey and clean laundry, two things that should not go together, like us, but somehow work. His touch lingers for longer than is strictly necessary before he drops my hand.

He's not intrusive as we walk through the bookstore, following behind me, occasionally stopping to pick up a book that I've looked at.

"I didn't take you for a romance reader," I say when he holds on to a title that I smiled at as I ran a hand over its cover. It was one of the ten books I read while at Elia's wedding and probably the one I enjoyed the most.

"I know you're not stereotyping me, Miss Robins."

I stop short and turn to look up at him. In my flip-flops, the height difference is a little more pronounced, but he's at a perfectly kissable height.

Damnit.

I take a careful step back, placing the book that was in my hands back on the shelf. "You're right. I'm sorry. I shouldn't have assumed."

He laughs a little, and I like that he's quick with a smile and a chuckle outside the office. "No, you're right. You had such a happy look on your face when you touched the cover, and *I* assumed you had read it before and liked it, so I picked up a copy for my sister."

"I did. I read it when I went to my friend's wedding. My last vacation for probably several years."

"Now, we do have those mandatory vacations. They are excellent for getting some rest and relaxation."

Cute of him to think that I can afford that, but there's no reason for him to think otherwise, really. I would probably spend those mandated vacation days picking up extra shifts at Claudia Jean's, the restaurant where I spent my years in business school working at. It's nice that the FDIC guidelines put this protection in place to prevent fraud and other financial fuckery, but it's going to be a few years till I can do what Charlie and Elia did and fuck off to Bora Bora for two weeks. The idea is that if someone is committing fraud, it's a lot harder to hide during two consecutive weeks off. The regulators prefer it this way, and we are nothing if not slaves to regulators.

"Ah, yes, the trip you just returned from."

"Yes, but at my level, we get three weeks."

"Go anywhere good?"

"Australia for a spell."

"What did you do on your trip Down Under?"

"I mostly just sat in my hotel room eating Tim Tams. It was winter in Sydney, and I'm not really a beach guy."

"So you...flew halfway around the world to what, sleep?"

"I did a lot of that too, you know we barely get any, and I *did* qualify that I spent *most* of my time in the hotel room, not all of it. I took a tour out to Uluru, saw the Opera House, and did the Bondi to Coogee walk."

"And ate Tim Tams."

"Lots of them. I actually brought back a whole suitcase full. It's how I bribe Quincey to be the best gatekeeper in the office and how I keep all my sisters happy."

"Smart man."

Carefully, I turn my attention back to the shelf in front of me before grabbing the first title that catches my attention.

"Because our job isn't the most conducive to relationships or having time for fun things. Isn't that right, Josh?" I say a little breathlessly as I turn to look up at him again. It's a reminder that our careers will stand in the way of anything that we could possibly be.

I'm not willing to forgo all I worked for because of a relationship, because of a man, even if he looks like he walked off the pages of a magazine.

"Taryn," he says almost as breathlessly as I did.

I want to tilt my head up to him and kiss him. It wouldn't take much effort to see what he tastes like. I already know what he smells like and what he feels like, even if it's just because of our first awkward meeting.

"Have you picked your book?" An almost pained look crosses his face as he steps back and looks down at what I picked up. It's some book about a princess getting dicked down, and I realize it's basically published fanfiction about the Crown Princess of Mondelia and her American beau before they went and got engaged.

"Yes, I have." I flash the cover at him with its cartoon drawing of a castle sitting on top of a small island nation.

"I happened to go to Mondelia on my travels." His voice is almost robotic as he tries again, switching to be courteous and almost bland.

I ask him questions about it, navigating to safe topics. He buys the book out from under me, offering to hold it when I run to make use of the bathroom. I don't love the charity, but I thank him profusely for the gift and make him promise to let me get the ice cream, which he also sneakily pays for.

The more time I spend with him, the more it feels like a date.

Needing the distance, once we're done with our cones, I make my excuses about having to get work done. Disappointment tips Josh's lips down, but he understands, and that makes it so much worse.

It's not the best idea because it only encourages these inappropriate thoughts, but when my roommate, Zelda, is out at a party, I make myself come to the idea of his mouth all over me.

Four

MY PLANS TO sit in my room and work the following weekend are shot to hell when Zelda confesses to having forgotten to pay the cable bill, which cut off our internet. She's working on getting it fixed as soon as possible, but I need to go to the office if I want to get any actual work done.

After my day with Josh, which was way too close to a date, I backed off. I avoided going near his side of the office, which wasn't hard because I had to spend most of the time redoing what Darren and Eric worked on over the weekend. The date that was not actually a date now lives rent-free in my mind, but I wish I could charge Josh rent for it. He took what was meant to be a calming day by myself and turned it into the kind of day most women dream of as a date.

I would know. I'm *still* dreaming about all the other ways we could have ended the date. Helping to squash my crush, it is not.

Since the offsite retreat is technically mandatory, I expect to have the office to myself. Even if Josh has work to do too, he's well-placed enough that he's probably sitting in several millions of dollars worth of a penthouse with a gorgeous view. I could text Elia and see if I could use her equally amazing, equally expensive penthouse, but I told everyone I had to beg off brunch for work, and while I know my friends would get it, I hate being the friend that perpetually has to work. Vivian, at least, also gets it, even if I am leaving her to the wolves, who are our very happy friends.

I grab what I can for clean clothes, which involves a cute jean skirt and a simple T-shirt. It's casual without being the shorts and tank top I originally grabbed. I'm not sure it's the smartest idea since all these offices are turned on max AC for all the men, never mind the women who are freezing their nipples off. But in case I run into anyone, I want to be dressed better than weekend Taryn.

It's fine. I'll be mostly alone, if not completely on my own, in the space. I wave to the security guard before riding up to my floor.

I settle in at my desk and throw on my massive noise-canceling headphones. I'm in the zone for several hours, not moving as I power through another proposal Manny wants, as well as fixing errors made by Danny and Eric.

When I lift my head, I nearly jump out of my skin.

"Looks like it's my turn to scare you," Josh says with a smirk twisting his lips. He looks just as playful and teasing as he did in Union Square. My heart goes wild for this look.

Even on the weekend, the man looks ready for a meeting. Granted, it's more like a casual meeting, but he's got a forest green polo on and shorts this time. I'm not sure who he's trying to impress.

"I figured you would have been working from home today?" I meet his gorgeous gaze. "How long were you staring at me?"

"Long enough. Working from home is nice, but I prefer to keep my home space separate from work. What do you say to taking a lunch break? We can go around the corner and get a nice meal."

I drum my fingers on the desk before looking up at him. I could do it. I could go out with him. It doesn't need to be anything more than two colleagues at lunch. Even if I want more. I wouldn't mind more, but I'm also not going to press him for more.

Damn it.

Is this what's going on in Eric's little pea-sized brain? The only difference is with Eric, I haven't made a move, and I haven't continued to press when that move was rebuffed.

Alright. Not the same situation at all. My morality is appeased by this turn of events.

I give in to the fantasy that Josh is offering, and I get up from my chair. "Let's go, then."

It's an awkward walk as we navigate down to the lobby. Josh's hand grazes the small of my back, and I feel that touch everywhere. I want it on my bare skin, but he maintains a respectful distance. It's like after our not-a-date, we're both too aware of the crackling energy between us that we're both avoiding.

Maybe I need to sign up for one of those dating apps just so I can get off and stop fantasizing about Josh. Oh wait, I would need actual time for that.

Once we're settled at the table, I fuss with the menu. "I think I'm a little underdressed for this place."

"Hardly. It's the weekend. I'm not exactly dressed up, either." Josh gestures at his get-up, which is honestly more appropriate for the golf course than this fancy steakhouse.

"Playing the back nine today?"

"Not today, but maybe next weekend if I can get ahead on this bullshit. Tell me your story, Taryn Robins, MBA." It's not the line of questioning we went down at Union Square, where our conversations naturally flowed through topics other than ourselves after that initial offering of details about our families.

A server drops by with our drink orders, and we both place an order for our lunches. Josh orders a glass of wine, so I do too. This isn't actually a working lunch, and it's the *weekend*.

"I mean, you seem to already know the basics. Why don't you tell me what you know about me, and I'll fill in the blanks."

Josh smiles and takes a sip of his wine. "Alright, I'll play. I know that you're Taryn Robins, who graduated summa cum laude from Dartmouth College. You worked for a few years at an accounting firm before going to Columbia Business School for your MBA. You were a hostess at Claudia Jean's while going to school. You opted not to take the offer from your internship, though I'm not sure why, and now you're working under Manny with Darren and Eric."

"You are quite the sleuth," I say over the rim of my wine glass.

"I can't take the credit. That's all because of Quincey. I don't think I could function without her."

"Isn't that the way of most men? Needing the women in your lives to manage it?"

Josh snorts into his drink. He has to wipe his mouth with the napkin, and all it does is draw my attention to his full, biteable lips. It's yet another urge I have to bury. This crush is getting out of control.

"I would say I resent that remark, but I just confirmed how important Quincey is to me. So, you've caught me."

"Have you two ever...?" The words are out of my mouth before I can think better of it. I don't want to know if Josh is the type of man who hits on his assistant. I don't want to find out that he's not the good guy I've started to believe he is. He also said as much to me himself when he asked if someone made me feel that way in the office, but it's still nice to get the confirmation.

"Me and Quincey? God, no. She's like an annoying sister who keeps me on my toes. I actually wanted to ask about that, and you can tell me that it's none of my business, but I'm trying to push leadership to take a more active approach to sexism and trading favors in the workplace."

There's a small alarm going off in the back of my head, a warning. Josh seems like he's everything he pretends to be, but he could also be playing good cop, trying to see if I'll talk shit about someone in the office. There isn't a single woman in a male-dominated office who doesn't have *some* sort of story, be it words that made her feel less than or actual action taken. All of it was something that was excused away as something that could have been worse. It doesn't make it true, but it makes it a sad fact.

"And?" I ask.

Josh focuses that laser gaze on me. It's just a taste of what I know he's capable of. There have been rumors of him turning that look on in meetings and walking out with everything he wanted and more. I'm surprised to see what amounts to a nervous gesture. He rubs his watch back and forth on his wrist while looking down at it. It's a false sense of security he's giving me before folding his hands on the table and re-engaging his focus on me.

"And I want to know why you thought I was going to demand you sleep with me over some coffee spilled on a shirt. I want to know if there are people in the office making you uncomfortable, and I want to get them fired for it."

I suck my lower lip into my mouth and then bite on it. "That's a bold assertion you're making for a woman you barely know."

"Trust me when I say this, Taryn. I don't believe anyone should be subjected to the whims of their boss, least of all when those whims involve sexual advances." He breaks eye contact to look at the table, jostling his watch again. "When I was sixteen, my parents divorced. Apparently, my father went through assistants like they were cheap underwear. When I was eighteen, I found out why when one of them confronted me. She asked if I was a predator like my father and then asked if I would like to get to know my new younger sibling. It turns out she was the reason my parents got divorced. She had gotten pregnant, and my father couldn't be bothered. He preached to me that I needed to take responsibility for denting the car, but he wouldn't take responsibility for my little sister."

I'm quiet as he says this, not sure what to say, but when he reaches across the table for my hand, I let him take it, squeezing it when he squeezes mine. "I had no idea."

"I know. No one does. I don't exactly lead with it when meeting people, but your reaction made me think that you needed to hear it. I don't know what your situation is here, but I'm not going to tolerate it. People who think the apple doesn't fall far from the tree are wrong because I hear that all the time in snide comments."

I wonder if it's the reason he can be so closed off while in the office.

"Do you talk to your sister?"

"Yes, she actually works at an accounting firm in the city. Once I knew she existed, I talked my father into doing something for her. Eventually, he paid for her to go to some bougie boarding school. I couldn't go back to pretending like she didn't exist after learning about her. To me, she's just my little sister. She's going to Tahiti or something for her high school reunion." There is a faint lift to his lips when talking about his sister.

"That sounds really cool."

"I mean, I want to do more for her. I know it's not my fault; it's on my father, but I still feel terrible for her circumstances. I still talk to her mother sometimes too, but that's harder. I just wanted you to understand where I'm coming from, and it's a place that knows that sometimes a choice isn't really a choice."

He's laid so much on the table in an effort to connect with me that I feel like I have no choice but to give a little. I'm not sure that was his intention, but I take a deep breath. It will be good to talk about it with someone who understands the industry. I haven't even really talked about it with my girlfriends.

"I didn't take a position at the firm I did my internship at because it felt like hush money. One of the partners I was working with offered to help advance my career if I only got on my knees." When I look up at Josh, there's tension in his body. The line of his shoulders looks rigid, and he's clenching his jaw. "I said no," I rush out. "I reported it, reported him for the abuse of power, because if he did it to me, there was no way he didn't do it to someone else."

"And the hush money?"

"Oh yeah, they offered me the job like a week later, and the salary was obscene. I mean, like nothing I should have been offered. If I didn't have scruples, I would have taken it, but I couldn't do it, even if I wanted to." Even if that amount of money would have helped my family get out of the precarious financial position they're in now.

Josh nods and then squeezes my hand again before drawing it back. The waitress comes and places our food in front of us before disappearing to refill our wine.

"I'm serious, Taryn. I know you don't know me well, and I know we're not going to work together much, but I want to know if this shit is happening. It's unacceptable and, frankly, disgusting."

I cut into my steak. "I appreciate your enthusiasm for making the workplace a safer space, but at this point, I would rather talk about my first period than being sexually harassed."

Chagrined, Josh blushes. "You're right. It's not exactly lunch conversation."

"No," I confirm. My tongue darts out to catch the small amount of steak sauce that drips onto the corner of my mouth. Josh's focus zeroes in on my lips, and the heat between us turns up to an eleven.

I can't look away from him, even as he takes a sip of his wine, even as he lifts his own cut of meat to his mouth. And now I'm thinking about having his meat, his cock, in my mouth.

As if we hadn't just been talking about abuses of power in the workplace. But he's not my boss; he's not even in my arm of business. So, I think I would be in the clear.

"You never finished telling me about you. And I shouldn't, but I want to learn more about you."

"Why shouldn't you?"

"Because I just finished telling you about how I won't stand for an abuse of power, and while you might be in a different business line than me, I don't want to court trouble."

"Am I trouble?" I ask, desperate to know that maybe this

attraction isn't one-sided. My heart is slamming in my chest at the idea that he could be on the very same page as me.

"I think you know that you are."

We avoid talking about the attraction that seems to be crackling between us. Instead, I tell him what Columbia was like and a little about my family. Josh fills me in on how he snagged Quincey and how he moved up through the company.

I stop drinking after two glasses of wine because...because... because I wanted a clear head and because at some point when Josh was telling me his story, I decided he was a good man that I could have a crush on. It might make me a hypocrite, but I haven't felt attraction this strong since, well, ever.

The walk back to the office is so tense it's almost awkward. Josh leans closer to me, then seems to remember himself and pulls back. When he steps back, it's my own reminder to do so because with each step I take, my body is drawn closer and closer to his orbit like we're on a collision course. I can practically feel the electric shocks between us when we do brush against each other. We're both so busy fighting it that I don't think we've stopped to consider the cataclysm that will come if...when...we give in. We do this dance even as we get into the elevator and ride up to our floor, but the only ride on my mind is one of a different kind.

"What made you pick investment banking?" Josh asks, startling me out of my thoughts.

"Money. A lot of money. Ivy league educations don't come cheap."

"Ah, the age-old issue of student loans."

I look away from him as the elevator approaches our floor.

Before I can think better of it, I lean forward and press a quick kiss to his lips.

Josh is stunned still, his hands braced on the bar in the elevator. When I pull back, I see how tightly he's clenching the metal. Fuck. Fuck. *Fuck.* Maybe I totally misjudged this, and now I'm the harasser, and I totally deserve to be fired.

The door opens on our floor, but neither of us moves. If I am wrong, I'll just have to avoid the part of the floor that has Josh's office and go to a friend's place to work for the rest of the day. I'm sure I could go crash with Charlie and Elia, and that Charlie could get me a new job so I never have to see Josh again.

The doors close again, sealing us back in. I look away from Josh to reach for the buttons, but Josh beats me to it, hitting the stop button before he slams his mouth over mine.

His hands cup my cheeks as he pulls me toward him, and it's like the fire between us is ignited.

Five

MY MOUTH OPENS TO JOSH, and he plunders it, taking what I have to offer.

And I offer him *everything*.

Josh's hands slide from my face down my body until he reaches my hips, and then he leans further into me and grips my ass. I wrap my legs around his hips as he backs me against the wall of the elevator, and somehow, doing this is even hotter than I ever imagined.

We crash into the wall, and rubbing against him causes an obscene amount of friction between my legs, causing me to moan. I thread my fingers through his hair as every nerve ending in my body comes awake.

"Taryn," Josh groans as he kisses my neck. His teeth scrape my skin, and I can't control how my body reacts. I'm rolling my hips, all but begging him to rip my skirt off and fuck me.

There is a crackle on the intercom in the elevator. "Excuse me, but, um, we noticed the elevator was stopped, and we checked the security camera just to make sure. Can you please confirm if you need any assistance?" The voiceover coughs.

Josh pulls back, and I press my forehead to his. Slowly, so

slowly, he releases me. My body slides down his, but we stay close, breathing the same air.

"We're okay," Josh calls, his voice cracking. He withdraws and goes to the panel to restart the elevator. We have to go down before we can go back up to our floor.

"I'm sorry," I say, needing to break the silence. We've retreated back to the separate sides of the elevator, and I feel cold without his warmth against me.

"You're sorry? *You're* sorry?" he repeats in disbelief. "I tell you that I want to avoid pressuring women in the workplace, and then I have you pinned against the elevator not an hour later. So, no, Taryn, you are not the one who should be sorry. I should be sorry."

"I wanted it, no, Josh, I *still* want it. I'm the one that owes you an apology. You made your stance clear, and I should have respected that boundary."

Josh chuckles. "I think we can both agree that it took two of us to blow through our boundaries."

"I'm sorry for that."

"I appreciate that, but it's unnecessary. I've been thinking about pressing you against a wall since you maneuvered that classic meet-cute in the kitchen."

I scoff at him, smoothing my hands down my shirt. I shouldn't have done that because I can feel the hardened peaks of my nipples. "You mean the meet-cute that *you* orchestrated? I had my eyes closed, so, clearly, you are the one that walked into me."

"It's possible I wanted a good reason to talk to the gorgeous woman in the office. It's possible I was a bit of a cad and wanted your shirt to be see-through."

Still feeling emboldened, I bite my lower lip and clasp my hands behind my back. It forces my breasts forward, and damn it if Josh doesn't drink his fill looking at my body.

"Only a bit of a cad?" I tease.

The elevator opens on our floor and we both pause before taking that first step onto the floor. We can write off what happened in the elevator and the bunch as a flirty, sexy one-off, but once we bring it onto the work floor, it stops being something that's hypothetical and starts to become real.

I think I want it to be real.

The heat in Josh's eyes tells me he might be feeling the same.

"Taryn." He clears his throat before grabbing my elbow and drawing me close to him. It's still deserted, as expected.

"Josh?"

He smiles. "I want to take you out. To dinner. On a date."

I open my mouth, suddenly unsure, and I know I'm gaping like a fish, but I don't know how I should answer. I turned down Eric, telling him that I'm not interested in dating someone in the office, but here I am, ready to climb onto Josh's desk and let him do whatever dirty thing he wants to me. For a second, I wonder just how creative he is.

"You're thinking about it," Josh says, putting a small bit of distance between us as he steps back. For a flash, I'm hurt, and maybe that should be my sign that I want this.

I've spent too long denying myself, too long putting aside my truer wants and desires in favor of the quick and easy option. I slept with my ex-boyfriend's brother because he was an easy lay instead of trying to put myself out there. Josh makes me want to try again, not just in general, but with him specifically.

What if, instead of overthinking it, I just went with what I wanted?

"Yes."

Josh pauses and watches me with wariness. "Yes, you're thinking about it?"

I close the distance between us, feeling my breasts brush against his chest, and he sucks in a breath. My nipples harden at the prospect of play.

"Yes, I'll go on a date with you." I'm not tentative in my words. I'm firm in my conviction. I want to go out with Josh, even if it's not the smartest decision I can make.

Josh nods. "I should be a gentleman. I should leave it at that, but I'm desperate to push this skirt up." His hand comes up and cups my cheek so he can rub his thumb over my swollen lips.

My chest heaves as he paints this dirty picture in my mind, and I can't help it, I lean into his delicious touch. "So, does that mean you're going to be a gentleman?"

I sound breathy and desperate for him, and the way his pupils widen makes me think that maybe he's just as into this as I am.

He's silent, no doubt deliberating how to proceed. He looks around our abandoned floor before shaking his head. I think he means no, he's not going to do this, almost like he's shaking common sense into himself.

"Fuck, no."

Josh bends and scoops me over his shoulder like I'm nothing but a bag of flour to be manhandled, and I am so on board with letting him manhandle me. He smacks my ass as I yelp at the sudden change in perspective, but I can't say I'm mad. The man fills out his pants very nicely, and if he wants to play dirty by spanking me when I can't do anything about it, then he's going to learn just who he's fooling around with.

I slide my hand into his back pocket and squeeze with everything I have, and it's like I've activated him because his sure strides become almost a sprint as he runs to his office, kicking the door closed behind him. Even in the short amount of time I've known him, I know he wouldn't do this if there were others in the office, but I like the edge of danger that maybe we *aren't* alone.

Josh gently sets me down on the edge of his desk, and there is a charged moment between us as we each take a breath and stare at each other.

I peel my t-shirt up and expose my small breasts to him, and the sharp intake of his breath makes me squirm on the desk. My breasts have always been a tender spot for me. They're smaller than I would like, than most of my partners like. I've been told how they wish my tits were fuckable and how they're just too small to be a handful. All really awesome things to be told about an insecurity at the height of vulnerability.

Feeling self-conscious, I try to cover myself, but Josh grabs my wrists and stops me.

"No, don't cover them. They're fucking perfect."

Then he's capturing just the tip of my hardened nipple in his mouth, and it has me arching my back as he drags his teeth over the sensitive flesh. I can't reach him without interrupting the attention he's lavishing on my chest, so I do the next best thing. I flick the button on my skirt and slide my hand in, finding it easier to go over the top than reach underneath.

The brush of my fingers against my clit has me moaning, but also the unfortunate consequence of Josh stopping what he's doing. I pause and look up at him. He's got this cat-who-ate-the-canary grin on his face as he steps back and away from me, crossing his arms while he leans against the window.

"What...What are you doing?" I ask, suddenly uncertain.

"Push that skirt up and show me how you please that pretty pussy."

Jesus fuck. My body is not ready for this man.

I suck my lower lip into my mouth. "You should do it for me. I would hate to stop what I'm doing."

He uncrosses his arms and does what I say. Josh might have used a bossy voice, but by being willing to listen to me, he's showing me that I'm *not* just an object for his pleasure. I should be disappointed by that because it's going to make things so much more complicated, but I like that he seems to be as invested as I am.

Josh may not be my boss in the office, but he's certainly the boss of *me* in *his* office.

He starts to pull my skirt down and off me, contradicting his earlier statements about taking it off, and I don't hate this for me. For the first time, I register the pain of having my wrist pressed against the metal teeth. It stings like nothing else, but when I lift my hips, and Josh starts to take my skirt off, he pauses and kisses the indentations on my wrist.

"Don't stop. Let me see you come all over my desk."

I'm so fucking bare to him right now that it's a little unfair, but then I catch him rubbing his cock over his pants, and the power I have floods me.

So, I go slow, opening my legs to him so he can see how I like to touch myself. I start small, rubbing little circles around my clit before sliding my hand lower and along my entrance. I'm so fucking wet for him right now. I can't even remember the last time I was this hot and bothered.

"*Josh*," I whine his name as I pump one finger inside myself before I bring it back up to my clit, swirling the wetness around. Usually, I hate touching myself without toys because I can never seem to get myself there. My fingers are too slim, too timid, too, I don't know what, but today, it's all I can do to *not* come with just a touch.

"Yes, my treasure?"

The pet name makes me feel so much. I feel gooey inside that he chose *treasure* of all things. Like I mean something, and this isn't...well, I don't know what it is yet, but right now it's fucking hot.

"Show me that cock you're going to be putting inside me, and I'll reward you by coming all over your desk just like you want."

Not to leave me all alone, he takes his shirt off by reaching behind him and dropping it onto the ground. His shorts follow soon after. There's something deeply erotic about the sound of his belt coming undone and his zipper sliding down. Last to go are his boxers.

Oh my god.

Oh my god.

It's pierced.

This buttoned-up boss has a tattoo and a pierced dick. I've

never before sucked a cock with a piercing. I'm ready for the challenge.

"I don't have condoms, so you won't be coming on my cock just yet."

"I'm clean, for what it's worth. And on birth control."

He strokes his cock and shakes his head. "I'm clean too. But not today. Today you're going to fuck your hand while I watch, and then I'm going to cum all over those pretty tits, and then you're going to ride my face until you come again."

"Is that how you think this is going to go?"

He smirks, and I start to circle my clit a little faster. "That's how I know this is going to go. I'm not the kind of guy who puts out on the first date. I'm going to make you work for it."

"Pretty sure that's supposed to be my line," I pant. My eyes are glued to his hand as it strokes all along his shaft, pausing only at his Prince Albert piercing.

"You don't have to fuck my face if you don't want to," Josh teases, slowing his movements, and I know just from that one move that he's going to be the type of lover who is going to draw every bit of pleasure from my body.

My hands and heart stutter over the thought of what it will feel like to have him fuck my ass with that piercing.

I'm done fucking around.

I become more focused in my movements, seeking that release I'm so desperate for. I repeat the motions I know are going to get me there while watching Josh grope his balls, alternating squeezing before releasing them and moving closer to me. I can feel the tension growing, and my hips start to roll against my hand, seeking all the friction I can get.

Then, like a freight train, it hits me, barreling over me. My head falls back as I shout Josh's name. Earlier, it was a tease, but this time, it's because I don't understand what he's doing to me. He's like some sort of sexual magician that has me under his spell.

"Taryn," Josh grunts, and I lift my head as I pant through the last of my orgasm. It's just in time to watch as hot ropes of cum jet all over my stomach. I want to tease him that it's not exactly all over my breasts like he promised, but the man is dropping to his knees and pulling me to the edge of his desk.

"You don't have–" I start, but then he gives me this look, his eyes narrowed. I shut up because he's licking me, and he's not tentative about it. He licks me from back to clit like he's taking that first long draw of an ice cream cone before he covers me with his mouth and uses his tongue on me in a way that has me falling back on his desk, knocking his lamp off it.

I want to care. I want to sit up and clean it up, but Josh bands his arm along my lower stomach and holds me down until I do as he wants. He sucks and nips at my clit until I'm crying for mercy, but he keeps backing off. Just when I start to really ride his face, ready for another O, when he slows down.

He's edging me, and I sort of hate him for it, while also loving the euphoria that comes when I'm close again. Then he spears me with two fingers, sending me over the edge. I grab whatever I can on his desk and squeeze as I scream through my orgasm this time, and his name echoes through the empty office.

I really hope no one else was here this weekend.

Josh gets to his feet and kisses me. His half-hard dick is right against my sensitive pussy, but I can't think of anything to say because every thought has eddied from my mind. There is just the sensation of Josh's mouth on mine, and I don't want him to go anywhere.

I want us to be fused together in this moment forever.

He tugs me off the desk and onto his lap as he sits in his much-nicer-than-mine desk chair. I'm curled against him, both of us still panting as we recover. What gets me is how at home I feel in his arms, pressed against him. I haven't felt like this in...well, I'm not sure if I ever have. I want to fall asleep in his lap, purring like a contented cat.

"Sorry I broke your lamp," I mumble into his chest. I'm not

going to fight against what feels right in this moment. We can deal with the complications later. Right now, I'm going to enjoy this feeling.

Josh makes this crush so much harder when his hand starts to stroke along my body, not in a sexual way, but in a comforting one from my ribs down to my hip and up again.

"I think we're both to blame for it. I'll let maintenance know on my way out that I need a cleaning person to come in and vacuum for glass."

"After we're dressed?"

He chuckles. "Yes."

He kisses my forehead, and I think I hate him a little for so much more than just being a sex magician, but for making feelings I've long thought dead start to stir inside me.

"I should probably get dressed and actually do more work today."

"No."

"No?" I lift my head to look at him.

"No. The whole company is supposed to be off at the offsite."

"You say that like it's supposed to mean something. Grunts like me still have to get shit done."

"*You* say that like SVPs don't also have work that they need to get done. I did just get back from a three-week long trip where I wasn't working at all."

"Sounds to me like you're just a slacker," I tease.

I want to learn more about him, so I adjust myself on his lap. It's weirdly intimate, talking without our clothes on with such basic get-to-know-you conversations, but I don't feel awkward about it at all. I do feel cold, so I slide off his lap and grab his shirt, sliding it over my head.

"Cold?"

"Very. Tell me more about you sisters."

"Do you want to get dressed? Warm up some?"

I consider his offer. I want to stay skin-to-skin with him, even if it's just the lower half of us, but the fear of being found out overrules that instinct.

"Yeah, I guess that would be the prudent thing to do."

I start to climb off his lap, but Josh stops me with a kiss. It causes me to melt into him entirely.

"Nothing about you makes me want to be prudent. I mean, fuck, Taryn. I've been pretty good about not mixing business with pleasure for the last fifteen years that I've worked in this industry, and yet I've known you for a week, and I'm ready to fuck you on my desk."

"You did fuck me on your desk, just with your tongue and not your cock," I point out with a grin.

"You're right, and one of these days, I'll fuck you with my cock too. I've asked after you. You're driven and smart. Other than your current team, you're well-regarded in the company."

My spine goes rigid. "What does that mean, other than my current team?"

"That means that Manny doesn't pay attention to shit, like knowing your actual name, and the other two on your team seem to think they know better than you."

It makes my skin crawl, and I climb off his lap to get dressed. I take his shirt off and toss it at him absently before sliding back into my clothes. All the calm and relaxation brought to me with those orgasms is gone.

"What just happened?" Josh asks while getting dressed.

"What? Oh, nothing; just...talking about work reminded me that there was a reason that I came into the office on a weekend instead of getting hammered at the company offsite. I have a slideshow deck I need to finish."

Josh grabs my arm, making me spin to face him. "Taryn, I know you don't know me well."

"You mean outside the carnal sense?"

"Yes, outside of knowing me carnally. Not many people know I have a piercing on the tip of my dick. That puts you in a very small group of people, which I think lends itself to a level of trust."

"There is nothing to say, Josh. You just reminded me that I have work to do. Truly."

Okay, that's only half true. He did remind me that I have work to do, but the reminder that Darren and Eric think they're better than me made me realize that I need to get back to work and that fucking a company higher-up is a bad idea. I can't prove them wrong about me if I'm too busy fucking the face of one of the SVPs of the company. It's a big company, and he's not directly my boss, but it's all the same thing.

He regards me with a narrowed gaze but seems to decide against pushing me on it. "Fine, but you'll need to break for dinner at least, and I want to go out somewhere nice. Do you have any food allergies or preferences I should know about?"

"You're not going to tell me where we're going?"

"No, I'll pick you up at your apartment, or here if you don't want me to know where you live. Dress up because it's going to be somewhere nice."

"That means there isn't going to be a lot of food." I drum my fingers on my lips. "Fine, but I have a shellfish allergy."

"I can work with a shellfish allergy." His lips brush my temple. "Go, get your work done, and text me where you want me to pick you up."

Josh grabs my phone from the floor and programs his number into it because I'm the dumbass that doesn't keep a lock on it.

"You're not...mad?"

"What am I supposed to be mad about? That you're driven and want to focus on your work for the time being? No, I'm not mad. Go get your work done. I'll be here. Just let me know before you head out."

My face relaxes because I never expected him to be so chill about, well, everything. But who knows? And that realization is another gut punch. Really, I'm the one who doesn't know. I hardly know him, and I've let him lick my pussy and cum on my stomach.

God, the depraved things I want him to do to me with that piercing. I wonder what it will feel like when I suck him off.

His light swat to my ass as I leave his office brings me out of the horny haze that I was about to walk to my desk in.

Everything is exactly as I left it. When I look at my clock, I see I have four hours before he's going to pick me up, and yes, I should do work just like I begged off to go do, but I also want to get dressed up. This is the first date I'll have had in... I don't even know how long. Yes, I've fucked, but I haven't *dated* in the longest time.

That settles it. I need to go home and primp. It's too late for a wax, and he didn't seem to mind that I was au naturel down there. But I could always do things like shave my legs. It is June, for fuck's sake, but since no one has been touching my legs, I can usually get away without it.

I can also appreciate that he didn't make a comment about the carpet matching the curtains. And I can appreciate his dick and his muscular body. God, I wish I had time to really look at his tattoo too.

There's a lot about Josh that I can appreciate, and that I do. But, mostly, it's the shocking kindness in an industry that values being a shark.

Quickly, I gather my things and make a break for it. As he asked, I stop in front of his office, but he's on a call already. I tap on the glass, not wanting him to think that I've abandoned him because his chair is spun around, facing the window.

He whips around to look at me, and the smile on his face isn't the kind that can be faked. It takes up his whole face, and damn it. Damn this crush that feels like so much more after two afternoons together.

Am I that starved for love and affection that I'm jumping at the first offering of it? No. That's not it. That's doing a disservice to how Josh treats me and how much I enjoy his company.

He taps his wrist, a reminder that he'll see me in a few hours, and I'm powerless to stop the little finger wave I give him as I leave the office.

I am so fucked for this guy.

Six

A QUICK SCAN of my closet when I get home reveals that I don't have anything to wear. I could grab the dress I wore to Elia's bachelorette party, except vixen red with my hair might have worked in Vegas or in a club, but it will *not* work at some swanky restaurant in New York City.

I shoot off a text before getting into the shower, but that reprieve is short-lived. The water is hot for all of a second before it comes through like ice pelting my skin. Nearly slipping after jumping in shock, I tear out of the bathroom with my towel secured around me.

My roommate, Zelda, is sitting in the living room smoking a bowl with her good-for-nothing boyfriend.

"Did you pay the landlord?" Our landlord, tired of late rent, will occasionally turn off the hot water or electricity to the unit until Zelda remembers to pay, which she usually will after two or three cold showers, but it's summer now, and she may not have noticed. What he's doing is no doubt highly illegal, but I've been on the receiving end of Zelda's absent-mindedness, so I can't say I don't blame him.

She takes a long hit before looking up at me. One could

confuse the blank look on her face for being high out of her mind, but I know that's just the mousy brunette's way of thinking. Her boyfriend takes the bowl, lighting it for himself as Zelda slowly releases the pent-up smoke out her nose.

"Nnnnnnoooooooo." She draws the word out before focusing on me and committing to her answer. "Yeah, no, I didn't. It's been so hot, I figured we could save."

"You do know we use the electricity for other things in the apartment, right?" That's when I realize that the lights are all off and so is the TV. The only other sound is coming from her Bluetooth speaker. Hell, I didn't even realize the lights were out because when the bathroom light switch didn't work, I automatically pressed the battery-operated light that we have for these moments. I failed to make the connection, and, sure, maybe it's a little bit on me for not noticing, but I'm just used to this bullshit.

"Yeah, but I just charge everything up at Dusty's place." She gestures at her boyfriend, and he raises a hand in greeting as if this is the first and not the hundredth time I've seen him.

"Hey, want a hit?"

I have the worst roommate ever, and if I want to actually get some work done before meeting Josh for our date, I need to find somewhere else to shower.

"You're the worst roommate *ever*, I think," I tell her, shaking my head. I should just be paying the landlord directly, but since I'm only subleasing to Zelda, I'm not on the lease, and the landlord doesn't want it to fuck with his taxes.

If I didn't need an apartment that was dirt cheap, I would move out, but I'm paying a criminally low amount for my child's shoebox in a shipping container-sized apartment. I'm not going to let Zelda and her forgetfulness smoke me out of here.

"I think a hit would help you relax. You're always so uptight," she offers the bowl in my direction again and my eyebrow actually twitches.

"No, thank you." I turn on my heel and go back to my room to towel off, glad that I already have texts back from the best people in my life.

I send one last text and sag in relief at the immediate response and agreement. Quickly, I pack my stuff up and head for the subway, grateful I have friends who are ready to jump in.

After waving to Elia's doorman, Benji, I take the elevator up to their apartment, and I visualize. I visualize myself being able to live in an apartment like this in five years. It's a beautiful dream, one I don't think I'll be able to achieve between my loans and wanting to help my parents with their mortgage.

The financial weight weighs on me. I know without a shadow of a doubt that my parents would not be in their position if it wasn't for me. Granted, I'm not the reason both my parents lost their jobs, but I am the reason they have two mortgages on their house. It's because they couldn't say no to me. Not for all the summer enrichment programs I did in high school and SAT tutors to ensure I got good grades and many extracurriculars for my college applications. They didn't say no when I asked for skiing lessons because all my friends were going to Killington for a weekend. They gave me the money for my sorority, for clubs, and for studying abroad.

I probably would have gone on willfully ignorant of their financial situation if their company hadn't made such a public exit from the town. I caught my mom wine-drunk one night, and she cried to me that they had no idea how they were going to keep their house.

My head hits the wall of the elevator, and I sigh. My mom's looking, trying to find other jobs as a secretary, but she's not the most technologically literate, and when she's applying against these twenty-two-year-old babies who can toggle from document to document without their hands leaving their keyboards, she doesn't stand a chance. Not only are they more proficient, but they're cheaper too.

My dad's skillset as a shipping room manager leaves him a little pigeon-holed because of his age. After a work accident left him with chronic back pain a few years ago, he was on light-duty restrictions, which makes it hard for him to find something with equal pay that's just as understanding of his pain. They say they can't discriminate based on age, but of course, companies are going to want to hire stronger, younger employees capable of doing more for a longer amount of time. My parents' severance only got them so far, and they decided to involve their daughter with a degree in finance well after that money was spent.

So, I send them money, as much as I can spare. I'll continue to put the bare minimum down on my loans, which will keep accruing more and more debt, until I'm sure my parents are in a good space financially. I'll give them my bonuses until they're stable, and then I'll take a look at my own living situation and hopefully find some way to get myself out of the hovel I live in.

The elevator opens, and Elia already has the door open, a smile on her face.

"I figured when you asked about needing our shower that Zelda didn't pay rent again?"

"No, I think she's paying the rent, but when she doesn't also pay for electricity, he cuts the power to the unit. I'm pretty sure that's illegal, but I'm not on the lease."

"It is definitely illegal," Vivian confirms from the couch where she has not only one but two of Elia's cats sleeping on her lap.

"Still not on the lease to do anything about it," I point out.

Ainsley saunters out of the guest bathroom, and I can't stop the smile that hits my face. I drop my stuff on the island and rush over, dropping to my knees in front of her.

"And how is my baby niece or nephew doing today?!" I say, not to Ainsley, but to her itty bitty bump that's just starting to show. She's hardly pregnant, possibly still in her first trimester if I did things like keep track of when in my life I am.

"They are a menace, but go shower. I heard you had no hot water."

I give Elia an accusatory glare. "I only texted *you*."

"We were all already here post-brunch," Vivian points out. "Not her fault you ditched us today, though I'm wondering if you have a good reason for that?" There is a smile in my friend's voice as she continues to stroke Mochi.

"What makes you think that?" I ask defensively.

Ainsley flicks at a raw spot on my neck. "You have beard burn. Shower, then I'm going to make you sing like a canary."

Elia shrugs. "Charlie took the hint and went golfing with Chad, Walt, and Ken. You are in safe company to tell us all about why you're looking so relaxed."

"Okay, well, let me shower first, and then I'll let my story loose, promise."

They let me slip into the guest room where I stay when I'm watching the cats while Charlie and Elia travel. Already laid out on the bed are three different outfit options. Elia has placed a strapless black jumpsuit, a yellow sundress, and a white linen skirt with a black crop top.

I'm quick in the shower, focusing on *all* the shaving. There is so much primping that I want to do, but I pause while the conditioner sits in my hair as I smooth a second helping of shaving cream on my legs so I can hit them again with another swipe for a closer shave.

I stop because Josh liked me with a big old stain on my shirt. He liked me today with my T-shirt and no bra. I don't *need* to primp and shave for him, but I want to. I want to get gussied up for him. I want to put in the effort for him to know that I'm trying. I may not be able to go Dutch on our date to show him I'm just as invested, but I can put the effort into how I look for now.

When I emerge, my hair is up in a towel, and I'm wearing the tank top I showed up in and the red thong I packed for the date.

"I don't know what to wear," I whine.

Three heads swivel to me.

Ainsley pops an antacid in her mouth before chugging some water. "Well, let's start with what happened today, and then we will get to the appropriate attire."

I fill them in on the last two weeks, from meeting Josh to today, and then lunch with the two orgasms he gave me on his desk.

"Ohh, an office romance. How tawdry," Elia teases, walking back into the room with three wine glasses.

"I mean, it's not an office romance. I wouldn't call it a romance, and like, sure, it started in an office, but we don't work together, so I hardly think that counts."

Vivian, who had been lifting her wine glass to her mouth, pauses and levels me with a look. "It is absolutely an office romance regardless of what you're trying to project right now. You fucked on his *desk*. If that doesn't say office romance, I don't know what does."

I purse my lips. "I think fucking on his desk during business hours would make it count."

Vivian lifts her brows. "You're in investment banking. Every hour is business hours."

"That statement is rude and correct, but it doesn't change that I don't like it."

"Can we focus on the whole face-fucking thing?" Ainsley asks. "The man, who is a superior to you, got on his knees and let you ride his face? Right there. And then he sat bare-assed and sweaty on his desk chair..." Ainsley trails off, and we all look at her waiting for her to finish her thought.

"The man what...?" Vivian leads.

"The man is obviously a keeper. I mean, I've fucked a few FiDi fuckboys in my heyday, and not one of them would go to their knees for a woman." Elia opens her mouth, but Ainsley shakes her head. "Before you say it, Charlie was *never* a fuckboy. Charlie is a serial monogamist. He went from serious relationship to serious relationship. Sleeping with Taryn was an aberration."

We all scrunch up our noses. "Actually, we were dating for, like, six months, but that's *not* the point, and it's old news. Josh... I mean, we haven't talked much, but he seems like a good guy."

"He has to be if you're giving up working hours to go on not one but two dates on the same day with him," Elia teases.

"It's not like I blow you guys off a ton for work."

"All the time," Elia confirms at the same time Vivian says, "Constantly."

"This is the third brunch in a row since I got back together with Ken," Ainsley says. "I don't blame you. You've got a monster job, but you've been a little absent lately."

"Et tu, brute?" I scowl at all three of them.

"Listen, we say this as your friends and as former workaholics. I'm glad you have this date, and you should get out there and date more. Didn't you say someone else at your office asked you out?" Vivian says.

The reminder of Eric makes me drop my head back, causing the towel to fall off it. "Yes, and I told him I have strictly a no office relationships policy."

"Why would you say something as stupid as that?" Ainsley asks. "You basically live in your office. How else are you going to date? And even if you don't want to date, how else are you going to find someone to fuck?" Ainsley shoves a cracker into her mouth and then rubs her stomach.

"First of all, I don't have to explain anything." I stomp my feet in a mock tantrum. "What am I going to wear?! I don't think anything you set out will work. He said to dress up."

"Did you bring any of your own clothes?" Vivian asks, setting her empty wine glass down. Even though it's illegal, she moves the sleeping cat off her lap to come see what the options are.

"Told you finance bros like to show off," Ainsley says, pushing to her feet.

"I don't think he's trying to show off." No, that doesn't feel like Josh. It feels more like he wants to do something nice.

"Well, come along." Elia beckons us into her master bedroom and then into their shared walk-in closet. Elia's clothes are busting at the seams, while Charlie's side even looks a little cluttered. She shrugs sheepishly. "I keep my out-of-season clothes in the guest room."

"Don't you think you're outgrowing this place? It's basically Charlie's bachelor pad," Ainsley says, dropping onto a bench.

This closet is literally the size of my apartment, and I can't help it; a flash of jealous rage passes through me. My friends are so good to me, and they don't deserve for me to feel like this, but it's hard not to when they have so much, and I'm scraping by with a roommate who doesn't pay the rent. I know if I asked for help, they would give it in a heartbeat. Elia has offered to even have me move in with them, but I can't accept that.

There is an awkward difference between the amount of help I'm willing to accept and the base jealousy that courses through me at such opulent wealth. You would think that I would be used to it, going to college with kids who drove around brand new Beemers not built for New Hampshire winters. Parents with mommies and daddies who would donate a new wing to the gym to get little Johnny out of trouble.

I don't hold it against my friends, and I'm grateful for their every kindness, like letting me crash here to watch their cats while they travel or use their hot water before a date.

I let my friends dress me like a doll. It's only fair. Once upon a time, we did the same to Elia before the gala that Charlie and Ainsley went to with their parents. Ultimately, we decide on a tight emerald green dress with a keyhole cut where the cleavage goes.

"I don't think I can fill this out," I say, gesturing to the flat of my sternum.

Ainsley steps up a sleeve of crackers in her hand and points a stern finger in my face. "First, we don't use that sort of language on Barbie.com. We love bodies of all shapes and sizes, and I can read your subtext. Second, it's all about what you do with the goods you *do* have. I don't know who got it in your head that all you have are mosquito-bite tits, but they're wrong. And, honestly, even if you did? Who cares?"

Ainsley sticks a cracker in her mouth before handing off the sleeve to Vivian. She's methodical as she opens drawers, looking for something.

"If you tell me what you're looking for, I can help you find it," Elia offers.

"Ah, but then I wouldn't find this." Ainsley turns around with a giant purple dildo and vibrator and waves it at our friend, who is turning violent shades of scarlet. "This is a little far from the bed, is it not? You need it closer at hand." She turns around and puts it back where she found it without another comment. "I am looking for...These!"

She has two things that look like chicken cutlets in her hand that I'm familiar with only because I've seen *Miss Congeniality*. It's because of that movie that I know what's coming.

Vivian looks amused as she stands in the doorway, a refreshed glass of wine in her hand. Ainsley unzips the back of the dress, baring my breasts to the room before she uses the silicone to force my breasts forward on both sides. With careful maneuvering, she zips me back in and turns me toward the mirror.

"Tada!" She flourishes her hands at me like she's some sort of magician.

"Isn't this... I don't know, false advertisement?" I ask, poking at the fleshy orbs.

"Hardly," Ainsley scoffs, tugging at the middle part so the hem rises a little.

"Besides, hasn't he already seen your breasts?" Elia chimes.

"I vaguely remember a promise to cum all over them." Vivian cackles from the door.

"Why am I friends with you lot, anyway?"

"Because who else is going to remind you that you're a ball-busting rockstar and that you are gorgeous even when you can't see it yourself? Now, sit your ass down. These fake lashes aren't going to apply themselves," Ainsley orders.

"You just said it yourself. She's gorgeous already. She doesn't need fake lashes. Let the poor girl do her usual makeup," Vivian says, giving me a wink.

Ainsley sucks her lower lip into her mouth, and I think I can see tears glistening in her eyes. "Okay." Her voice is so small that we all give Vivian a look. I haven't gotten to spend much time around my newly pregnant friend, so I'm only guessing this is just part of the hormones.

"Ainsley," Vivian slouches.

"No, no, it's okay. I'm fine. It's just *hormones.* Ken came home from the bar to find me crying over a video of ducks in raincoats that was just so *cute* and *stupid*. They're *ducks;* their feathers are meant to get wet. But then the baby one came over, and I was just thinking about my little baby." She breaks off, the tears coming in earnest. We all move to comfort her, but she throws her hands up to stop us, and we all halt in our tracks. "*No!* This will pass. We need to get Taryn ready for her hot date."

"I really have time. We were going to meet at eight," I hedge.

"Meet where?" Ainsley asks, perking up, tears forgotten. She grabs the crackers from Vivian and pops another in her mouth.

"He didn't say. He just said that I could let him know where we could meet."

"Let him pick you up here," Elia suggests.

"No, I don't *live* here, in case you've forgotten, and if you want to talk about false advertising, letting him think I live here would totally do that," I remind them.

"I'm going to echo Ainsley: who gives a shit? He works with

you. He knows roughly how much you make. Who cares if he thinks you live here or in Westchester or in Jersey or in your current apartment? You are stressing, and I get that, but, babes, you've already let him lick your pussy. You're past the awkward stage."

I plop onto the bench and look up at them. "But doesn't that make it more awkward like...you know how I taste, but I don't know your middle name and if you even have one."

"Can't be more awkward than waking up with no memory and moving in with the guy who hit you," Elia chirps.

"Or fucking a guy and his wife only to find out that they were your new clients for divorce."

Vivian's face distorts for a second. "Hold, please." She whips her phone from her pocket. "What do you want? It is a Saturday, and this is my personal number." She pauses while listening to the person on the other end of the call. "You are welcome to *try* to move the closing, but then I'll be sending you a Time is of the Essence letter, and then you can explain to your client why you cost them fifteen million dollars in a deposit after you ignore my TOE letter. You and your client have been pulling this shit for the last eight months, and my client is tired of it, and frankly, so am *I*. So, call your grandma back and say sorry you have to miss her party, but you have to work. You've been bullying me for long enough, and I'm done, Knox. I want this file done, and I never want to hear from you *again*." She hangs up the phone and lets out a calming breath before turning to look at us. "It's a lot more satisfying when I'm in my office, and I can slam my phone down on him. I'm okay, really." She takes another calming breath before finishing her wine.

"When are you going to hate-fuck?" Ainsley asks, batting her big eyes at Vivian innocently.

"There will be no hate-fucking Knox Benedict. He's a royal pain in my ass, and the sooner I never have to speak to him again, the better. Anyway, this isn't about me." But we all hear her phone vibrating in her pocket. Her eyes widen with disbelief, and Elia goes over and extracts Vivian's phone before rejecting the call.

"I vote you just have him pick you up here. The whole point is it's a *date*. You're supposed to talk to each other and get to know one another anyway. Sure, Charlie and I cheated because we spent all our time together, so by virtue of that, we had to get to know each other, but it's just a date. You're not marrying the guy," Elia points out.

Vivian's phone goes off again, but this time we ignore it.

"This is why I hate dating. I'm too busy to consider each and every word I say. I have to be careful enough when I'm at work, let alone when I have a few precious hours to myself."

"Why do you think I'm still not dating?" Vivian asks.

"Because you're twice burned," Elia volunteers, and Vivian shoves her.

"Because you're waiting for Knox to punish that pussy for hanging up on him?" Ainsley suggests a grin on her face.

"Enough about sleeping with Knox–hard limit, I'm not kidding."

"Got it, sorry. I won't mention it again," Ainsley rushes to apologize, even as tears spring to her eyes.

"Ainsley," Vivian says, exasperated.

"No, no, I'm okay. It's just the hormones. You know I'm tougher than that." Ainsley opens her eyes wide as she fans them with her hands.

Since I left my laptop at my apartment, and I'm not going to sit here and work while I can spend some time with my friends, I grab my phone, which rests next to my glass of wine, and shoot off a text before I can change my mind. I'll have Josh pick me up here.

I catch up with my friends, getting to hear where Charlie and Elia have planned for their next trip and how Ainsley is feeling about her new job and pregnancy.

We're not spending a long amount of time together, but it's long enough that I can feel some of the tension ease from my body. Yes, I have some concerns about work, a few things that I don't love being left in limbo, but Josh was right. Today was meant to be a no-work day, anyway. Let Darren and Eric figure it out.

Under the guise of leaving at the same time, the three of them come downstairs, trying to wait to see Josh, but I shoo them away. Only Elia remains.

"I'm legitimately waiting for my husband." She gives me an innocent smile that I see right through.

"Uh-huh. Sure, and the Pope is a stripper."

"You don't know his private life." A grin cracks Elia's face, and she runs away from me. The sound of metal hitting the lobby floor has me turning around to see a sweat-glistened Charlie catch his wife as she jumps into his arms.

"I was just gone for a few hours." He laughs before kissing her. They're so cute it's gross.

His golf clubs are all over the floor, and once he sets her down, they both gather his clubs up.

"Good to see you, Chucky," I say, giving him a little finger wave.

"What's the matter? You don't want to give me a big hug too?" Charlie moves in for a hug, but his wife puts a hand on his chest.

"She has a *date*. No getting her all sweaty."

"You didn't seem to mind," he points out to her but turns his appraising gaze on me. "A date, huh? Who is the lucky guy?"

"No one you know," I tell him, but it could very well be that Charlie does know Josh. Charlie didn't have to cut his teeth on investment banking before jumping into private equity, but that was thanks to good old-fashioned nepotism.

"Sure. Is he coming to pick you up here?"

My phone buzzes in my hand, and I'm glad to be saved by the bell.

"Nope, that's my ride!" I move toward the lobby doors, but then Josh walks through them. I know he doesn't see me right away because his gaze is scanning all the faces, and I prefer it this way because I get to see that first moment when he does find me.

It's subtle, the change in his face. His eyes brighten, widening as he looks me over from head to toe. We decided to put my hair up in a bun with tendrils framing my face. Thankfully, black pumps go with just about everything, so I had those myself. Let's just hope these heels don't snap.

A smile splits his face as he takes a step forward, but he hesitates when he sees Charlie and Elia. Unsure of what else to do, I wave at him, and he continues walking toward us.

Charlie turns around and sees Josh, and I see the flicker of recognition on both faces. I don't think I like that at all.

"If it isn't the most disappointing Breckinridge. You know your father is still cursing having contributed DNA to your birth?"

"Is that so, Joshua? I find that interesting because your dad called me on Father's Day asking when I would be sending him a card since at least I managed to live up to his expectations."

For a second, I'm afraid they're going to come to blows and that this will be the end of whatever budding feelings were growing between Josh and me because things might be electric between us, but I've known Charlie longer, and my friends are not negotiable.

There is a tense moment before both men crack a smile and do that stupid bro hug.

"Long time no see. I heard since the last time I saw you that you went and got married! My dad took great pleasure in telling your dad all about it at lunch."

"You were at that lunch?" Charlie's stance widens as he crosses his arms, leaving Elia and me completely forgotten.

"It was my quarterly tribute to the old man. Your dad just happened to be at the restaurant. My dad enjoyed being able to show him up with that, at least."

"Who knew there was a competition to be the least worst father? Sorry, forgive my manners. This is my wife, Elia. And it seems you already know our friend Taryn. This is Josh. Our dads have worked together for years. Josh was supposed to be the other heir apparent but went into I-Banking instead of private equity just to spite his father. If only I had been so smart."

"It's a pleasure to meet you, Elia, but I have reservations for dinner with Taryn. We should make time to catch up soon."

Elia claps, "Oh! Like a double date! I love that!"

"We'll make plans for sure, but first, let me convince Taryn I'm worth a second date." The charmer that he is, Josh gives Elia a wink and then offers his arm to me. "Our chariot awaits."

I slide my arm in with his and wave over my shoulder at my friends. "Tell me you are not driving in New York City," I say to Josh. "I don't care how much money you have, driving is such a waste of time."

Josh coughs into his hand as we step up to a black town car. "You really know how to cut a man off at the knees. No, *I'm* not driving, but once you told me where I was picking you up, I knew it was going to be easier to have a town car take us across town."

He opens the door, guiding me in before walking around and climbing in himself. He's clearly already communicated to the driver where we're going because the driver easily navigates away from the curb.

"I still think driving in this city is stupid."

He quirks a brow. "So, you *never* drive?"

"Well, when it's late, I'll get a PickMeUp! or use one of the company cars and expense it, but I usually either walk or take the subway."

He seems to consider that. "Why won't you drive?"

"Too many streets are shut down all the time. Too many cars. Too many pedestrians. I was running late one day and thought, hey I'll take a PickMeUp! to work so I won't be late. Then my car got into a fight with a bike messenger, and guess what? I was late."

"I saw that coming."

"I bet you did." I relax into the seat and study him, glad I don't have to wear heels on the subway for all my bluster.

"So, how do you know Charlie and Elia?" he asks.

"I actually went to college with Charlie, and then I met his wife through him. She's really sweet, and he's a great guy. You're a little older than us, right? Or is that impolite?"

Josh snorts. "I don't think it's impolite, but yeah, I'm a few years older than Charlie. He was a snot-nosed kid that my dad would tell me to befriend because he was friends with Charlie's dad. Eventually, he got a personality, and we became actual friends."

"How old are you?" I ask. I know he's on track to be the youngest Executive Vice President in our company.

"I'm thirty-eight, just a touch older than you. Is that a problem?" He studies me in the interim.

"Not even a little bit. We're adults. I don't have a problem with age gaps outside the truly icky, like adults and children."

"Good," he says with a smile.

I give him a smile back. "Good."

He slides his hand in with mine, and we hold hands the rest of the way to the restaurant.

Seven

HE'S TAKING me to one of the most exclusive restaurants in New York City. It's owned by a retired chef who, if the rumors are to be believed, came out of retirement because his wife was tired of having him home. So, the compromise is that he opens every day for one dinner service with thirty tables. He's reportedly very selective about who gets a table because he doesn't want any problems like people sending their plates back or asking for dietary accommodations.

"I confirmed that the menu tonight has no shellfish. There's actually no fish on the menu at all this evening," Josh says, holding the door open for me.

The room is large enough that people can be sitting apart from each other. I glance around and think I see a few celebrities enjoying glasses of wine and cocktails.

"Thank you for that," I whisper to him, afraid to disturb the peaceful ambiance created by carefully placed candles and lights.

After giving the host our name, we're led to a table in the corner. It's small, but it gives us space to look out at the room. It's more intimate than I expected. The booth is rounded, forcing us to sit side by side instead of facing one another.

There is no ordering tonight, not even wine. I don't know how much this costs, but I can't imagine being able to afford it. I can't even offer to go Dutch, but something tells me that Josh would see that as an insult. The idea of letting him pay for anything makes me twitch, like when he ran away with the book I wanted last weekend or covered the ice cream while I was ordering mine. Both of those things made it feel like too much of a date. But tonight is technically a date, so I guess I can be okay with it.

I squirm in my seat.

"Did I mention you look stunning tonight?"

"Really? I feel a little underdressed." Especially when I know for certain that's an Oscar-winning actress walking past our table to the bathroom.

"Tell me more about you, and stop worrying about everyone else."

I look up at him, twisting a little so I can face him. "That's very easy for you to say. I'm still trying to feel like I can fit into this world. I didn't grow up the way that you and Charlie did. My parents own an old farmhouse out in the suburbs. My mom still drives the same minivan she drove when I was a kid."

"My mom still lives in the same house out on Long Island that I grew up in," Josh tells me." She stayed there because my older sister lives a few blocks away, and she helps with my nieces and nephew. My youngest sister, who is twenty-two, still lives at home despite my dad offering her an apartment. I know you think I lived this silver-spoon life, but if you give me a chance, if you let me show you who I am, not just who I show to the world, I promise you might actually like me."

"I like you, probably a lot more than I should," I confess.

His smile feels soft and private, meant just for me. "So do I."

"Tell me about your family."

"Alright, I have four, technically five, sisters. My youngest sister, Gigi, was a last-ditch effort to save my parents' marriage, or was an accident in the midst of their divorce. My oldest sister,

Connie, has three monsters, my nieces and nephew, who are spoiled rotten. I love them so much, but they're a perfect case of like and love not being the same thing, and maybe that makes me sound callous and hateful, but my nephew, who is nine, cut his little sister's hair right before her school picture and again the night before her dance recital. She's seven and retaliates by regularly destroying his cell phone and tattling on him for the dirty mags he manages to buy. The youngest is just a baby still, so thankfully, not getting into too much trouble."

"I had no idea they still printed those," I say with a laugh.

"I didn't either, but I guess since his sister is always destroying his stuff, he has to get it from somewhere."

"They sound awful. I'm sorry."

The server deposits our first round of wine and a starter.

"They really are, and my sister and her husband just indulge them. Like, 'Oh, Canada microwaved your cell phone and nearly burnt the house down? Here is a new one. And he'll be like, "Oh, Tennessee cut your hair so now you have to go to the dance recital with a bald patch? Have a new American Girl Doll.' No punishment for either of them."

"Wait, their names are Canada and Tennessee?" I ask, enthralled.

"Yep, named for the place of their conception, which is a thing I always wanted to know about my sister and her husband. Their youngest is named Nolita."

I can't help but laugh, and I'm graced with a responding smile.

"Tell me more about this minivan."

"Well, it was top of the line when I was eight, one of the first cars to have those push-button closers. My dad was so proud when he got it for my mom, but he made the mistake of imitating all those holiday car commercials."

"Yeah? What's that?"

"He made a major financial investment without talking to his partner. I guess he expected it to be like the car commercials. Get a big hug, maybe some nookie later, but my mom turned as red as the giant bow sitting on the car, and she slammed the front door in his face."

"Ouch."

"Yes, and, you know, cars depreciate in value as soon as you drive them off the lot and without there being something catastrophically wrong with it, there really aren't any returns, so she had to get over it. My dad did sleep on the couch for a few weeks after that. And he couldn't even get her jewelry to make up for it because he spent all his gift money on the car."

"She forgave him, though?"

"Eventually. There was groveling. I was young, so I don't remember it clearly, but they always had a solid relationship. Needless to say, he never bought her another car without her permission, and she refuses to get rid of the old boat because it was a gift, so she can't be expected to give it up."

"Wow, he really walked into that one." Josh laughs as our first course and second round of wine are delivered.

"Indeed he did. It's got to be over twenty years old at this point. I wish they would just replace it already." My smile fades as I think about why they can't replace the old clunker that probably needs a new transmission.

Josh takes my chin in his hand and turns my head to look at him. "Where did you just go?"

"Nowhere. It's not a big deal. I just miss my parents. I don't get to see them often with my work schedule, even though they're just outside the city. They live fifteen minutes from the GW Bridge on a good day."

"They must be proud. Two Ivy League degrees and a prestigious job at one of the top investment banks in New York City."

"That doesn't mean much to them. I mean, obviously they're glad I'm succeeding, but it wouldn't have mattered to them if I went to a state school or to an Ivy League school. To them, education is education."

"They sound incredible."

"They really are."

The rest of the date passes with ease. The food is amazing. The conversation is terrific, flowing from similar college experiences to travel to our shared love of campy thriller movies. He tells me more about having so many sisters, and I regale him with more of my father's well-meaning blunders. By the time we get to dessert, his hand rests on my thigh, and I love the proprietary feel it evokes.

No check is delivered. Josh just confirms I'm done, and he rises, offering me his arm.

"What do you say we take a walk and burn some of these calories off?"

I stand up and move into his space. "I have a better idea of how we can burn these calories."

Josh's hands rest on my hips, and he tugs me even closer. "I have the same idea but, treasure, I need to take a walk first. Otherwise, I'm afraid the first time I'm in that pussy will be a disappointment to us both."

He's whispering directly in my ear, and it makes my body tremble with excitement.

"Then, by all means...lead the way."

When we exit the restaurant, Columbus Circle is a hotbed of activity. Tourists are still filtering in and out of Central Park while darkness settles over the city like a blanket. It does nothing to quash the overwhelming heat, and maybe that is why there are still so many people out and about. They have emerged, seeking something to do now that the oppressive sun has moved on to another part of the world.

We walk along Central Park West, headed uptown. It's a quiet walk, and I'm grateful because if I had to walk and digest and talk at the same time, I might throw up all the delicious food we ate. I expected our meals to be sparse the way that high-end meals are. I expected it to be all about the presentation and less about the quantity. Not that I could afford it, but Ainsley and the rest of my friends have told me enough about places like this for me to think I knew what I was getting into.

This restaurant was not like that. We had a dozen courses, each paired with a half glass of wine, and there was a decent amount of food on each plate. I'm also super thankful for the walk because I want to be able to have hot, acrobatic sex with Josh, and I know that if I'm too full, that won't happen.

I wonder briefly what it could be like for us to be more with regular dates where we end the night going home and just enjoying each other's company. I find the more I talk to Josh, the more I like the sound of his voice and the stories he has to tell. There's more than just sexual chemistry between us, and I don't know if I dare to imagine a world where we could freely explore it.

We turn when we get up into the 90s, and we're faced with a row of gorgeous townhomes. I've been letting Josh lead the way the whole time, but now I'm curious. Does he have a place along the water?

We're barely half a block in when he stops at a brownstone and opens the small iron gate, leading me up the stairs. I pause a second, looking up at the space, somewhat surprised. I expected him to have some hot bachelor pad with sprawling views of New York City. I didn't expect some a homey place. I mean, Ainsley has been looking at the brownstones around here because she's about to light all of Ken's stuff on fire.

"Did you change your mind?" Josh asks as he pushes the front door open. He puts his hands in his pockets, watching me.

"No, this just isn't what I expected for you."

"Did you expect me to fuck you against a window looking out

on the city in one of those garish pencil buildings on billionaire's row?"

I bite my lip, and he laughs. "Well, maybe. Am I that transparent?" I walk close to him and pause on the step below him.

He withdraws his hands from his pockets and runs them down my face as he looks into my eyes. It's such a tender thing that I'm glad it's not my turn to say anything because it takes my breath away.

"No, not that transparent, but it's what I would expect from most assholes who work on Wall Street. But if you're going to learn only one thing about me, I want it to be that I'm not like most finance bros." He kisses my forehead, then the tip of my nose, before giving me the softest brush on my lips. "Come get the grand tour."

He walks me through the whole building from top to bottom, showing me each and every room, including guest rooms and a second living space on the second floor. The whole third floor is his bedroom space, which feels so gluttonous that I sort of want to scream. It's not until he shows me his closet that I realize my entire apartment could fit in the space he has dedicated to his closet and bathroom.

"This is..." I do a full circle to get a complete look at the room. "Not enough space if you ever want a woman to move in here. You're using all of the available closet space." I gesture to the racks and racks of clothes and shoes. At the center of the closet is a dresser with about forty watches, including at least three Rolexes, and I don't even want to consider what other brands.

He tosses his head back as he laughs. "I'll be honest, I need to clear about eighty percent of these clothes out, and my sisters rail on me about it all the time."

"Why haven't you?" I ask, running a finger along the top of the dresser. I'm not surprised there is no dust.

"If I only had time," he says, tapping on the watch display.

"That was *awful*," I tell him, leaning my back against the dresser in an open invitation.

Josh takes it, moving so he can brace one hand on either side of me. "But it got you to smile."

I lean in to kiss him, but he pulls back abruptly, and I'm confused. He offers me his hand and leads from his bedroom, only adding to my confusion.

"I haven't even shown you the best part."

"Are you about to take me to your red room of pain?"

Josh laughs again, leading the way downstairs. He stops when he gets to the bottom and looks up at me. "Would that make you change your mind about us?"

"Us?" I ask, not daring to hope.

"I would like there to be an us. An us that goes on dates that end with kissing and more. I would like there to be nights where you're naked and under me and nights where you sleep by my side."

"Do you want to...*date* me?" I'm unable to keep the smile from my face and voice. The idea of dating at thirty feels like such a weird concept. You have a boyfriend and girlfriend when you're in high school or college, but in your twenties and thirties, you date around. The idea of being his girlfriend, being the girl that this man, who I know has such little time to himself, would choose to spend that free time with, is invigorating. He looks vulnerable looking up at me, and damn it, my heart melts when he nods.

"Yes, I'm not getting younger, and maybe once upon a time, I would have felt you out a little more first after feeling you up a lot, but I like you, and I'm not interested in wasting either of our time if this isn't something you're interested in pursuing."

I appreciate his directness. I owe him at least a little candidness in return.

"I like you too and want to get to know you further." Now is the moment I should tell him that I'm worried about the possible impact that a relationship with him would entail for me professionally. The thought of how this could impact my career makes my stomach swoop. I know what happens to women who date in the office. They're seen as loose and easy. If the women pick the right guy to fuck, it means promotions and raises as long as they keep putting out, but once they stop, suddenly their performance reviews tank too. I don't think Josh is that type of man. If I did think that, I wouldn't be here with him. But I could be seen as sleeping around to get ahead, and since Josh has no sway in my review process, I would fall into the latter group of women who are made an example of by *not* getting promoted. I can't let my career suffer, not when my parents are counting on me to help them financially. They've already sacrificed so much for me. "But if we're going to be a thing, we can't be a thing in the office."

His brow furrows. "Why not? Our firm doesn't have an anti-fraternization policy. They know the only place we will ever meet someone is in the office."

"And honestly? Not having that policy in place is a mistake. There are way too many possible pitfalls with it. Regardless, I don't want people to see us together and think that I'm sleeping my way up."

"But you're not even in my line of business. We're never going to work together."

I move to take a step back up the stairs. "This is a boundary for me, and if it's not one that you can follow, then I don't see why we should bother moving forward."

He hooks his arms around my waist, lifting me off the stairs so I have to lean into him, even if it means pressing my breasts against his face. Because he's not a thirteen-year-old boy, he doesn't take the moment to motorboat me. Instead, he sets me down on the floor.

"Understood, but only while we figure this out. If we become serious that this is something that's going to stick, I don't like the idea of hiding. It feels like there's something we should be ashamed of, and I'm not ashamed of you, Taryn Robins. My dad kept all his affairs and women in the office a secret, and I don't want to be like him."

"Deal, but it's something we have to talk about first before going public."

"Deal," he agrees readily.

"Great. Now, take me to your red room of pain."

He gives me a deadpan look. "You never answered if that was a problem for you."

I stand up a little taller, thinking over his words. "No, it wouldn't be, but is that where you're taking me?"

"That's good to know. I don't want you to be my Sub. There will be no spankings or belting in your future."

"And if I ask for it?"

His gaze goes molten, and I think my panties burst into flames. Slowly, Josh walks me backward until I hit the wall behind me.

"Then I will have no choice but to be a slave to my mistress and give her what she wants. Is that something you like? Do you want me to take all the power out of these pretty little hands?" He slides his hands in with mine, bringing them above my head to pin them against the wall by the wrist.

My breath is coming out in pants as he slowly drags his hand down my side, stopping to roughly grab my breast. I moan at the contact, arching up and into him. Eyes dancing with delight, he lowers his mouth over mine, but he doesn't kiss me. He's not holding me hard or being rough with me by any stretch of the imagination, but it makes my pussy clench with need.

"I didn't hear an answer, treasure."

Without breaking eye contact, I pivot us using my body so we roll along the wall. Josh moves effortlessly with me, releasing my wrists as soon as I take that first step. Now, his back is against the wall while his hands rest on my hips. I reach for his belt and slowly unbuckle it, letting the sound fill the tension between us.

I slowly slide his belt through each rung of the loops until it's free in my hand, and I snap the sides together before dropping it to the side.

"Maybe sometimes. Maybe sometimes I want you to be rough with me and hold me down as you take what you want from my body. But sometimes..." I undo his button, then slowly drag his zipper down so we hear the release of each zipper tooth before I can't go any further. It's torture for me as much as it is for him until I slide my hand into his boxers, moaning as I feel the hard length of his dick in my hand. "Sometimes, I want to make you a mess. I want you to be the one begging to come."

I drop to my knees before him, gazing up at him through my lashes. He looks like he's struggling to remember his name, let alone the English language. I can't help but lick my lips as I stare at the bulge that's eye level.

What he's packing isn't going to be a surprise, but as I tug his pants and boxers down just enough that they settle on his tree-trunk thighs, I can't help but swallow thickly at the sight of his red, swollen cock. It was one thing to watch him jerk himself off all over me, but it's going to be another thing to take it into my mouth and let it abuse my throat because that *is* what I want. I want him to fuck my face like he's going to fuck me, hard and merciless, leaving me a teary mess.

Tentatively, I lick the underside of his shaft right up to his piercing, where I swirl my tongue around the metal, laughing a little when I hear his head hit the wall, followed by his fist.

"I can think of something better you can do with your hand." I grip his cock and give it a slow stroke as I feel him out.

"Yeah? What's that?" he asks, his voice so low and gruff I can barely hear him.

"You can use it to pull my hair while you fuck my face until you can't tell if it's tears, drool, or cum streaming down my face."

"Fucking Christ, Taryn," he says, threading his hand into my hair.

"No, I'd rather be fucking you."

His chuckle is the last coherent sound he makes before I take him into my mouth all the way, testing how far down his shaft I can get before he hits the back of my throat.

It's all the way.

I've always been told I have a big mouth, but most guys don't realize how true that is.

"If I get too rough, tap my leg, and I'll stop." It's the only warning I get before he shifts his hips back and then thrusts forward, bumping the back of my throat. It causes tears to well in my eyes, but I don't dare tap his leg.

I like it a little rough, but I like being a little rough back. I also like being held and cherished and having someone make love to me like I matter and I'm not just a vessel. I'm in a quandary of desire, but right now, all that matters is that I can feel the tears running down my cheeks and the spit on my chin as I take it, take every thrust.

I move my hands to his ass so I can feel the power he uses as he moves into me. It makes me want a toy to play with myself while I play with him. I want to reach between my legs and strum my clit until I'm choking on my orgasm and his cock at the same time, but how he's abusing my mouth right now, I don't dare.

"I'm going to come, Taryn, and it's up to you if you're going to swallow it down like a good girl or if I'm going to come on your pretty face or your perfect tits. Grab my ass if you want to swallow, or snap if you want me to come on your face. If you want me to paint your tits with my cum, squeeze my balls."

Maybe another night, when I'm not wearing someone else's dress, I'll let him cover me in cum. I use both hands to grab his ass and hold him in when he starts to convulse while I swallow every drop he gives me.

Josh releases my hair only to grab my shoulders and guide me onto the hardwood floor. It takes me a second to realize that his face is between my thighs, and my panties are tossed somewhere over his shoulder.

I'm already a bomb ready to detonate, and when he licks me nearly from my asshole all the way up to my clit, I cry out, this time fisting my hand in his hair. When he spears me with two fingers, I arch off the floor as my orgasm rips through me.

I moan, unable to think a single coherent thought as I fade into nothing but the feeling of his mouth on me.

When I come down from my orgasm, we're both panting messes on the floor. Josh sits up and helps me into a seated position.

"And to think I didn't even get to my favorite part of the house."

Eight

IT TURNS out his favorite room in the house is a basement theater that he had built out with surround sound and a bar in it. The sound is completely insulated, a fact he's proud of because he loves to watch movies with explosions in them and has yet to get a complaint from his neighbors.

So, while I expected our night to be a full-fledged fuckfest, instead, we spend it on a lush sleeper sofa. The couch is really a glorified bed with a sofa back and armrests. He gets me off two more times, but he still doesn't fuck me. I fall asleep in his arms after another orgasm leaves me boneless and sated in his arms.

Because we're in the basement, I have no idea what time it is when I finally wake up. It's only because Josh is extricating himself from me that I do wake up, and I'm confused because of how dark it is.

"What is it?" I hear him whisper into the phone.

I roll over in his direction, guided only by the brief light from his phone before it goes out again. Rubbing my eyes, I sit up and realize he can't see me either. "I'm up," I whisper to him, not wanting to interrupt his conversation. "You can turn on the light."

I can hear him fumbling with the light switches before a gentle glow around the edges of the room illuminates the space.

He's only in his boxers, and judging by the ache in certain spots on my skin, I slept in the probably way too expensive dress I borrowed from Elia and can only hope I didn't tear it anywhere.

"I can't come pick you up." A pause while the person on the other end of the phone responds. "Not everything is about you. I have a life and things I enjoy doing while not working on weekends. I told you the last time was the last time." Confusion crosses his face, and then he lowers his hand, the home screen bright on his phone. My guess is whoever was on the other end hung up on him.

"Who was that?" I croak, rubbing my eyes a second before remembering that I did my makeup, so I probably just smeared mascara and eyeliner all over my face.

"My baby sister, Gigi. She went to a party in Westchester and wants me to pick her up and take her home."

"Where is home for her?"

"Long Island. Do you have anywhere you need to be today?" he asks, leaning over to cup my cheek.

"Why? Do you need to go get her? I can go home or something," I offer, even though I don't want to do that. I want to stay with him and go get her if that's what he's going to do. I'm already selfish for his time because I know it's so limited.

"No, she's an adult and needs to learn that I'm not going to bail her out all the time."

"It's okay if you want to bail her out."

Josh crosses back to sit beside me. "No, eventually she needs to learn. She has our other sisters to call or, if she's really desperate, our parents. Dad at least still feels guilty about having been fucking his secretary when she was born, so he enables her the worst. I think she doesn't call him because she wants someone to set her straight."

No lie, his father sounds like an awful man.

"Do you still talk to your dad?" I remember him mentioning

that he's had lunch with his dad since Charlie and Elia got married, but I don't know what that entails. Josh sighs long and heavy, and it's the kind of sigh that tells you there is a whole story behind that question. I rush to continue. "You do not have to tell me if you don't want to."

"No, it's just barely seven in the morning, and I want to drink some coffee before we get into it. Do you want to shower first or at least put on comfier clothing? I should have offered before coming down here, but I didn't expect you to see *Anaconda* and get so excited we had to put it on."

"I mean, it's no *Tremors*, but it does in a pinch. Yes, I will take you up on the offer of softer clothes. I'm chaffing in all uncomfortable places."

His lips are soft when he leans forward to kiss me. "We don't want that."

I take the offered shower because the amount of bodily fluids on my body makes me feel a little dirty. Waiting for me in the bedroom is a fresh T-shirt and a pair of sweatpants, and fuck if it doesn't make me swoon for him just a little bit. Apparently, being taken care of is one of my love languages.

When I come downstairs, Josh has similarly changed into something more comfortable, with a pair of basketball shorts slung low on his hips and a t-shirt.

"I asked you for one thing, just *one* thing, Jessica, and you couldn't do it," a voice from Josh's phone whines.

"Don't act like you don't ask me for shit all the time, Gigi. It's always, Josh, can I crash at your place. Josh, can you loan me money? Josh, can you pick me up? Josh, can I borrow your car? So, please, spare me the dramatics. You can always order a PickMeUp!"

"*Jessica*, who is the dramatic one now?"

I'm silent as I listen to what must be a sibling argument. I'm not mad about taking in this view of Josh as he stands beside his stove with his back to me. The oven is on, filling the room with the scent of bacon cooking.

Not wanting to be caught eavesdropping, I make sure the stool I pull out is loud, alerting him to my presence.

Josh whips around, grabbing his phone and taking it off speakerphone just as I hear that same female voice speak. "Who is there with you, Jessica? Did you have sex last night?! Oh, ew, but also, I'm calling mom."

"Don't you dare, Copycat. I'll talk to you later, Gigi." He hangs up the phone and tosses it across the counter, away from me, before advancing toward me.

"Jessica?" I ask, looking for an explanation.

"Do you know how incredible you look in my clothes?"

"Don't think you can distract me with sex," I warn him, even as I tilt my head to the side as he begins to kiss my neck.

"How about I'll tell you, but only if you agree." He scrapes his teeth against my collarbone. I'm thankful he's been careful about only giving me hickeys in places that can't be seen, like all along the insides of my thighs and on my breasts.

"What would you have me agreeing to?"

"I have two tickets to the Met this coming weekend. Think I can convince you to be my date?"

I've never been to the Met, and the idea is enticing, but it has the potential to blow up our whole situation. Still, finding out why his sister called him Jessica might be the right sort of bait.

"What if someone sees?" I turn to look up at him, my pointy chin digging into his chest.

"No one is going to see because no one cares that we're seeing each other."

"Can I think about it?" I offer nervously.

His lips brush the top of my head. "Of course."

"You still have to explain the Jessica thing to me."

He scoffs. "Because I am a consummate gentleman, I will answer your question, but only while I finish cooking, so if you decide to leave while listening, I won't have to see it."

"Sorry, but you're stuck with me," I tell him affectionately.

"We'll see," he says skeptically. He leaves my side to go back to the counter, where he starts dicing a pepper. "I'm only two years younger than my older sister, Connie. She desperately wanted a baby sister and refused to call me Josh or Joshua. For a while, it was Joshwena because she was only two. Eventually, she started calling me Jessica because I was the only boy in a house full of estrogen. As each of my younger sisters got older, the nickname stuck, sort of how Gigi is Copycat because she would copy *everything* we did."

"And so your nickname became Jessica?" I ask with a laugh.

Josh sighs and pulls out a small loaf of challah bread, which he slices with deliberate cuts. "Yes, and if you dare breathe a word of that in the office..." he puts the knife down and leans across the counter toward me, "I will edge you for weeks, and you will never know when I will finally let that pretty pussy come."

I can't stop the startled noise of outrage that escapes as he turns back to what he was doing with a calm expression.

As he puts dirty dishes in the sink, I get up and take over the cleaning. He continues dipping the bread in egg batter and dropping it on the skillet.

"You don't have to do that," he scolds, but I give him a glare and worry only about scrubbing the dirty plates.

"But I want to."

We work peacefully in tandem until breakfast is ready, and we sit down to eat. He's whipped up a French toast benedict and managed to sneak some prosciutto under the eggs. It's decadent in a way that I didn't expect, but I'm not going to complain.

Josh clears his throat. "To answer your earlier question, I do still talk to my dad. As horrible as a husband as he was, he does *try* to be there for us. We don't talk a lot, but maybe once or twice a month I'll call, and we try to get lunch or dinner quarterly. My mom knows but doesn't love it for obvious reasons. She supports us, even if that means having to see him at my sister's weddings."

"I'm guessing your mom knows about your other sister?"

"Yes, she does. That took some navigating, but my mom is a good woman and thankfully doesn't blame Kayleigh for her circumstances."

I can't say I would ever be strong enough to not hold it against someone for being my husband's illegitimate kid, but I hope I never have to find out.

Not wanting to pry any further, I change the subject. "So, you like to cook?" I ask, knowing that even if he doesn't like it, he's certainly good at it.

"My mom was nothing if not determined to send her kids into the world able to fend for themselves. I think she was always frustrated that my dad was always helpless in that regard and would then blame working long hours for why he didn't do things."

"So, all of you know how to cook?"

"No, Imogen is a disaster in the kitchen, and I could never figure out if she was willfully fucking things up for if she really just is that bad, and Gigi never had the focus for it. She's grabbed hot pans and had to go to the emergency room for burns because she just wasn't paying close enough attention."

"Well, if I ever meet your mom, I'll be sure to thank her for making you such a good cook." I push my empty plate away and stand next to him. He places his fork down, turning his hungry gaze on me.

Grabbing his knee, I twist his stool so I can settle myself between his legs. Just as I'm about to kiss him, there is a knock on the door.

I lick my lips and pull my bottom lip into my mouth.

"Ignore it," he instructs before leaning down, but the knock comes again, more insistent this time.

"Joshua James Bartlett, you open this door right now. I know you're home."

"Joshua James?" I ask as he drops his head on my shoulder.

"Looks like you'll get to thank my mom a lot sooner than you probably expected."

"Oh, no. I'm not meeting your mother dressed in your clothes after a night of...*that*."

His gaze heats, and he gives me a lascivious grin. "Oh no? We didn't have sex."

"Just because you didn't penetrate me with your cock does not me what we did last night wasn't sex."

The knocking comes a third time. "You've left me no choice," his mom's cheery voice calls. I hear the sound of keys jangling.

"She has keys to your house?" I whisper-hiss like she might hear. "Do you have like...a back door I can escape?" I start to frantically look around because the morning after is not how I want to meet his mom.

"Yes, she does. Sometimes if I'm out of town or she's out late in the city, she'll stay here because most of the time I'm working late."

I try to escape, but he catches me around the waist and pulls me against him.

"If you don't want to meet her, you don't have to. But you will be meeting her eventually. She'll be a good ally when it comes to my sisters."

"You mean your sisters are worse?" Jesus, how long is she going to take with the keys?

"Much."

The door pushes open and I don't get a choice in the matter anymore. It's almost a relief that I'm just going to meet her now.

I'm so glad I showered because meeting his mom with...no, I can't even think about it.

I turn and find a tall woman standing there, looking at where I'm positioned between her son's legs. One arch eyebrow raises.

She has a full hourglass body that's in well-tailored slacks and a tank top. Her silver and black hair is gathered in a knot on the top of her head.

Josh shuffles us from the kitchen to the front of the house, where his mom is standing in the entryway.

"I understand you didn't want to pick your sister up. I can see why now." She doesn't sound any particular way about my presence, and I'm not sure if that's better or worse. At least her voice isn't dripping with disdain.

"Mom, Gigi is 22. At a certain point, she needs to figure out how to do things on her own. If she can get herself up to Westchester, she can certainly get out of it. She's still in the same state, for Christ's sake."

"But it's *upstate*. It might as well be another country. Did you know she called your father before either of us, and he couldn't get his dick out of his new underaged girlfriend long enough to help her? So, she went to ask *you,* and then you said no. She's *only* 22. Do you remember the stupid shit I had to bail you out of at that age? If I remember correctly, I had to wire money to Mexico for–"

"*Mom!*" His tone is harsh, but then he starts to laugh, "Maybe we don't air my dirty details in front of my girlfriend."

I'm torn between swooning like a teenager at being called his girlfriend and wanting to hear more.

"It's not like you introduced her or anything. You just had a woman wearing your clothes in your home. How was I supposed to know you were serious about her?"

As much as I want to know more about this trip to Mexico, I can tell this is going to be a conversation where Josh gets scolded by his mother no matter what happens.

"I should go," I say, reaching for where my purse was dropped on the couch when we first got here. The dress I borrowed from Elia is slung over it as well, and as much as I want to leave Josh's clothes here, I want to steal them so I can snuggle into his scent all day.

"Please, don't leave on my account. But if you're leaving because my son has terrible manners and doesn't want to introduce me to the woman he clearly spent the night with, that's understandable. I thought I did a better job raising him, but alas."

"Janet, this is Taryn, my girlfriend. Taryn, this is my mom, Janet, for whom the word 'filter' has never existed."

She shrugs as she approaches me. "It exists. It's just meant for coffee or water purifiers, not for me or my words. Enchanted to meet my son's *girlfriend*." She sounds positively elated as she puts emphasis on the word "girlfriend," and I have to worry about what I have just gotten myself into. She shoots a look over her shoulder at her son before offering me her hand, which I take.

"It's a pleasure, but I didn't exactly finish my work last night since we had our date, and I should get to it."

Josh and I look at each other awkwardly. I don't know what sort of affection he's comfortable showing in front of his mom. I'm prepared to walk out of here without a kiss or anything, but Josh snags my hand, making me twist toward him. I open my mouth to say something, but he's cupping my face and planting his lips right on mine. He wastes no time plundering my mouth for everything he wants. His other hand comes to my waist and pulls me against him so our bodies are pressed tightly together.

I melt against him because there is no other option when he's holding me like this. It's the type of embrace you get from a long-time lover, but Josh and I are so new. I was never *not* looking for a relationship. I just chose not to pursue one because work is crazy. Never in my wildest dreams did I anticipate finding someone who not only understands the crazy hours I have to work but also works just as hard as I do.

"Ahem." Janet clears her throat and we break apart, grinning like idiots.

"Text me when you get home?" It's a question, but I can also tell it's a demand, and I can't very well deny the man.

"I'll text you when I get where I'm going," I agree, and even though it takes a considerable amount of strength, I turn and leave, closing the door behind me while I press my fingers to my swollen lips.

Sitting on the stoop of the house next to Josh's is an older woman with grey hair. She checks me over from head to toe, a wide smile splitting her face.

"It's about time," she says with a laugh before looking back at the street and taking a sip from her coffee.

I know she's talking about Josh, but I can't help but agree that it's about time I found someone right for me.

Nine

ELIA AND CHARLIE ARE SAINTS, not pushing me about my date and letting me work at their dining room table since I don't know if the internet is going to be back on at my apartment. It's clear from the way that Elia keeps glancing at me that she wants to ask about my date, but she thankfully keeps her questions to herself. I'm not in a super sharing mood, not when it's clear that Charlie and Josh know each other.

I do, however, get blown up in my text group while I'm trying to work, but I made the wise decision to leave my phone in my bag on silent so I wouldn't be harassed by my friend who is sitting in the same room as me.

Elia: She's not saying anything, but she came over at like nine this morning.

Ainsley: That's my girl.

Vivian: Give her a break, guys. Not all of us can be in happy monogamous relationships, and we don't drive the third degree.

Ainsley: Something you want to tell us, Viv?

Elia: Oh, leave her alone already.

Ainsley: That's right. We're still waiting for her to hate-fuck that Knox guy. Do we know what he looks like? Is he even hot?

Vivian: Ainsley...

Elia: She did say hard limit on this.

Ainsley: Well, if Taryn isn't responding, who else am I supposed to torture? I think I'm already popping, which they say isn't supposed to happen until later in pregnancy.

Vivian: Maybe because of your size? You are teeny.

Ainsley: I prefer fun-sized. And also, let's not be sizest here, though I would love to know what this guy Josh is packing. Elia mentioned he was handsome. Does he have the goods to back up the looks?

Taryn: Oh, for fuck's sake, you assholes, I am working. If I promise to kiss and tell at brunch next weekend, will you all please shut up so Elia will stop looking at me like I'm sitting on the location of the holy grail?

Vivian: Deal

Ainsley: Sold

Elia: But you're sitting in my apartment right now. Will you at least give me a preview?

I slam my phone down on the table and look up at Elia, who's watching me with these big owl eyes from her spot on the couch.

Charlie glances up from his iPad, looking between his wife and me before refocusing on whatever finance article he was probably reading. Or maybe it's porn; what do I know?

"What?" Elia asks innocently.

I point a finger at her. "Don't play the victim here. Yes, Josh has a great-sized dick. It's not a monster cock, so I don't have to choke it down when I'm giving him head. I can't tell you how it feels because we didn't have sex."

"I think I'll go into the bedroom and put some headphones on," Charlie announces to no one in particular, giving his wife a kiss on the crown of her head before disappearing into their bedroom.

Once the door is closed, Elia turns to look at me. "You mean, you wore that dress and he *didn't* fuck you?"

"He ate me out like he was a starving man licking the last of the sauce off his plate. I was not left unsatisfied, and that man has a God-given gift for going down on a woman, but no, we didn't fuck. He took me back to his palatial townhouse, where I got the grand tour, including his red room of pain, but he told me that's second date material only. We didn't even make it into a bedroom before I was on my knees in front of him, letting him fuck my face, and then, like I said, he ate me out. We went down to watch a movie, where he came on my tits again, and I fell asleep to him fingering me."

"There is way too much in there for me to pick apart all at once. But he can't be all that good if you fell asleep while being finger-fucked."

"Okay. Well, Miss Smartypants, it was like my fifth orgasm, and my body said enough was enough."

"And in the morning? Were there more orgasms?"

I groan in frustration, wanting to go back to the financial model I'm building. "No, there were none because his little sister called and woke us up. I took a shower while he made breakfast, and then his mom showed up. And that's why I was at your apartment at nine. So, can we *please* leave it alone until next weekend? I have one last chunk of this project I want to get done with before I have to see the Tweedles tomorrow."

"Yes, of course. One last question."

"*Fine.*"

"Hey, it's my Wi-Fi you're using and abusing, missy. But, red room of pain?"

The interest in her voice makes me scowl. "Fuck off, Elia."

"Just as long as you remember your safe word!"

She's smart to duck when I throw my pen at her.

I don't know what to expect from Josh on Monday, but he drops me a message that he's in back-to-back meetings all day and he'll stop by my desk if he can. Which is really fine by me. I don't know how I'm going to be able to look him in the eye when surrounded by colleagues. I know what his cock feels like in my mouth, and I'm going to have a hard time not salivating at the thought of it.

Listen, I'm well aware I'm a hypocrite, but I also can't stop the thought of going into his office and letting him bend me over his desk while knowing there is an office full of people who have no idea exactly what we're doing. The thought of getting caught thrills me, even if I know it would be catastrophic to my career. It's riding that edge that has me squirming.

Eric and Darren have thankfully been quiet, a little too hungover after the offsite this weekend. They haven't even made a single inappropriate comment or tried to insinuate that my worth as a woman is being able to get fucked in my holes. They haven't exactly said that to me, but I've overheard their conversations when they think my headphones are on or when they're just whispering to each other about their conquests. I can't exactly make a complaint because they'll say I overheard a private conversation or deny it outright, and the money at this job is just so damn good. I'm sure this company knows about the problem at my last job. They no doubt heard about it when calling for references. The last thing I want to be is seen as a woman causing problems for the menfolk.

For all the steps forward made during the Me Too Movement, it seems to have mostly had the effect of pushing the misogyny behind closed doors. I can only hope that the more senior I get, the better it becomes.

Around nine that night, I get up to stretch my legs and relax my eyes because after fourteen hours of staring at my computer screen, I need a break.

It's only natural that my legs take me toward Josh's office. Quincey isn't at her desk, and if that's because she went home for the night or is, like me, taking a walk, I don't know, but the light is on in Josh's office.

I tap gently at the door in case he's snoozing again and poke my head in. He lifts his face, and the stony, haggard expression melts away into a soft smile when he sees me.

"There's my girl. I've only got twenty minutes before I'm supposed to call Tokyo again. I was only supposed to help with this deal for a few weeks, but the guy I'm covering is taking an extended leave of absence."

I cross the room and perch on the edge of his desk next to him. "What for?"

"The official story is that he's needed out of town to care for his ailing mother. The actual story is that his wife found him hogtied to the bed while his mistress shoved a carrot up his ass after coming home early from taking care of *her* ailing mother."

"Wow, I don't even know where to start with that."

Josh swivels his chair so he can face me while running a hand up my thigh. I went pantsuit today because all of my skirts are in the wash because laundry is a foreign concept.

"Ordinarily, this wouldn't have even been a thing, but this particular SVP's wife plays bridge with the CEO's wife, so it became a problem. Which is why I'm thirty-eight, and I'm playing what feels like a game of telephone."

"Don't get me wrong, rock your kinks, but I don't see how it's a work thing."

"It is when your mistress is the CEO's daughter."

I can't help the startled laughter that escapes me. "Well, that is a lot of complicated nonsense."

"She's an adult, full stop, so it shouldn't make a difference, but that's what happens when you get your rocks off with the boss's daughter."

It's hard not to think of what happened at my internship and how the manager who propositioned me took a leave of absence before being fired just so it didn't look totally awful for him.

Josh starts to tug me onto his lap, but I resist. "No, someone could walk in."

"No one is going to come visit me. I sent Quincey home an hour ago. The only regular fixture around my office is you."

"Are you complaining?" I ask, leaning toward him, hoping to steal a kiss.

"No, but if you're taking suggestions, I'd rather have you spread out before me naked."

"I'll take it under advisement." Then I kiss him. I want it to be chaste and quick, but Josh grips the back of my neck, giving me a panty-incinerating kiss.

Well, fuck.

I can't complain as his hand threads into my hair, twisting until he has a good grip on it. I'm ready to start panting for him, but he's pulling me back off him.

"Miss Robins, are you trying to compromise me in my own office?" he asks teasingly, but I can see in his eyes. If he could strip me out of my clothes with a look alone, he would.

"That depends, Joshua. Can I compromise you?"

"In a heartbeat."

I'm about to kiss him again when I hear my name being called. I pull back and away from Josh, smoothing my hands down my pants. I hope he can't see how they tremble from just one kiss.

But then again, maybe I do want him to see how he affects me. There is so much about being together that we have to hide. Why should I have to hide how into him I am? Just to protect my feelings? If anything, doing that would cause more problems. I want him to see how badly pulling away from him hurts me too. If I could lay out before him the way he described, I would, in a heartbeat, but I've seen what this industry will do to women who are perceived to sleep their way to the top.

Eric pokes his head in and says, "Oh, there you are. Darren has some questions about the deck and said you've been gone awhile."

My eyes roll so hard I think they might get stuck like that. He has questions on the PowerPoint I sent him eight hours ago that he's been allegedly reviewing all day. It would be as soon as I get up that he wants to call me back to his desk to discuss it. "Tell Darren I'll be there in a minute."

Eric's gaze shifts between Josh and me. "He said it was pretty urgent. There were few slides he wanted rewritten."

I push off the desk, but before I can say anything, Josh pipes up. "I believe she said she'll be there in a minute." The tone he's using sends a delicious shiver down my spine.

I can see the question on the tip of Eric's tongue, wondering what I'm doing talking to an SVP who's not in our line of business, but he can't exactly question Josh about it, and he's smart enough to not question me in front of Josh.

"Manny wants the deck by 11."

"Oh, for fuck's sake," I mutter, wanting to say so much worse, but I also know that while I'm dating Josh, I shouldn't put him in an awkward position because I reamed out my coworker. All of it is bullshit. "I'll catch up with you about that thing tomorrow," I say to Josh, knowing full well there is nothing I need to follow up with him about, but I need to at least pretend like I had a legitimate business reason for being in his office. His face is perfectly impassive as he nods at me, but when his focus turns to Eric, he narrows his eyes.

As Eric and I make our way back to our desks, I can feel the tension radiating off him. If he has any comment on what he walked in and didn't see, he's welcome to voice it. I wait for him to say something, but the words never come.

"I found her in Josh Bartlett's office," Eric says, dropping into his chair like a sullen child.

Turning to my laptop, I roll my eyes. "What did you need fixed?"

"Fixed?" Darren asks cluelessly.

"Yeah, Eric said you came looking for me because you needed slides fixed."

There is a beat too long of silence, and I turn around to find Eric and Darren giving each other looks. I roll my eyes and look at the fifteen emails I missed while walking to and from Josh's office.

"Riiiiiight, slides twenty-six through thirty need to be redone," Darren tells me, and I really wonder why I'm taking orders from him, but then I remember why. He and Manny bonded at the strip club they went to with our client at the start of the project and named him the unofficial junior manager of the project, which isn't even a real thing. It's like assistant to the regional manager. Manny isn't even supposed to do events like that, and our compliance team would probably flip out if they knew, but Manny *insists* that everyone paid their own way.

"*You* did those slides," I point out, spinning to face him.

"Right, but you're so much better at prettying up the data. Don't worry. I did the hard math. You just have to do the girly shit like making sure the colors all match."

"You're too kind." The sarcasm in my voice is obvious as I turn back to my laptop.

"I figured that you would appreciate something that isn't too trying. After all, you spent all that time and money to get an MRS degree, and making something pretty is what you're best suited for."

Slowly, I turn and glare at Darren. There are women who have flaunted that they only went to college for an MRS or missus degree. Their goal was to find a high-earning husband in college or shortly thereafter so they could be set up as trophy wives. I have no issues with women who do this, but I am not one of them, and the insinuation that I'm not working my ass off and that those women aren't working *their* asses off in the meantime really butters my biscuit.

"You know what, Darren? You can kindly fuck off."

"Miss Robins."

My head snaps up, and I see Manny standing there with a frown on his face.

"This is what I've been talking about, Manny. She's uncooperative and dismissive. I asked her to do her part on the deck, and that was her response," Darren says emphatically.

"Manny, if I could explain," I plead, rising.

"There is no need to explain. Clearly, you've been working too much if your temper is this short, Tara. Maybe you should head home for the night and let Darren and Eric work on the last few slides, and whatever is left, you can approach tomorrow when you're fresh."

"But really, it's not what you think–"

"What I think doesn't matter, Tara. I know you were doing some work this weekend. It's okay to ask for help when you're out of your depth. I appreciate you trying to put on a good face, but really, go home. You need to rest those bags under your eyes." Manny doesn't give me a choice to refute his claim. "I have to go ask Josh Bartlett if he has any thoughts on my proposal from last week."

Manny waits, gesturing for me to pack up my stuff, and I'm

stunned stupid for a moment that I'm being sent off to bed with a pat on my head.

It's fucking bullshit, and I want to give him a piece of my mind, but pushing will only make it worse. Manny has made his mind up and knows that Darren is the good ole boy, and if I fight or complain about the injustice of the situation, I'll look like the whiny, emotional woman.

Since I need this job and I haven't started looking for a new one yet, I'm going to do as I'm told and leave. I'll pretty up the deck and fix their mistakes while I pull my hair out at my apartment.

Manny nods at me before strolling in the direction of Josh's office. I want to text him and rage about this, but I can hear Josh greet Manny amiably, and the last thing I want to do is get in the middle of his working relationship with a managing director, so I grab my bags and walk out with my back straight and my head high.

Ten

IT'S a little unfair to dodge Josh during the week, and maybe it makes me a shitty girlfriend, but I'm still so livid about how Manny treated me, and worse, that I didn't stick up for myself that I don't want to be in anyone's company.

I ignore the barbs that Darren throws my way and Eric's attempts at catching my eye. Even if I was willing to date someone I work closely with, it would never be Eric. He's proven that he's spineless and will follow along with anything that Darren tells him to do.

If I was in Josh's department, I wouldn't be willing to go there with him, but it's not something I need to worry about since he's not on my team.

My cheeks are still flushed from the gym when I get a ping from Quincey asking me to see her, so while the Tweedles aren't here, I get up and go to see Quincey.

She looks up at me. Her brown hair is styled like a 1950s pinup girl, and she gives me a wicked smile.

"Joshy would like to speak with you in his office. I was asked to summon you." She gestures toward the closed door with a smirk, which makes me wonder how much she knows.

When I walk into his office, Josh is sitting behind his desk with his phone to his ear. His gaze follows me with interest, and I get why. I hadn't let myself, but I've been missing him all week. Just seeing him makes me want to climb into his lap and kiss him senseless.

He beckons me toward him with a crook of his finger, and while I want to run to him, I make sure his door is closed and locked before I saunter toward him, pulling my skirt up. He meets my gaze with an elegantly raised eyebrow, but he doesn't tell me to stop. Instead, his hungry gaze follows each inch of leg I expose as I move to sit on his desk. I picked one hell of a day to decide on silk stockings and a garter. Maybe, no, definitely some part of me wanted this.

"I'm going to have to call you back, Parker. Quincey is flagging me down like a woman possessed." Pause. "You're right. I don't pay her enough, and if I stay on the phone with you any longer, she's going to start demanding hazard pay. We'll talk soon."

He hangs up the phone just as I get to him.

"You *summoned* me?" I ask. I want to inject some malice in my tone, but I can't find it in me to be legitimately annoyed.

"You say it like I've conjured some dark witch."

I climb onto his desk, planting one foot on either side of his chair. Since I'm in a skirt, he's free to run his hands up the outsides of my thighs between the fabric and my skin.

Fuck, this is why I didn't want to get involved with someone I work with because all I want now is to slide off this desk and onto his dick.

"Who says you haven't?"

"Well, I think my dark temptress would be better served actually here and tempting me. It feels a little like you've been avoiding me, and I can't tell if it's because you just have a lot of work, which I totally get, or if you're trying to avoid having to tell me if you want to come to the opera with me tomorrow. If not, I'll give

Quincey the tickets, and we can spend the night at your place or mine."

Shit, I completely forgot about the opera, and now that he's brought it up, I'm not sure what to say about it again.

I lean toward him, spreading my legs just a little now that I have more space to maneuver with my skirt sliding up. Josh, bless his heart, does not let his gaze drop to where I can see the tempting hot pink of my panties.

Panties I picked out with him in mind. Panties that I imagine him peeling down my legs.

"Definitely not my apartment. It's roughly the size of this office, and I have a roommate. Why don't we just go to your place after work tomorrow and forget the opera?"

Josh places a kiss on each of my knees, and I can't help but wonder why that's so damn sexy.

"Are you ashamed to be seen with me? Is that why you don't want to put on a pretty dress and come out with me?"

He leans back in his chair, like a king expecting worship, but I know him well enough to know that he doesn't actually want me on my knees before him, not while he's waiting for an answer to his question. Well, maybe that's not exactly true; he does love when I play with his piercing while sucking his dick.

I chew on my lower lip, wondering how I can explain this to him without sounding like I'm playing the world's tiniest violin.

"I don't know if I have anything that's nearly on level with The Met."

"You mean a dress?" he asks, sitting up and sounding genuinely curious

"I mean a dress. I have dresses, and they're pretty, but I don't know, going to the Opera feels like such a grown-up thing, and I feel like I don't have any clothes that are grown-up enough for that." I also don't mention that what I do have will look like dirty dish rags next to the Valentino-wearing women that will no doubt be in the section we're in. "And I'm not angling for my rich boyfriend to take me shopping, but the dress I wore last weekend was borrowed. My disposable income goes to work clothes." And food, really, but I don't want Josh to know just how dire my financial situation is.

Excuse me if I want to just have a boyfriend and not throw all my troubles at him fifteen minutes after we start seeing each other.

"So, you say you're not angling for it, but I'm going to do it anyway because if you're going to learn one thing about being my girlfriend, it's that I like to do things for the people in my life, be it getting lunch for Quincey or being there for my sisters or getting my girlfriend a dress for the opera."

"That's emotionally aware of you," I point out, biting my lip.

"Let's call it growing up surrounded by estrogen because it's definitely not because of my father. Tell me what you need, and I'll get it for you."

I squirm on his desk, and not because I'm so turned on it hurts. I don't want to be a charity case. Ainsley has offered to help me before, and I know I could ask for help from my friends, but mixing money with a new relationship or even a friendship doesn't feel right. But letting my boyfriend buy me something nice...I don't love it, but that's what people in relationships do, right? They get gifts for one another and treat them to nice things, like new dresses and the opera.

"You know I'm not doing this with you because I'm interested in your big fat wallet."

"No, you're just interested in my big fat–"

I silence him with a kiss, which might have been his goal all along, because he pulls me into his lap. If we get caught like this, there is no excusing it as me dropping into his office for something.

I tense in his arms right away, but he's relentless with his kiss until I relax into it.

"You don't think this is moving too fast?" I ask when he lets me up for air.

Josh laughs. "Too fast? I'm barely allowed to admit that we're dating to the woman I spend ninety percent of my day with. You're fighting me on taking you to the Opera. I don't think there's any slower. I'm not complaining. I don't want you to feel like you have to do anything just because. While you may not be *my* subordinate, you are a subordinate at the company. I don't want you to feel like I'm putting you in a difficult spot." I start to withdraw from his lap, but he holds me close. "But, I'm almost forty. I did the fuck around thing through my twenties and thirties. I'm not interested in doing blow off someone's ass or carving time out of my day for an hour-an-a-half date during which I'm just going to be stressed about work because I'm not compatible with this person. I like you a lot, Taryn. You're driven and smart and gorgeous. Let me be invested in this while you'll let me,"

"All this to buy me a dress?"

I don't know how his words make me feel because I like him too. I'm also enjoying spending time with him, and his reasons for not really dating are mine too. But will he be happy with me like this forever? Keeping our relationship quiet? As much as idealistic Josh would like to say it won't make a difference that we're together in the office setting, I know what gets said about women, and if anyone manages to find out about my internship? I'm not sure I'll be able to get another job.

"All this to buy you a dress. Say yes to me, Taryn. It's the easiest yes in your life."

I can imagine other circumstances with him that might be an easier yes, but it is much, *much* too soon for that.

"Fine, yes, buy me a dress."

"Excellent. Now get. I have work to do, and this vixen in my office has been distracting me."

"Quincey really doesn't know about us?" I ask, climbing out of his lap. I have to tug my skirt back into place.

"No. Does she have her suspicions? Yes. Will I be all but confirming them for her when I tell her to go get you a dress? Yes."

"You're bossy," I point out, leaning up to give him another kiss.

"But you like it when I am."

My cheeks warm. "I think you like it when I am too."

He fights the smirk, but I watch as it slowly takes over his face with heat dancing in his gaze. "You're not wrong."

"I'll see you tomorrow," I promise him.

"You'll see me sooner than that, treasure."

I keep my head down and focus through the rest of the workday. Manny still frowns at me like a disappointed father every time he glances in my direction while we discuss strategy. I want to kick him in the shins for it, but I need to get a positive review on this project if I want any hope of getting out from under this team.

Quincey sends me a ping that I have something to pick up from her desk before she leaves for the night, so while Darren, Manny, and Eric sit in the conference room to eat dinner together, I slip back toward Josh's office.

His door is closed and it leaves me a little disappointed, but it was Quincey who asked for me, not him.

She starts talking as soon as I'm in earshot of her. "I guessed your size just by looking at you, which I'm very good at, but the dress has a little stretch. Do you want to slip into Josh's office and try it on first, or are you going to just take me at my word?"

"Is he on a call or in a meeting?"

"On a call, but I love the idea of him getting all flustered because you're in there taking your clothes off."

I can't help but cough and glance around surreptitiously to see if anyone heard her. There is no one within earshot, but that doesn't mean she couldn't have been heard. Quincey waves her hand dismissively.

"No one gives a shit what I say. I'm just an assistant who is overqualified for this job, so what do they care?"

"Overqualified?" I ask as she hands me the garment bag with Sak's written across it. No doubt Quincey saw this as a challenge to spend as much of Josh's money as she could.

"Yes, well, I also have an MBA, but because my schools didn't have some stupid plant growing on them, my degree is worth less to some higher-ups here. It suits me just as well. Josh saw what value I could bring him, so in exchange for working under him as his assistant while also doing some actual finance work. I get paid more than adequately, and I get bonuses and a promise of a glowing letter of recommendation should I choose to leave. But I won't ever leave that man unless I'm forced out." Jealousy burns hot in me for a second, but the black-haired beauty only laughs. "He's not my type, honey. I like my men a lot more unattainable than Joshua Bartlett. No, Josh is like a little puppy I don't want to kick."

I don't know where to start with all the information she's just thrown my way, so I go for the low-hanging fruit. "It's bullshit that your degree isn't worth as much as mine."

"Like I said, I still make six figures, and Josh makes sure I have weekends off. And when my birthday or the holidays come around, somehow I always find myself with one more Chanel bag, so I can't complain. Though buying clothes and shoes for his new girlfriend is going to get me that Louis Vuitton luggage set I've been eyeing for years." She rests her chin on her hands while she looks up at me. "Now, are you going to try it on or let him be wowed by you tomorrow?"

"I think I'll let it be a surprise."

"The dramatic reveal; I adore that. You don't talk much," she points out.

But what am I supposed to say? It's not like she lets me get a word in edgewise. "I'm just used to having to keep quiet for the male egos on my team."

"Oh, I heard you're with that Darren Williams man. He's the worst."

"You say that like you have experience working with him."

Quincey waves me off. "Hardly, but word gets around in the assistant pool, and there are times when we tend to go the malicious compliance route for some people. He's one of them. Likes to make snide comments about assistants wearing clothes that are more befitting their role, i.e., short skirts, button-downs that are bursting at the seams, you know the type."

"A misogynist that belongs in the golden age of the mediocre white men?"

"Exactly. I've never had to deal with him, and I count my lucky stars that I don't have to. Josh wouldn't stand for it."

Knowing that Josh would stand up for the assistants or other women in the office warms my heart. I'm glad to know that he's the type of guy that will shut that shit down. He made that clear to me when we first went to brunch after being concerned about how I was treated in the office.

But how do you explain to a man who has never had to experience it that it's not all the time that sexual harassment takes the form of some older man telling you to get on your knees or grabbing your ass? It's in snide comments about what you should be wearing. It's in "hugs" and similarly "innocuous" touches that, to an outside observer, seem to be innocent but leave you feeling like your skin is crawling. It's also the discrimination of your manager taking the males on your team to a strip club and not inviting you because they assume you wouldn't want to go or because it would be awkward while they talk about "manly things."

I, too, can hold a business conversation about better investments while looking at a set of bare tits; probably even better because while I can admire their shape, I won't be getting as hot and bothered as the guys would. Though I can't say I've ever tested that theory for myself.

"Well, I should probably get back to my team of miscreants before they notice that I was gone too long."

Quincey nods. "If they get out of line, you know you can tell Josh, right?"

And that is exactly why I won't let my relationship with Josh become office gossip. I can't be seen as the little lady who cries wolf to her more powerful boyfriend. Not only would I be slutting my way up the corporate ladder, but to then get my male colleagues in trouble? Forget it.

"Of course. I'll see you next week, Quincey."

I stash my stuff at my desk before going back to the conference room.

"What's the matter, Tara? Had to change your tampon?" Darren asks when I walk in.

"No, sorry, I don't have any of the extra large ones for a heavy flow. You wouldn't happen to have any on you since you're being extra bitchy? I figure it must be your time of the month too."

Darren turns red with rage and slams his hands down on the table, but Manny chooses that moment to walk in. "Where were we?" he asks, going right back to his desk, having missed the entire exchange.

I'm counting the hours until this project is over, especially because Eric once again fails to say anything to Darren about his behavior. At this point, I'd be surprised if he did.

I'M glad I let Vivian talk me into using her Urgent Hair blowout credit. Sitting in the chair at the salon reminds me that it's been too long since I've taken the time for self-care. I'm trying so hard to scrimp and save that I'm wearing myself down financially, and it's taking its toll.

While walking back to my apartment, I check my bank account to see just how bad things are looking. After my parents finally came clean about their financial situation, I gave them each a credit card to use for groceries. They're usually good about not spending more than a few hundred a week on food, but when I check the current balance, I break a cardinal New York City rule and stop dead on the sidewalk to call my parents right away.

"Hey, Honey!" my mom greets sweetly, but there's something lurking in her voice that sounds a little like nervousness.

"Can you tell me why there is a charge for six *grand* on the emergency credit card? Did someone steal it? I need to know so I can report it to the bank."

"Let me get your father," she says and immediately hands me off. I can hear the shuffling on the other end of the phone. I resume my walk, hoping that it can calm me down. Between my parents' mortgage and my student loans, my six-figure job isn't enough, and while this amount shouldn't ruin me financially, it feels like it's going to.

"'lo?"

"Dad," I start.

"It's the car. She broke down on the side of the road. We needed to pay for the tow and the repairs. You said the credit card was for emergencies, and this is an emergency."

I can appreciate that he cuts through the bullshit, but it still crushes me to know that things are this bad for them. I know it probably hurts my father just as badly to have to rely on me for things.

"It is for emergencies, and you're right, you need the car. Have you had any luck talking Mom into *selling* the house?"

That's going to be the fastest way for my parents to break free, but it's been hard to convince my mom, who grew up in the same home I did.

"We had a realtor come and look at it, and, bumblebee, it's not good."

Taking a soothing breath, I nod, not that he can see me, but I have to gird my loins to hear it. My parents' home is a gorgeous rustic farmhouse that sits on two acres of land, which is unheard of in the suburbs where they live. But in this case, rustic is code for old.

"The realtor says we can't even talk about selling unless we get someone in to give a quote on the roof and the electrical. She also says that for us to be able to even consider selling, we would need to do about a buck fifty in renovations, minimum. The house has what she calls charm, but I think she just means it's broken down."

"What about a flipper? Would a flipper want it? I mean, it's got all the hallmarks of one of those shows. I'm sure they could even find a body in one of the walls."

I unlock my door and climb the five flights to my apartment, going slow so I don't sweat through my blowout.

"Problem with a flipper is they wouldn't want to pay what we're askin', so she says we're better off puttin' in the changes ourselves."

"Got it. So, I guess without the car, that means the job hunting has been stalled?" It's a statement, not a question, but I pretend anyway.

"After we sold my car, being down to only your mom's car makes it hard for all this job hunting."

The company restructuring has left them both struggling to look for something new when they were mere years away from retirement. Now, instead of winding down how hard they had to try at work, they have to reformat resumes that they wrote in the 80s and learn buzzwords they can use in interviews. Bad isn't a good enough word to describe what I feel for my parents, whose mortgage rivals my student loans.

At least they get equity from what they're putting into the house. I have two pieces of paper that make me more attractive in an industry where my gender is held against me.

"Most job hunting is done online these days, Dad. Did you post your resume on all those sites I told you about?" I have to fight to keep my voice from cracking.

"It's just so impersonal. Your mother and I got our job because we walked–"

"I know. You walked into Mr. Freebaker's office and told him what a good fit mom was for the company and that if they wanted her brilliance, they had to hire you too, but that's not how things work anymore."

"I know that, but...I'm sixty years old. I just want to be able to spend the winters somewhere warm with your ma. I don't want to have to look for jobs."

"Dad, I know, and I don't want you to have to either, but I'm not yet in a position where I can take care of everything, even though I so wish I was. I just need you and Mom to do it for a few more years, please." I hate how my voice catches, but there is no avoiding it. There is no avoiding how much it hurts to not be able to do all the things for my parents. They did everything they could raising me and ensured I never wanted for anything, including school programs. To them, it made sense to take out a mortgage on the house for the most they could get.

But I got to study abroad and have all my textbooks covered, and I didn't need a job while in college. I was nineteen and never questioned where all this money was coming from until it was too late.

"I know, bumblebee. I'm sorry. This isn't your burden to bear. I know I have another credit card I can use. I just have to make sure your mom didn't already take a pair of scissors to it."

"No, don't do that. I can cover it. I just need you to use your computer and look for jobs. You worked in your industry for decades; you have to have contacts."

"Don't you worry, Taryn. I'll see what I can do about getting some pokers in the fire. Are you doing anything fun this weekend? I hope not working more."

"I actually have a date tonight that I need to finish getting ready for. Let me know if you need anything, Daddy. And please just let me know before you put another big charge on my card. I just about had a heart attack."

"Of course. Enjoy your date. Let's hope this is one you actually bring home to us."

Nothing against having Josh meet my parents, but I don't want Josh to meet my parents for a while. As evidenced by his mother airing dirty secrets, I'm not ready for Josh to know bitchy teenage Taryn quite yet.

"Not a chance, Daddy. I love you."

"You too, bumblebee."

It's a testament to how shaken I am by the call that I don't even think twice about giving Josh my home address when he asks to pick me up.

I'm sitting in my robe, staring at the dress I'm supposed to put on, when I faintly hear the buzzer to my apartment go off.

The dress that Quincey picked out for me is stunning, but it almost cost as much as fixing my parents' car, never mind the matching red-bottomed shoes she picked out for me. It's a black trumpet-style dress by Oscar de la Renta, which I would never have picked for myself, opting to lust after one so pretty. I have other little black dresses I could have worn, but none this nice. They're all just this side of sad from having been washed so many times.

My makeup is done, and my hair is still pristine from when I got it done a few hours earlier, but other than pausing long enough to put my face on, I've been bent over my laptop working out new calculations to make sure I'm going to be able to pay this car bill.

"Yo, T, some dude is here for you?" My head snaps up to see my roommate at the door, and my eyes widen.

"Did you let him in?" I ask, looking over her shoulder like I'll see Josh, but where my bedroom is doesn't have a line of sight to the front door.

"Well, duh. I didn't know you wanted him back here too. My dude, this is her room. She's waiting for you if you know what I mean. I've got some good noise-canceling headphones. I'll throw them on. You won't even know I'm here." She gives me a wink before pushing my door open wider so Josh can walk in.

He stumbles over the threshold, his focus fixed on me. His gaze rakes over my skin. I can feel it everywhere.

I'm wearing a black robe from when Elia got married that has my monogram on the front.

"Josh."

"If I had known you just wanted to wear a robe, I wouldn't

have splurged on the dress." He says it to be charming but that just makes the tears well in my eyes.

I drop my head back and open my eyes wide like that's going to keep them in. I can feel one escape and slip down the side of my face.

"What is it, treasure?" I hear the one step it takes him to make it to me. I fan my eyes, a trick I learned from a girl who used to do beauty pageants.

"Nothing, I'm fine. I just... The dress is too much, the shoes, it's all just too much. You're too generous."

"Right, generous. It's all a gift. Is that the problem? Am I playing into the power imbalance between us, not just from a work standpoint but a financial one? Help me see the problem, Taryn."

I frown and give him a light push. "Stop being so in touch with your feelings. It's freaking me out. Most men don't have the emotional maturity to figure out why I'm freaking out before even I do."

"The benefits of dating an older man."

I snort at that, finally starting to level out emotionally a little bit.

"Stop, you're, like, six years older than me." I relax a little and let Josh wrap me in a hug, one that I desperately needed. He keeps anticipating my needs before I even know them.

"Apparently, that's lifetimes compared to the fuckboys you've been seeing."

Another snort. "Like I have time to actually see anyone. More like I'm used to working with emotionally stunted children."

Immediately, I want to claw the words back. What we're doing is too new for me to be complaining to him about Darren, Eric, and Manny.

Josh's eyes narrow, but he must decide against pushing me. "Tell me what the problem is, and let me fix it." His thumb swipes under my eye, gathering the remaining wetness.

"You can't fix it." When I look up into his stricken face, I rush to continue. "It's not a you thing; it's a me thing. It's a my parent's thing. They're going through some stuff financially, and I can't help but feel guilty since it was my college that landed them in this situation. So, I'm trying to help them out, and they had a setback today."

I see his brow dip down before he smooths it out. "Then it sounds like you *really* need a night out. Pack a bag and spend the night at my place. Put on the pretty dress and come out and enjoy the night before we're both too high to do anything about it."

"Is she smoking again?" I ask, glancing toward the door.

"You can't smell it?" He laughs out the question.

"Honestly, I'm nose blind to it at this point. Go wait downstairs. I'll be ready in two shakes."

"And miss seeing what's under that robe? No fucking way."

I push him toward the door. "All the more reason for you to wait downstairs. I want what's under here to be a surprise."

Josh tenderly grips my chin and tilts my head back before giving me a soft kiss. "Hurry up. We can't miss the start of the show since I know I'm going to be dragging you out during intermission."

He slips out of my bedroom, closing the door softly behind him. I rush to put together a bag, wondering what I'm going to do with my clothes while we're in the show.

When I reach Josh downstairs, he's lounging against his car, thumbing through his phone. As I close the security door behind me, he stops what he's doing and looks at me, which gives me a chance to really look at him. He's magnificent in the tuxedo he chose for the event. In my earlier upset, I didn't even notice, and I'm sort of glad I didn't.

If I had seen just how incredible he looked, we would have never left my apartment, roommate be damned.

"I...do we really have to go?" I ask, eyeing him up and down. The clothes fit him so well, really, too well. I want to lick every inch of him and then ride his cock while we see just how many times he can make me come.

"We do, although I am sorely tempted by you to say no. We don't even have a private box, so I can't tease you all night long."

"What are we going to see, anyway?" I ask, stepping into the car as he holds the door open for me.

"*La Traviata*. Are you familiar with the opera?"

"Vaguely. That's the inspiration for Pretty Woman, right?"

"It is, but don't go reading into it. You're hardly a courtesan."

I laugh, waiting for him to go around the car to sit next to me. When he finally closes the door, he leans over and kisses my cheek.

"I wasn't going to say it, but you went there first," I tell him.

"I just happened to have the tickets already."

"You just happened to have two tickets?" I twist in the seat to face him, wishing I could raise an eyebrow to convey my skepticism.

"Right, we're in a box on the Parterre, which seats eight."

I interrupt him before he can go any further. "Let me guess: you know the other occupants of the box?"

"I do. They happen to be a few old friends, but it's not like I'm introducing you to my core friends. These are just other friends that I associate with on a regular-ish basis."

I grab his hand and squeeze it, careful not to dig my nails into his skin. "Give it to me straight, lover boy. How good are these friends that you're ambushing me with? Because let's be honest, this is nothing short of an ambush."

"Two of them are women who also work in finance. The other two are old family friends. The last two were supposed to be my sister and her husband, but their sitter canceled before I even asked you, so they let the tickets go. Everyone was an afterthought; bringing you somewhere nice was the forethought."

I reach forward and grab his jaw, tugging him close to me. I'm not as mad as I thought I would be, especially since I'm comforted by the knowledge that at least two of the people attending are women.

"You can make it up to me with orgasms," I tell him sternly, but I can't keep the smile from my voice.

"Ma'am, yes, ma'am."

I squeeze my thighs together at the delicious thrill his submissive tone gives me.

"Now, what am I supposed to do with my pot-smelling clothes that you asked me to bring?"

"You're going to leave them in the car so I can ravish you thoroughly later."

"Ravish? What are you, some eighteenth-century pirate?" I tease.

"If that's what it's going to take to get you into my bed later, then I'll be whatever you want me to be."

I bring his hand up to my mouth and bite his knuckle gently. "So, you want to do a bit of roleplaying then? Stealing away the fair maiden onto your ship?"

Josh leans forward to kiss me. "What have I gotten myself into, courting you?"

If I spoke, my voice would sound squeaky and high, and I doubt any words would actually escape my mouth. Instead, I bring my mouth to his, kissing him with way too much gusto, but I hope enough to convey just how much that idea appeals to me.

The car comes to a stop, and I realize that we're at the Met. As much as I don't want to leave this bubble that we've created on the ride uptown, I'm actually sort of excited to meet Josh's friends. Because without even realizing it, this went from a fun, casual thing to the sort of arrangement I could see myself relaxing into. And that scares me most of all–the idea of falling in love with Josh Bartlett.

Twelve

IT'S my first time at The Met, and I'm trying not to look like a tourist as I stare up at the gorgeous chandeliers. They look like a burst of light or what I imagine it looks like when a star explodes. All around us, finely dressed people are chatting amiably about their excitement or making their way up the stairs toward their seats or the nearest bar. The show doesn't start for another hour, but we had to get here early to meet his friends.

I'm feeling just a little lost when Josh slides his hand with mine, and it settles the achy feeling in my soul from being so far out of my element. With a gentle tug, he pulls me against him before we mount the red carpet staircase toward our seats.

"My friends are going to love you."

"Sure, sure, but what happened to them just being business associates and not really friends?"

"Well, it might be more complicated than I initially said."

"You're late." A stern voice interrupts us from the landing just above. A short, round woman is scowling at Josh. Her hair is pin straight and pulled away from her face, allowing me to really admire her stunning makeup. It's like she wanted a smokey eye and leveled it up to a thousand with a perfectly winged eyeliner. If she said she got the lines perfect using a knife, I would believe her a thousand percent. Her lips are painted a bright pink that matches her strapless pink jumpsuit perfectly. I would *kill* for the confidence she's exuding right now, not only for her bold color choice in a city where black is the norm, but for the way she's staring Josh down with a look that could shrivel balls.

"I am *on time*. You said to meet here at seven. It is seven."

"I know you're glued to your phone, Joshua. I said six forty-five."

"Darling, let's allow Josh to make it up the stairs; he's caused a traffic jam," another woman dressed in an ethereal gossamer blue and gold gown says, coming to the other woman's shoulder. Her makeup is much more natural, but I think I keep catching flecks of gold around her eyes as she moves. There's something strikingly familiar about her, but I can't place it.

"Bex, I appreciate your attempts at managing our time, but this is New York City. You're lucky we got here by seven."

"And who is 'we?'" The shorter woman asks, looking me over. There is nothing cruel in her tone, just curiosity as she looks me up and down.

"I'm Taryn Robins," I say, reaching my hand out to her once we get to their level.

"Taryn, please meet Bex and her lovely wife, Han." Josh pronounces Han's name like Han Solo, and I wonder if it's short for something.

Bex gives me a warm smile and shakes my hand. "I expected Josh to bring one of his thirteen sisters tonight, not such a lovely creature like you."

I look over at Josh and give him a sly smile. I already like Bex despite how intimidating she seems to be. Then again, Josh mentioned she also works in finance. You can't be a woman, a short woman, and survive without having to be the loudest voice in the room.

"Did you go to Columbia by any chance?" Han asks as we shake hands.

"I went for my MBA. I graduated last year." I try to study her more closely, but Josh's hand settles on the small of my back, and all I can think about is where he's touching me. Both women glance at where his hand disappears behind me, then at each other before focusing back on me.

"That's where I know you from. Did you take Professor Cohen's class on Foundations of Valuation during your first year?"

I take a step back in surprise and nearly step off the landing, but Josh is there, making sure I don't fall. He takes us a few steps forward, and as a group, we shuffle to the bar.

"I did, actually."

"Right. I probably look a little different."

"What my woman is trying to say is that while in business school, she didn't want to shine, so she stuck with her messy-hair-don't-care attitude and had these obnoxiously thick glasses."

Han looks at her wife affectionately. "It's more like I wasn't interested in attracting any more attention than was necessary."

"Because look at her. She's a fucking smokeshow, and she was still getting asked out every other week in her leggings with holes in them."

"That's because you were the one asking me out all the time," Han says, beaming at Bex. "Even though we were already married."

"That's right. I wanted to remind that pussy who has it on lock."

"They're disgustingly adorable, aren't they?" Josh whispers in my ear. He's close enough that with each word, his lips are a caress against my skin.

I nod and glance at him out of the corner of my eye.

"I take it you two have been together awhile?" I ask, looking between them.

"It started when she took that last oat milk from the fridge at my bodega," Bex starts.

"*Our* bodega, and you said yourself that you could have supplemented with soy milk but that you wanted the oat milk. I have an allergy."

"I'll get drinks while you recount. I've heard the story a time or two," Josh offers, slipping away toward the bar.

"I should hope so; he was our officiant," Bex jokes. "Anyway, of course, I said that. It was the only way I was going to get the attention of the hot chick I saw there all the time. I was a little stalker, checking her out when she was there. One time, she showed up late at night with lipstick smeared on her neck that disappeared into her shirt, and I knew I had to have her."

"So, Bex here decided the best way to shoot her shot was by buying all of the oat milk from the bodega–which only carried it because I requested it. I swear, the guy behind the counter *knew* you were hoarding them too, because he gave you this *look*." Han is smiling at her wife, brushing the long dark locks of Bex's hair over her shoulder, exposing a tattoo in the shape of lips.

"I knew I had to get this woman alone, so I told Han that if she *insisted* on buying the last of the oat milk, the least she could do was invite me over for a cup of coffee."

"We never did have that coffee," Han says affectionately.

"Because oat milk is disgusting, and putting it in coffee is a sin," Bex counters.

"And the oat milk Bex was hoarding that she apparently hates?" I ask as Josh comes back with four glasses of champagne.

Han takes one but doesn't take a sip after we clink glasses. "Eventually, I did drink it when I went to her house. She was kind enough not to dump them all, so when I spent my nights at her place, I drank it, and some I took back to my place *and* my office to drink. Sometimes, I had to just have a glass of it so I could finish them all before the expiration date."

"What do you do, Taryn Robins, date of Joshua Bartlett?" Bex asks, taking Han's glass while Han looks in her purse for her phone, which she produces and looks at before putting it away and focusing on me. I notice she doesn't take the glass back from Bex.

"I actually work in investment banking at the same firm as Josh."

"And is this how you met? Bedding the young associate... how uncouth, Joshua. I'm disappointed in you," Bex teases.

Josh scowls. "Taryn is an adult and capable of making her own decisions. We went into this with our eyes open before going down this path."

Han waves her phone. "I just got a text from the others. Their flight from London was delayed, and they won't be making it in time. They've only just landed at JFK now." She looks at her wife. "And quit teasing them."

Bex scoffs. "They knew when their flight was first delayed that they weren't going to make it if they were flying into JFK. What did they think was going to happen?"

I appreciate the shift from Josh and me as the conversation moves to how JFK is the worst of the three neighboring airports. Bex hands her empty glass to her wife, but I don't comment on it. If Josh notices, he keeps the observation to himself as well.

I want to ask about the others that were coming but I bite my tongue. Bex and Han are enough for me to focus on without adding people I haven't met into the mix.

When there's a lull, I turn the conversation around. "You both work in finance, right?"

"Bex works at the Federal Reserve, and I'm a consultant," Han says. "I actually just started my own firm after business school. I spent my twenties at one of the big firms, getting just shy of partner before I went to b-school. I was going to go back, but it didn't make sense."

Josh shakes his head but stays silent.

"Partner. Isn't that the goal, though?" I ask.

"You would think, but it felt like the perpetual carrot and stick. I wasn't bringing in enough work. They didn't see the drive in me. Really, what they didn't like was that I wasn't working my managers and associates to the bone. I let them have personal lives as much as I could. All the other partners and directors were pocketing all this money that was a surplus from how their associates traveled, and I frowned at that. So, I decided the only way to do it the way I wanted was to start my own company.

"My Way Consulting was born after a night of sitting on the floor of my apartment in my bridal shower dress, bemoaning that I needed to get on a plane and travel for a client who didn't actually want us there to begin with. From there, I started to spin out all the ways I would change consulting if I had my own firm. I was starting at Columbia in a few months, so I took my time while there to build connections and make sure when I graduated, I could be sure I was up and running."

"Helps that she has a sugar momma," Bex teases.

"It does, but things are a little more complicated now that I'm–" Han seems to catch herself before rushing to say, "On my own. Things are complicated on my own. I can really only have one client at a time until I'm able to build out my services and my firm. Fortunately, my one client is also a female-led small org, so she gets it."

"It also helps that she has other business minds that she can pick when she needs a hand or is in a pickle," Josh interjects, finally adding something. He seems content to just let me vibe with Bex and Han, which I appreciate so much. I have my core group of friends, but it's clear that these two mean a lot to Josh if he officiated their wedding.

"So, how did you all meet?" I ask, glancing up at Josh, who smiles at me before placing his hand on my hip.

"Josh is my cousin, actually," Bex tells me with a grin. "Our moms are sisters who thought it would be fun to get pregnant at the same time. Josh's mom already had one, and my mom decided on one and done. Once you have perfection, there is no getting any better, and my mom recognized that at least."

Cousin. I turn to look at Josh with a glare that he has the decency to look ashamed of. He knew he was ambushing me with his cousin and her wife without telling me.

"She just has my mom's brood of children to hang out with," Josh says. "She got the best of both worlds–only child syndrome with a gaggle of cousins."

"It's so cute. They vacation together and do weekly dinners together," Han gushes.

I turn to look up at Josh. "Weekly dinner?"

"Don't look at me like that, treasure. We've been dating for a week. It's not like I've had time to discuss it with you, not to mention I severely lack the time to actually attend. I'm missing this week again because of work bullshit."

I don't point out that he missed last week because we were together, although maybe he didn't if he went after his mom showed up. The idea that Josh spends that much time with his family brings me an obscene amount of joy. I'm close to my parents, but I'm also an only child. It means that I have no one to commiserate with when my mom is driving me crazy or when my dad is on my case about something. There were times when I wished I had a sibling. Someone who would understand what it's like to have my parents as parents. Someone who could share the burden with me now as they face financial ruin.

The lights flicker, letting everyone know it's time to get to their seats. Before we start, Josh pauses in front of me.

"Where did you go just now?"

I meet his gaze, forcing a smile. "What makes you think I went somewhere?"

"Your shoulders sort of hunched, and you, I don't know, you went somewhere else. I could just tell."

"It's a long, long story." I realize then that as much as I've been trying to play at keeping him at arm's length because I don't want to dump all of my emotional baggage on him, I want that. I want someone I can tell my worries to. I want someone in my life who can help me problem-solve and work out all the things that I can do to fix the issue.

To get that with Josh, I need to be all in with him, and I want to be all in with him. He's given me every indication that he does too. And maybe that just means having to play it smarter at work, but I want him in my life in all the ways. Meeting parents and talking about worries before going to bed and waking up to delicious, slow sex.

I want it all.

"We don't have to go in," Josh offers. "I would be more than happy to explore what's on your mind and your body instead of sitting through the opera."

I give him a gentle shove before taking his hand. "No, sir. You told me that I had to be a good girl and sit through this opera and that we couldn't just have sex tonight. So, later. I promise we can talk it through it later. After the show. You wanted me to meet your friends, so here we are, meeting your friends. Or maybe I should say, your cousins."

"I don't remember using the term 'good girl' when I said that, but you can call me 'sir' anytime." He gives me a little swat on my ass before gesturing me toward our box.

During the first act, I try to enjoy the show. Really, I do. The theater is gorgeous, featuring more of the sunburst chandeliers that slowly rise just before the curtains are drawn. Bex and Han sit in front of us, and between reading the translation in front of me and the way Josh has his hand resting on my thigh, I feel like I barely actually watch or hear the show. During the intermission I nod along like I understand. I know that when I'm in a better financial position, I want to come back and really enjoy it. Maybe catch the show twice–once so I can read the words, and a second to just watch it while knowing what is happening.

A moment that transcends the words for me is during the second act when Violetta gives Alfred a chance to be the one who could love her by offering him a flower to be returned to her when wilted. My eyes flick to the screen to read her words as she sings about how he is maybe the one for her. And her willingness to take a chance on love. My hand squeezes Josh's involuntarily, and while I may not be a famed courtesan, I can see the parallel to my own life with my resistance to even try to get involved with someone. Violetta takes a chance with Alfred the way I'm taking a chance on Josh.

At some point while watching Violetta find out that her tuberculosis has worsened and that she will never get her happily ever after, my worries about my own life slip away. I've mastered being able to watch the production and read the words in front of me. I don't fancy drawing parallels between this show and my life, but the feeling of loss is pervasive. I know it's not a competition to see who has it worse. I mean, yes, my family is on the verge of financial ruin, but I also still have them together and whole, and I have a man who I want to be with beside me, regardless of what that could mean for me in the workplace. He's shown me that he's generous, kind, and loving with those in his life.

I would be honored to be one of those people.

By the end of the third act, I'm so engrossed in the production that as the final curtain falls, I'm surprised to find Josh cupping my face as he wipes my tears away.

"It's so tragic," I whisper, looking into his eyes as the clapping in the room comes to a close. I'm glad to find I'm not the only one crying when Han turns around, her face similarly streaked with tears.

"It's bullshit is what it is," Han chokes out before the tears turn into a full sob. Bex pats her shoulder when Han refuses to be consoled.

"PMS. You know how it is," Bex explains.

"Yes, that," Han agrees. "I think, maybe another time we should do drinks or something, but not...not tonight. It was lovely meeting you, Taryn. Hopefully, we can do this again sometime."

Neither of them waits for us to respond before Bex ushers Han out of the box.

Josh turns to me. “Han is trying to get pregnant. It’s a whole...thing.”

“It’s really none of my business,” I hedge as he leans against the seat. The theater is emptying slowly, and if we leave now, we’ll just get caught in the hoards, so I don’t mind sitting and waiting.

“They would tell you themselves, I’m sure, but they probably wanted to wait to see how our conversation about it went first.”

“What difference would our conversation have on the situation?”

Josh tugs me toward him so I’m standing between his legs. “Because they asked me to possibly be a sperm donor. They want to keep it as close in the family as they can. A male cousin on Bex’s other side of the family is their current donor, but it’s been a few cycles with no results. They asked me because it’s not working out, and they’re getting frustrated.”

My heart goes out to them. When Ainsley wanted to get pregnant, she said she started to look into getting a donor. She even went as far as getting an appointment at an exclusive sperm bank before Ken swooped in with a solution that seems to be working very well for them. Collectively, Vivian, Elia, and I were all prepared to do what it took to support Ainsley as she moved toward her goal of motherhood.

“That has to be really difficult for them. What are your thoughts on it?” I know why he’s telling me, but we’re so new, and my thoughts on it should have no bearing on what he wants to do. At the same time, the idea of a tiny human with Josh’s face running around intrigues me.

It’s not that I don’t want kids. I think they’re great, and I’m excited to be an auntie for Ainsley, but at the same time, I’m not sure I want to be a mom. I have this career that I think I’m great at, and for now, I’m doing what I want to do.

I don’t think that motherhood completes a woman, but I’m

also not opposed to the idea of growing a new life. Which is the *exact* worst outlook to have because while I'm all confused about my feelings toward it, I have a biological clock that's ticking in my womb, telling me I need to make a decision about what I want. But I suppose at a certain point, no decision is a decision of its own.

Josh clenches his jaw as he seems to sort through what it is he wants to say on the matter. "I want to help my cousin. It's also not like she's some random woman out there with my child. I would still be around, and I would still get to be cool Uncle Josh. I appreciate Bex because she's not pushing me on it at all. She was very straightforward and matter-of-fact that she wants to have a baby, and she wants the baby to be a blood relation to her. But at the same time, I'm undecided if I want to have a child. So, I struggle with wondering how I'm going to feel in ten or fifteen years if I don't have a child of my own or when that kid has their kids. I would love to say I'm this well-adjusted man who would be able to compartmentalize my feelings and think of it as nothing more than jizz in a cup, but I'm only human. What if I look at this kid and they have my eyes or nose? What then? It's not fair to the child."

Josh waves his hand dismissively before settling them on my hips. The chatter outside our box has dulled, and I'm glad because it gives me a second to really think about how to respond without the chaos outside distracting me.

In the theater below, the ushers are walking through, checking for lost belongings, and starting the cleaning process.

"I'm sorry. That was a lot to dump on you for what equates to a second date. Maybe I should have stuck to my strengths and focused on getting you naked."

I shake my head, turning to face him. "Stop it. You're allowed to have thoughts and be complex and to want to think about this huge life-changing decision. You're allowed to talk out loud about it to your girlfriend, and even if that's too much for a new relationship, you're allowed to talk to your friend. What do you say we go back to your place so I can stop worrying about ripping this dress that costs as much as my pre-tax paycheck, and we can have a real, deep talk?"

"What happened to me ravishing you?" He leans forward to kiss my pulse point on my neck.

"What happened is someone decided to have an existential crisis that I can only manage with wine and/or ice cream. So, let's go back to your place, take our clothes off, and cuddle while we reveal all our deepest, darkest secrets."

Josh stands abruptly so we're chest to chest before giving me a long, decadent kiss.

"If you insist on taking your clothes off, who am I to deny you?"

Thirteen

"ANY CHANCE of your sister cockblocking us again this weekend?" I ask as we step into the townhouse.

Josh gives a low, dangerous chuckle. "Not a one. She's visiting her friends from college in Napa for a girls' weekend. None of my other family members will be a problem either since they're busy with various other things. Bex wasn't kidding when she said she thought I was going to bring one of my sisters. I was originally going to ask Kayleigh when we booked the whole thing."

I stop where I'm standing and drop my arms down at my sides. "Joshua, you are just so wholesome."

Josh nearly growls when he turns around to face me. He moves quickly, knocking my bag out of my hand before grabbing me around the waist and hauling me against his body. "Wholesome is not the word I want you to be thinking about when my name comes to your mind. That is the *last* word, actually."

The fancy panties I got for just this sort of occasion are so wet from that declaration that I feel like I need to go to the bathroom just to dry them out.

Or, I could let Josh peel them off my body like he was born to do it.

Yeah, option two works.

"Really? What word would you prefer I think of first, *sir*?"

My smartass response gets the exact rise out of him I wanted. I can feel his cock stir against me where we're touching. His mouth captures mine, and there is a momentary battle for dominance before I yield to him. I yield in every way that matters, letting my body mold around his.

Josh doesn't wait for me to claim him back. He scoops me up behind my knees and holds me to his chest.

"Josh!" I exclaim as I hold on to him. He's taking the stairs two at a time until he's pushing his bedroom door open with his foot.

"Taryn!" he mimics before throwing me onto the bed. "I have been waiting a week to sink my cock into that pretty pussy. You teased me at the office with those hot pink panties."

I swallow around my suddenly very dry mouth. "You didn't seem all that affected."

He scoffs. "Is that a joke? Not that affected? You made it very clear the office is the office, not a play space, but are you walking that back now? Would you rather I had peeled those panties off you and kept them all for myself while you went back to your desk with your cunt wet after I ate it for breakfast?"

I moan at the picture he's painting, and it's so damn wanton that I feel my cheeks heat in embarrassment in response.

"I want an answer, my treasure. That wasn't clear consent. Because if you said yes, I don't know if I would have been able to stop myself from fucking you on my desk with someone in the office next door. Does that make you hot to know that you could have been caught at any moment? Do you trust that I wouldn't let that happen?"

"Yes." The word comes out of my mouth immediately, and I look up at him, finally able to open my eyes because I was too busy picturing what it would have been like to be spread out on his desk while Quincey answered the phone right outside his door. "Yes, I trust you."

I trust him not just because he's done nothing but prove to me how he would take care of me but also because he knows the risks of an office relationship. He knows the perception of women and the possible consequences.

"Does that mean you want me to do that? Make you suck my cock while I'm on a call? Or maybe I'll be balls-deep in that sweet cunt while I go over an earnings report. Get off the bed."

For a second, I'm startled, but then I comply, rolling off awkwardly because of the shape of the dress. Thankfully, he doesn't make me flounder for long. Josh takes my hand and helps me to my feet before he carefully spins me around with his hand on my hips.

He reaches up to where the top of the zipper rests before he pulls it down so slowly that I might expire before he does anything. But I should know better. Josh is going to take care of me. He's going to take care of my pretty little cunt.

It's not a word I love to use to describe my vagina, but when he says it, it feels so dirty, so filthy, so right.

Josh's hands slide over my shoulders before pushing the dress off me and leaving it in a crumpled heap on the floor. A dress that costs just under ten thousand dollars, and it's lying on the floor like yesterday's underwear. He takes my hand and helps me step out from the circle of the dress, and I melt a little more as he holds my hand while he looks me over from head to toe.

I did do a little shopping for today once I agreed to go with him. I wanted something sexy for Josh to unwrap and find me in when we did finally get here because getting to feel his cock moving inside me is something I've been trying to avoid dreaming about, but I couldn't help it.

I went and found a black thong, garter, and bra set that took my Bs and made them look like Ds. From the way Josh is looking at me, I want to cover up, but it's not like this is anything he hasn't seen. I lower my arm from where I was trying to hide myself and let him see me, let him see all of me.

"Jesus Christ. Taryn. Why did you let me talk you into the opera?"

"You're very persuasive, sir." I add that last bit for a little dramatic flair.

"You keep up that attitude, and I'll be fucking your mouth instead of your cunt."

"No," I tell him, shaking my head, seizing on my moment to take control of the situation. "You can fuck any other part of me *after* you've given me three orgasms, at least one while balls-deep in my cunt," I say, echoing him. "I need you inside me tonight. I need your dick inside me tonight."

This time, a sly grin splits his face. "Yes, ma'am."

Josh scoops me up, this time spreading my legs so I have to lock them around his hips before he falls onto the bed with me on my back. He kisses me, burning me through with passion until he slowly reigns it in, kissing down my neck and along the cups of my bra. He gives each breast attention like he knows that it's something I'm sensitive about. Josh's mouth covers the lace as he captures my nipple, causing me to cry out.

"I love your breasts. They're fucking perfect, and I know you don't think it's going to be possible, but I'm going to fuck them and cum all over your face while you say 'thank you.'"

The mild degradation in this image makes me grind against him, and he gives me that grin that tells me he knows I like what he's saying.

"Josh." I grab his arms, stopping his descent. He must hear something in my voice because he stills and lifts his head to look at me. I want to tell him about all the dirty things I do like, but I think that should come during a less sexually charged moment. Maybe later, when we've gotten past that initial fucking to see if we even have chemistry like that, not that I doubt we will.

The sincerity on his face only makes me smile at him. "You're wearing too many clothes."

He looks down as if just realizing he's still in his tuxedo. "You would be right about that, but I have to ask, treasure, what are you going to do about it?"

Finally all that running and working out I've been doing comes in handy. I tighten my legs around his waist and roll him so I'm on top. The man is smart because he gives in to my desire, rolling with me instead of fighting against me.

Falling for him is as easy as falling backward onto a bed, swift and comfortable, knowing that I'll be safe where I land.

It's my turn to tease him, though I'm still winding myself up as I grind down on his rigid length where it rests, trapped in his pants. I'm methodical, undoing each button slowly, watching as his breaths get more shallow. There is a biological need in me to reward him for lying there while I rub against him like a cat in heat with his hands just resting on my thighs. It's without a doubt that I'll have bruises from where he's gripping me so tightly, but I actually relish it.

When I've got all the buttons undone, I run my hands up his bare chest, slowly peeling his shirt open so I can see his bare, rippled skin. I can see the side of his tattoo peeking out again, and I realize that I told myself I would lick it.

I refuse to deny myself any further. I let my tongue start on the edge of the ink, and I trace it. Now that I can look more closely at it, I see that it's the bow of a ship. I can't get at the rest of it since the vast majority of it is on his back, but I vow to return to it, slowly kissing my way up to his mouth.

He's silent except for the harsh sounds of his breath when I hit a particularly sensitive patch of skin. Josh seems content to watch me as I have my way with exploring the ridges of his body, pausing when I get to one nipple. I run my tongue along the outside, slowly working up to the peak of the stiffened skin before gently blowing. His response is immediate in the form of him bucking his hips up into me. Josh is reaching behind him, but I'm too focused on my task to pay attention to what he's doing. I might actually expire when he sinks his cock into me finally.

I'm starting to make my way over to his other nipple when he rears up to wrap his arms around me. I can't help but yelp as he rolls me over so I'm flat on my back.

"Stop fucking around, treasure."

Josh discards his shirt before working down his pants. He seems to hesitate once his cock is free, but he resumes stripping, barely kicking them off.

I want to wrap my lips around his dick just to remind myself how great it feels in my mouth. He's paused like we're on the precipice of something, and I know we are. I know that it's something I absolutely want.

I want to come home to him when I'm done with work. I want him to be there when I complain about problems I'm having. I want to be able to take his burdens and meet his family. I lean up to grab his face to pull him down to me.

"Why did you stop?" I ask, the moment morphing right before my eyes, all the frenetic movements have slowed into something more tender.

"Have you ever been afraid to actually get the thing you want? Like you worry that maybe you've built something up in your head too much, and it won't be like you imagined?"

My heart lurches, and I'm afraid I've been reading this wrong the whole time. "Yeah," I say, my heart getting caught in my throat. All of a sudden, I feel too vulnerable lying naked under him.

"This is nothing like that, but I'm afraid of not meeting your expectations." It's such an honest thing to say that as much as I want to make this a tawdry thing, reach between him and guide him inside me, I don't.

"You're already more than I ever expected in my life."

Josh kisses me then, slow and sweet. His cock brushes against my clit as he presses against me, and the roll of my hips isn't a conscious decision.

"I don't think you can know that until I've properly fucked you," he teases, rubbing his nose against mine.

"Then what are you waiting for? An invitation?"

His body stretches over mine as he grabs for something over my head.

"What's that?"

"My invitation," he teases, and I see it's a new bottle of lube. Josh applies some to his hand before rubbing it on his dick, and I can't help but watch as he strokes himself. For a second he appears to be very invested in his self-love, and I don't hate it. I'm getting worked up too, watching him.

He positions himself at my entrance and slides into me in one easy stroke. His piercing drags along my inner channel, and I bite my lip to stop the whimper from escaping. When he's fully seated inside me, we stay like that for a second, just breathing in the new sensation of being joined before he starts to fuck me in earnest.

Each thrust of his hips has my body jerking, but his iron grip on my hips keeps me from moving across the bed as he chases release for us both. I'm meeting his thrusts, trying to get just the right amount of friction on my clit when he slows down.

"Do you need something more? Is it not just your pussy that's needy? Do you need me to give your clit some love too?" He readjusts how he's positioned on the bed, being careful not to leave the warmth of my body.

He leans forward, gripping my face as he gives me a slow and languorous kiss before his hand trails down the length of my body so he can strum my clit. I cry out from the assault of sensation. He takes his time, varying pressure and how he's touching me until I go off like a bomb under him.

My eyes slam shut, but I can still hear the pained groan he lets out as my body clenches around him. The sound matches the one I'm making because he's made my body feel so good I'm afraid of what comes next. There's no way I'm going to be able to survive being away from him. I spent a long time grinding the right combination of sex toys to get me off. Knowing what it feels like to choke his cock with my pussy means I might never be able to self-love again to satisfaction.

"Cum in me," I demand, opening my eyes. Now that my orgasm has subsided, he's slowly rocking his hips against me.

His gaze shifts from watching where he's fucking me up to my face. "You want to take it the way I want?" Josh threads his hands into my hair, exerting some pressure. "Is this okay?" he asks, watching me closely.

"I want you to ruin me," I tell him. I expect something fierce in response, but instead, there is something tender in his eyes when he grabs a fist full of my hair and forces my head back to expose my throat.

"Be careful what you wish for." Josh doesn't kiss or lick, but he drags his teeth down the column of my neck hard enough to cause a spike of pain that has me clenching around him all over again. He finishes his trail with a kiss on my collarbone. "If, at any point, it's too much, just tell me."

"This is my only wish."

Josh pulls out of me so he can flip me over like I'm a rag doll.

I'm ass up when he trails a finger down my spine until he reaches my asshole. I shiver with delight when his finger circles the rosebud hole there.

"Have you ever been fucked here?" he asks before spreading my cheeks.

I feel so fucking vulnerable spread out like I'm a piece of property he's inspecting. It's a little bit degrading and a lot hot.

"Yes," I tell him truthfully. "But not as often or as well as I would like." It's an honesty that I haven't afforded many former lovers. I tried it once in college because who didn't experiment then? It was about as lackluster as you would expect from a college boy trying the same thing for the first time. After that, I was left with half-hearted attempts to get the job done if I wasn't made to feel ashamed for this preference. It's okay for a guy to like fucking ass, but for a girl to like it, that makes us weird.

"Treasure, another night; I'm going to make sure you love it." I can't see what he's doing, but he slides into my pussy in one smooth, slow thrust until he's chasing his pleasure. I have to hold on to the headboard with one hand while the other rolls slow circles around my clit until my orgasm grabs me, and I'm spasming around his grip. It's like he was waiting for that second orgasm. He moans through his own release, and I hold on to the headboard with both hands while he pounds into me.

He collapses onto the bed, turning just enough so he's not crushing me under him when he lands on the mattress. I can feel his softening cock slide out of me, his cum dripping onto my leg. I feel filthy and treasured all at once.

Josh keeps his arms around me, kissing along the back of my shoulder before I need to get out of bed and deal with the aftermath. It's the opposite of sexy, but I also don't want to lie in bed covered in juices.

"Are you alright?" he asks, a hint of worry in his voice as I climb out of bed toward the direction of his bathroom.

"I'm okay," I assure him, striding naked across the room. I have nothing to be embarrassed about. He's seen all of me and keeps wanting more. Hiding would just be false modesty at this point.

The bathroom is obscene, and I hate him all over again while thinking about my shoebox-sized apartment when he has space for a separate soaker tub and full-glass shower enclosure. The tub looks like a carved-out egg, but it's higher on one side and perfect to settle in. A tub like this is wasted on a man like Josh, who definitely never takes baths. Not because he's a man but because he's never home. There's space around the floor to set candles burning to create a romantic glow.

I moan at the injustice, taking a second to run my hand along the edge of his tub. We could both easily fit in there to soak for hours. If he let me, I think I would spend my time just lying in there between when I get home from work and when I need to go back.

"I heard–oh, you saw the tub."

I spin to face Josh. He's standing with his arms pressed against the door frame, looking deliciously naked as his cock continues to seep cum. I lift my gaze back to his face.

"You kept this a secret from me," I say, almost a little mad.

He grins and walks over, pulling me against his body. His cock grinds against me, but I don't break my glare.

"Can you blame me? I wanted to be sure you were with me for me and not just my tub."

"It can be both. I can be with you for you and for your tub. Those two things are not mutually exclusive."

He herds me in the direction of the shower, and I scowl at him, even when he presses me against the wall. I yelp at the bite of the cold tiles against my back, but Josh captures the noise with his mouth.

"I wanted to be sure that it was me. Can you blame a man for being a little insecure? I saw the look on your face. I think you're a little bit in love with my tub."

"Because I am. It's perfect. Bitches love tubs. Ask me how I know."

Josh laughs, and I can feel it everywhere, not just because we're touching but because it's infectious and spreads through my body.

"And how do you know, Taryn Robins?"

"Because it's me. I'm bitches. I love that tub. I want a bath."

"Now?"

I bite at his pec. "Yes, now. Well, after I pee. I am leaking cum."

"I'm not sorry about that. I thought we would shower and then lie in bed; maybe I could wring another orgasm or two out from you, and then we could fall asleep."

I give him a light shove, and he steps back. "Or we could shower off the sex and then get in the tub, where you could wring another orgasm from me, and then we could go to bed?" As the words leave my mouth, I realize I'm assuming he wants me to spend the night, so I quickly backtrack. "I mean, I could also go home if you don't want me to spend the night."

"Tell me what you want, Taryn."

"I want the tub," I tell him honestly, and he playfully grabs my sides, tickling me.

"You know that's not what I meant in the slightest. I said we could fall asleep, meaning you could stay here. If you're not comfortable with that, or you don't want to, you don't have to."

"Want. As in, I want that. I want to stay the night. Would you just start the shower and the tub while I pee already?"

"You're okay with me being in the room while you pee?" he asks while he twists the knob on the shower.

I slow my steps and then narrow my eyes at him. "Are you not okay with that? Does it detract from the sexy if you see me pee?"

"I don't know. In the past, women have gotten weird about it, so I'm not going to assume."

I walk over to his toilet and sit before peeing. "I think this is answer enough."

The look he gives me stops my heart in my chest, but I tell myself I must be reading too deeply into it. Because the look he's giving me feels like he's telling me he loves me, and I don't know if that could be true when we're still so new.

I would be okay if that's what his face was saying. Because I'm feeling it myself for sure. Maybe not love exactly, but that fragile feeling of a bond between two people. I just want to nurture and protect it as we move forward. I want to see that feeling and that bond grow between us, and I'm ready to do what I can to protect it.

Maybe I shouldn't have peed in front of him the first time we had sex, but it's normal. And the man was ready to finger my asshole, and I think he would have too if he had been better prepared. The lube was right there, but maybe he just wanted to get used to the idea that I'm even into that.

Stop. I need to stop analyzing everything so closely.

Our shower is just that, a shower. Josh is careful to wash my back and my ass. The way he was going on and on about my boobs, I would have thought he was a boob guy for sure, but now I'm wondering if I was wrong.

"Is this okay?" he asks as he runs a finger between my ass cheeks, pressing further until he's right at my asshole again.

"Mhmm," I agree, biting my lips, too afraid of him stopping. No. Josh is also an ass man.

Dare I think it? Maybe it's not that he's an ass or boob guy; maybe it's me. Maybe it's all of me.

"Just relax, treasure," he whispers with his wet lips pressed to my face. The rainwater shower is pounding down on us, and I relax as much as I can while standing. He bends me forward just enough before slowly pressing the tip of his finger into me. His mouth captures the moan that escapes as he slowly enters me. I press back so his finger can slide deeper, and hot fucking damn. He withdraws it, then pushes me back under the water to rinse all the soap suds from our bodies.

I can appreciate a man with a focus on hygiene.

The tub is almost overflowing when we finally do get out of the glass stall. We've both been pretty silent as we focused on just being together, and our time in the tub is much of the same. He climbs in first, hissing at the heat of the water. When I go to get in, I do the same thing.

Our skin is hot and flushed, and when he reaches between my legs with one hand idly stroking my clit while the other plays with my nipple, I give a soft cry as he manages to get me off.

We settle quietly after that, enjoying the peace of the moment.

"Will you tell me about your tattoo?" I ask sleepily.

Josh kisses the back of my head before tugging me closer to him. "What do you want to know?"

"Is there any significance?" Josh goes quiet for a second before I rush on. "You don't have to tell me."

"No, I want to. Part of it was that I was a punk kid. I was mad at my dad for abandoning the family. I was put in this role of protector, and even if it wasn't expected, I felt it was my duty to care for my sisters and mom. I was going off to college and just so angry. So I went and got my dick pierced and had this ugly little troll tattooed on my side just for the sake of being an asshole. When my dad saw it that summer while we were at a beach, he hit the fucking roof and told me I ruined my chances of being a professional. That was very obviously not true."

He pauses for a moment while rubbing my arms. "Please go on," I urge.

"When I graduated college, I was sick of explaining the tattoo, and I wanted something more meaningful to cover it up. So, I went and got a ship to represent the journey that I made from being this kid who thought he knew what responsibility was to still a kid, but one with a better idea of the complete journey he wanted to make to be a better man."

"Thank you for sharing that," I tell him, lifting his hand, which is clasped with mine, to give it a soft kiss.

We lie in the tub until we both turn to prunes, and I can only wonder what I did to wind up with such a wonderful man in my life.

Fourteen

IT'S another weekend in the office, and I'm thankful that, for the most part, it's quiet. Josh has started to take me home with him after work, and while his townhouse is far from the office, I appreciate having a non-weed-smelling space to sleep. I appreciate that I can fall asleep in the car on the way to and from the office, and Josh will wake me up.

What I think is killing him is that I'm making him let me out of the car a block from the office so I can at least look like I've been on the subway and had to walk instead of looking like we arrived together.

At least now I know how he does it. How, in the middle of June, he's able to show up at the office in a full suit without looking at all weathered.

But today, it's a quiet Saturday, and I decided to wear a dress. It's not tight like my skirt was, so I'm looking forward to hopefully tempting Josh into giving me an orgasm. That's the thing about our jobs; we might be having sexy sleepovers, but they're *just* sleepovers. I shower and sleep at his place and occasionally make a protein shake on my way out the door.

We haven't had sex since the night of the opera. I was nearly late for brunch with my friends where they demanded all the down-and-dirty details that I gave them only because it's fair when I demanded it from them.

Josh is standing in his office, his phone held up to his ear. He's not facing me, which makes it easy to slip in and take my panties off. I shove them into the couch with just a little bit of the royal blue fabric sticking out, a gift for him to find later. I'll have to remember to warn him about it before I leave.

He must hear me because he spins around and raises an eyebrow. Holding a finger up to his lips, he pulls the phone away from his ear, hitting a button on the phone before settling it into the cradle.

Another man's voice comes over the speaker, but I'm not even bothering to listen because Josh just pointed at the ground. I raise an eyebrow at him, confused, but then he points at me, then at the ground. My blood heats in my veins, and I can feel the flush as it works its way through my body.

If he wants me to suck his cock like it's a thick milkshake while he's on a call, I'm going to rise to the challenge. Or, he's going to rise, and I'm going to get on my knees like the good little slut he wants me to be.

I have to bite my lip to stop from moaning when that thought skitters through my mind. I'm not sure we've exactly decided on what sorts of games we're playing here. I've never been heavily into the BDSM community, though I'm aware of it. I think we're exploring what feels right to us. At this point of knowing Josh, I know that if I was uncomfortable with something, I could say so, and he would respect that.

That's why I do as he wants, and I get on my knees. I patiently wait for him to approach me, even as the old carpet digs into my knees. I wonder how long he's going to make me wait because while I would wait forever, I also have team partners who are here. I'm just lucky that they decided to go out to grab lunch instead of ordering in.

Josh crooks his finger at me and then points to the ground right in front of him. And damn it. I want him to fuck me so hard right now because the idea of crawling, again, feels like it should be so degrading. I'm not some dog at his beck and call. But then I'm placing my hands on the ground, and I fucking *crawl* to him.

The pleasure in his eyes when I stop just before him is enough to soak my panties. That is if I was still wearing any. As it is, I'm acutely aware of just how wet this entire exercise is making me.

His hand grips my chin gently before gesturing for me to rise.

Once I'm on my feet, he pushes me back onto his desk, and I get on it, sitting just at the edge. I wonder if he's going to reward me for being so good and doing exactly what he wanted.

Josh leans forward and presses his mouth right next to my ear.

"I'm on a call with the CEO of a company I'm working with. I'm not on mute so you need to be *fucking quiet* when I fuck you, or else."

I can't help but shiver, wondering what "or else" would look like, but I nod. I almost want to find out, but the same way I would be pissed if he fucked with my career, I know he would not appreciate it if I did make a sound.

He squats just a little so he can grip my calves and work his way up my legs to my thighs. His hands stay on the outside of my thighs until he reaches my hips. I'm watching his face carefully, and I know the exact moment he realizes that I'm not wearing panties because he goes still and lifts his gaze to mine.

I don't know what I expected, but him mouthing "good girl" at me was not it. As quietly as he can, he slowly slides down the teeth of his zipper. I'm sure whoever is on the other end of that call can hear it. The same way I'm sure they can feel the tension crackling in the air because I'm certain that all I want is for him to fuck me hard enough on his desk for everything on it to fall off with the roughness of his motions.

When he frees his cock, I take a second to look at the swollen flesh as he pumps himself a few times. Josh reaches out and grabs my hand, licking my palm before setting it against his cock. I bite my lips to stop from making a sound, and I'm reassured when I see that Josh has to do the same.

I want to kiss him, but I know that as bad as sex sounds can be, kisses can also be equally loud and breathy. So, I focus on not making a sound as his fingers find my wet heat. I spread my legs wider for him, even if it means grinding my teeth down into nothing as he slips one, then two fingers inside me. Josh uses my wetness to move up to my clit, spreading it around so that when he does jerk me to the edge of the desk, he can position his cock against my entrance.

His movement into me is slow. He makes what feels like a million micro-thrusts, gradually moving deeper inside me, and each jerk of his hips is driving me wild. I'm holding onto his shoulder with one hand and biting into my other one.

When he's finally fully seated inside me, I'm so close to the edge that I'm amazed that he was able to get me there with his cock. Josh's hands find my hips, and he grips them hard enough that I'll get to marvel at the bruises he leaves on me later.

His thrusts are so careful and measured as he moves in me that I bite my lip until it bleeds as I shatter around him. It's not wholly unexpected, but I keep holding on to the feeling of him moving even as tears slide down my face. Josh buries his face in my neck when his own release hits him. I can hear the low groan he makes as his movements become jerky and erratic.

That's when I realize that no one is speaking any longer. Josh doesn't seem to notice or care because he presses his forehead against mine, stealing a kiss that feels like he's stealing my very soul with it.

I'm trying to breathe as quietly as I can, which honestly gives me a newfound appreciation for people in horror movies because it's a lot harder than I gave them credit for. Josh withdraws from me, and I give myself a second to mourn the loss of him inside me and the connection that came from that.

But then this man, this powerhouse of a banker, gets on his knees before me. He pushes my dress up so my bare pussy is exposed to him. I wonder if he just has a thing for watching my pussy leak his cum, when he does something so unexpected.

He licks my pussy from back to front before going all in on my clit. I don't know for sure that the call has ended, but I was told to be silent, so that's exactly what I'm going to do. I'm going to sit on the edge of his desk while he eats me out.

When his two fingers slide into me, curling so he can stroke at my g-spot, I let out a little whimper, and he stops. It was *barely* audible, but I get it. He meets my gaze and gives me a mischievous grin, my previous release all over his face.

"My call might be over, but there are still people in the office. One more sound like that, and I swear I'll have you over my knee, and you'll need a standing desk for a week."

"What makes you think I don't want that?" I ask, but we both know that I'm too worried about my job to even entertain it.

"If you want me to spank you, all you have to do is ask. But for now, I can't do it, so let me eat this pussy. I missed lunch."

I thread my fingers into his hair, nearly ripping it out when he makes me come again. When the aftershocks have abated, he gets to his feet, carefully stuffing his cock back into his pants. He grabs a few tissues from his desk and gently places them between my legs to catch what is still dripping. I should go grab my panties now that he's decided to cum inside me, but I can deal with the discomfort for a little while if it means he has a surprise waiting for him.

My breathing is too heavy for me to even think of something witty to say. Josh looks like a mess. There are spots on his pants that are clearly from fucking someone. All around his mouth is wet, and his hair is sticking up in a million directions from my tugging.

"You look freshly-fucked," I tell him quietly, not wanting our conversation to be overheard.

"I look freshly-fucked? Treasure, you have blood on your chin from where you bit yourself hard enough to bleed, and while I did my best to clean up the mess I made between your legs, you definitely have a wet spot on your skirt from where you've been sitting." I didn't even register the pain, but sure enough, when I wipe around my mouth, it comes back with just a little blood smeared on it.

"Since you did me the courtesy," I start, leaning forward to kiss him, "I guess I should pay it forward." Using my thumbs, I wipe the excess of me from his face while kissing him deeply.

"You really are a treasure, you know that?" he says when he pulls back.

"I hope that call wasn't important," I quip, hopping off the desk.

"I was on mute the entire time. It was just an informational call and not one that I needed to actually be present for."

I give him a light shove, but he captures my wrist and pulls me against him. "And all that nonsense about needing to stay quiet?"

"Well, you did need to stay quiet. How much longer do you need to be here?"

"If Darren and Eric are gone, I could just leave now and tell them I'm working on it at home. We're not terribly collaborative."

"Have you talked to Manny about it?"

I scoff as I try to finger-comb his hair. "Yeah, *okay*. He wouldn't believe me even if I did."

"That seems unfair to Manny. From what I can tell, he's a good enough guy."

I sigh. Josh is never going to get it because he's a man in a man's world. I could try to explain it to him, tell him all the ways that he's wrong, but at the end of the day, it doesn't matter because there's nothing he can do about it.

"Sure, Manny is good enough," I say, attempting to placate my boyfriend. Getting into all the ways that Manny is a shit boss is just going to ruin this postcoital glow, and I want to hold on to it for just a little longer. "I'll message you if I'm good to go."

Josh nods and presses a kiss to my cheek. “If there is something specific, you should talk to Manny. If he doesn’t know, he can’t do anything about how Darren and Eric are treating you.”

I give Josh a curt nod before walking out of the office for the bathroom to clean up the mess he made of me a little better.

Part of what he said is right. If Manny doesn’t know there is a problem, then he never has a chance to fix it. But talking to Manny is just going to look like a worse conversation than the one I just had with Josh, and I know Josh is on my side. Manny won’t believe me, and as soon as Darren comes in with his explanation, I’ll be the one treated like a pariah because there is no way that Darren or Eric could be the ones in the wrong.

Unfortunately for me, Darren is already sitting at his desk when I make it back from the bathroom.

“Where the fuck have you been, fire crotch?” Darren asks, flinging a paperclip at me. I manage to snatch it from the air before it hits me, which earns me a begrudging respect, not that I want it for that. As sick as it makes me, I want Darren to recognize me for being able to do my job and do it well. Part of me doesn’t care at all about Darren, but I want him to realize that I am good at my job.

“Does it matter? I don’t question you when you have to take your daily wank sessions.” I sit at my desk, but Darren slides his chair across the small walkway so he’s next to me.

“What’s the matter, red? Jealous of my hand? If you want, I’m happy to take some of this stress you’ve been holding on to. I know you’ve said no to Eric, but maybe that’s because you want someone else to pay you some attention. I’m happy to see if a good fuck makes you a little less of a bitch.” His hand rests on the inside of my knee, and he starts to slide my dress up as he pushes between my legs.

I get to my feet, shoving him back before I slap him across the face. Darren seems just as surprised as me at what just happened, but he gets to his feet as well. I want to shrink back and away from him, but he'll only see it as weakness and press his advantage. I can't let that happen, so I stand my ground, even if it terrifies me.

"What's going on here?" Eric asks, walking over as he wipes his hands with a paper towel before tossing it away. He glances between Darren and I.

"Little miss isn't feeling good, so yet again, she's going to take the coward's way out and leave us to work. Maybe you should go home, Tara." Darren's voice is full of venom.

Stiffly, I nod, not willing to be in his presence anymore. I don't want to be in anyone's presence anymore. I turn to my computer and shoot Josh a message that I'm going to be heading to my apartment to do some laundry and that I'll see him on Monday before I pack up my stuff. I'm too shaken to even care that I've sent that message on the company messenger service instead of a text. I know he'll see it faster this way.

Eric follows me to the elevator. "Tell me the truth. Are you running away because Darren said something stupid? You know he's all bark and no bite."

Indignation rides me hard as I spin to face Eric, palm itching to hit someone again. "Which is nothing at all like you, right, Eric? All whimper and no bark?"

"What do you want me to do, Taryn? You don't want to date me, so why should I put my neck on the line for you?"

I'm thankful when the elevator shows up quickly. "Because it's the right thing to do, Eric."

I step into the elevator and let it close me off from this toxic place.

In a shocking turn of events, Josh is confused about why I left without him, and he's wondering what's wrong. I shoot him a text, letting him know that I just realized I have a lot of work that I still have to do before the end of this project. We have one month left, and it's four weeks too many.

I do a few more hours of work from my room, thankful for noise-canceling headphones because there are people over when I get there. I start to contemplate what it would look like if I got another place, and I vow to look into it as soon as I'm in my room.

But being away from Josh and the office just reminds me of all the other stressors hanging out in my life in the form of my student loans and my parents' mortgage. When trying to look at my finances to see how much of an apartment I could afford, I realize I can barely afford this place. My student loan balance somehow only grows despite my making regular payments.

It feels like nothing I do is going to be good enough, not to impress Manny and get out from under him, not with the finances I'm trying to deal with. Maybe in a few years when I'm bringing in bonuses that are over seven figures, but until then, I have to find a way to make this all work.

When I'm finally turning in for bed, I see I have a text message from Josh.

> Josh: I have to be in Boston for a meeting next week. What do you say to taking the weekend and we can play tourist for a few days? I promise to make it worth your while.

The idea of getting out of Manhattan feels refreshing. Elia's wedding was months ago, and while it was paradise, it was for a wedding, which meant needing to make sure that Elia had everything she needed for her big day.

This would just be a weekend of Josh and I. Sure, I would still have some work to do, but it would be easy enough for me to work on the Acela up to Boston, and if he had work to do on the weekend, I'm sure I could get work done then too.

I look at my credit cards to see how bad the outstanding balance is, and I cringe, knowing that the round trip could be costly. Josh knows enough to know I worry over money, but asking him to pay for my tickets doesn't seem fair.

Like he knows what I'm thinking, the next text comes through.

Josh: I'll buy your plane/train ticket, and in exchange, you'll let me see if oysters are really an aphrodisiac.

I laugh in spite of myself.

Taryn: Only if you want to see what it's like fucking a closed throat.

Josh: Fuck, that's right. You have an allergy! Okay, then we will avoid all the shellfish, and I'll still fuck your throat.

Unable to resist him, I agree to this trip.

Fifteen

MY FUCK-OFF VIBES must be on point because Darren doesn't dare address me directly. There are no snarky comments when I tell the team that I'm going to be taking the weekend for the most part and I don't want to be bothered by them at all. Manny seems to take it well too, nodding when I say this. I get the feeling that it's not going to stick for him, but I was always going to answer emails from him regardless.

"Tara!" Manny shouts my name, and I lift my head from the spreadsheet I'm pouring over.

"Yes?" I ask, my gaze tracking as he moves around the wall of cubicles before coming to stand in front of me.

"I have a proposition for you, and I would like you to come with me."

My cheeks burn, and I glance around, catching Darren giving me a smirk before he pantomimes a blow job. Manny never struck me as the type to demand a blow job in front of others in the office, but maybe I'm wrong. Regardless, I get to my feet and follow him. He doesn't head in the direction of his office but down another hallway I've often traversed. My steps want to slow as we get closer and closer to Josh's office.

Does he know that we've been fucking? Does he know that I'm planning to go to Boston with Josh for the weekend?

"Is he in?" Manny asks, stopping in front of Quincey's desk. She lifts her head to see who is asking. Her attention flicks to me for just a second.

"He is, but he only has fifteen minutes before he has to leave if he has any hope of making his train." Quincey is nearly shouting at the end.

Josh comes out of his office looking like a tall drink of water on a hot day. His hair is combed back and smooth while his suit jacket rests perfectly on his shoulders. Everything about him makes me want to crawl into his arms and stay there, but he's respecting my boundaries as he gives me a casual glance.

"Manny," Josh greets, holding his hand out. "As Quincey here said, this has to be short. You mentioned having something you wanted to discuss."

Josh gestures for us to step into his office ahead of him. He gives me a questioning look and I shrug, unsure of what Manny wants, but it's making me nervous. Josh's hand smooths down my back to pinch my ass as I pass him.

I can't even seriously glare at the man as he closes the door because it just makes me want to be frisky. Manny walks and sits on Josh's couch, shifting the cushions, and that's when I see it: the royal blue of my panties that I left there last weekend. The ones I forgot about until this very moment because of the haze of anger after Darren's come-on. But I've already moved to take a seat in the chairs in front of Josh's desk, so I can't sit next to Manny and try to grab them.

It takes considerable strength to not pantomime to Josh about the panties because pointing them out will just draw more attention to their existence. What the fuck was I thinking?

"Yes. I wanted to discuss Tara with you. I know it's unorthodox having this conversation with her in the room, but I would rather get things moving in the right direction instead of wasting any more time."

"Taryn," Josh corrects. He's leaning against his desk with his hands braced on the wood behind him and his ankles crossed. The power he's exuding is painting a filthy image in my mind. I want to get on my knees in front of him and lick his cock until he begs me to suck on it. And Jesus fucking Christ, this man is both good and terrible for my libido. It's like Josh is purposefully avoiding looking at me because he knows what I'm thinking.

"That's what I said. Anyway, I was thinking that it might be a good idea for her to transfer to your team for that new project you're about to start. I've already been having her run some of the numbers and she's familiar with it. I think it would be a good idea for her to get more exposure to the different lines of business that we offer."

There is no controlling the expression on my face. My jaw drops, but I'm quick to close it before looking over at Josh to see how he's reacting to this. In a blink of an eye, he looks at me before looking at Manny.

"Respectfully, sir, I'm not sure that's wise." His formal approach to this reminds me that Manny is technically above Josh for the time being, and it could become a what-I-say-goes situation.

"Is it because she's a woman? Because I can guarantee she's a good worker. Not as strong as Darren and Eric, but what she lacks in skill, she makes up for in effort."

Lacks in skill?

"Excuse me?" I demand, turning to look at Manny. It's unbelievable. I could say I don't understand where he's got this impression of me, but I know exactly where it's from. Darren and Eric have been in his ear from the start, and I never had a chance to impress Manny. I try to reroute my brain and what I actually wanted to say because I can promise it wasn't going to be anything productive. "Have I made a mistake or done something wrong?"

Manny shifts on the couch, and my panties become more obvious. So far, Manny hasn't noticed, but I'm not even worried about that at this point. "Besides your attitude issues toward Darren and Eric? I know you think I can't see it, but I do. You act like you have a chip on your shoulder when it comes to them, but they're just trying to help you." He focuses back on Josh. "Again, this is not to say that Tara has done anything wrong, because she hasn't. She's a delight to work with, and when you need a softer touch with clients, she's perfect. I think it would be a better move for her career."

Josh pushes off his desk, but his face is unreadable. "You've given me a lot to think about. Obviously, I had plans for who I wanted to bring onto my team, but I would like to think about what you've said tonight. If it's alright with you, I'd like to take the weekend to consider it, and perhaps when I get back, we can have a more in-depth conversation without *Taryn* present."

Manny waves Josh off. "It is all things she would hear during her review of this project. I think it's good for associates to know what they're facing when it comes to what is going in their files. I think this would be a better move for Tara."

Can they try asking *Tara* what she wants, maybe? Or at least get her side of the story in this awful he said/she said drama. Darren had to have run to Manny and told him that I struck him. God, it makes me wish I *had* told Josh when it happened, but telling Josh would have meant making a formal statement, and I don't think my career can survive me making two sexual harassment claims.

At a certain point, the question from everyone in the room will be, "What is she doing to encourage this?" or "Are we sure she's even telling the truth?" And I can't face that. I won't face that. I need this job. There's a desperation that I didn't have when I made my first complaint. I can't say that I would have made a different decision knowing what I do now about the financial situation my parents are facing. I try not to dwell on what could have been or should have been because there is nothing to be gained by that, but right now, I'm wondering if I had gotten on my knees to get ahead if I had accepted the hush-money job offer, where I would be now.

Immediately, I kill the thought. *If* I had, I wouldn't be with Josh, and I would choose him every time.

"Her name is Taryn, and as I said, we can discuss this later. I have a few things I need to finish up before leaving for Boston."

Manny presses his hand down on the couch to push off, and it's a credit to how shaken I am that I don't even register that my boss's hands are on my underwear. Manny notices them and pulls them out of the couch.

"Josh, I didn't think you were the type, you fox. Have you been raiding the hen house? I guess the apple doesn't fall too far from the tree, does it?" Manny says it like it's a legacy to be proud of.

The look on Josh's face breaks my heart, but he reaches forward, grabbing the underwear, and stuffing them into his pocket. "My sister dropped by the office over the weekend and was repacking her overnight bag. She must have left them behind," he covers smoothly.

Manny winks at him. "I don't blame you. Quincey seems to have the right qualifications for the job."

Josh's temper has to be bubbling over. "That's enough, Manny," he snaps. Letting out a slow breath, Josh lifts his chin. "I don't think it's appropriate to speak about any woman in the office like that. I'd like you to apologize to Taryn."

I look up at Josh with hearts in my eyes, but he's only making it worse.

Manny gives him a light punch in the arm. "Lighten up, Josh. Maybe if that was your secretary's thong, you wouldn't be so uptight. I'll choose to overlook that disrespect as protectiveness."

My boss doesn't spare a glance at us as he walks away. Josh

reaches out for me, but I dodge his grip. "We'll talk this weekend," I assure him before going back to my desk.

The entire train ride to Boston, I go over my options. I think I can push back enough on Manny to not be transferred. It would be a blow to not only my standing on the team but also to my confidence. Manny is all but broadcasting that he doesn't think I'm good enough for my job, which hurts when taking into account the amount of work that I do.

Josh has texted me what hotel he's staying at and that he's left me a key to the room at the front desk while he finishes up a late meeting. It's fine by me because I still don't know what I'm going to do. After the meeting Manny and I had with Josh, it was like Darren knew what happened. He had a smug smirk on his face for the rest of the day, and since I wasn't blowing off steam with Josh for a few days or crashing at his apartment, I ran myself physically into the ground at the gym.

The hotel room we're in is stunning, if a little modern for my taste. The floor-to-ceiling windows offer amazing views of the construction site next door, but as long as they don't work weekends, I'm not complaining.

There's a tray of chocolate-covered strawberries and champagne on ice in the room, along with a note from Josh telling me to relax. The soaker tub is calling my name, so after filling it with piping hot water, I carry my strawberries and champagne over to it before I sink in.

Being alone without my work in front of me is giving me time to think. I'm genuinely jealous of Han going out there and deciding to break the toxic cycle of how hard we work in this industry. Consulting is one area that I always thought about, but they often work the same hours, just with travel and a lower salary.

Groaning, I take another swig from the bottle of champagne. Every time I question why I'm putting myself through this, I remember that my parents might be kicked out of their home.

I'm done with the bottle by the time Josh walks into the room. With a tired smile, he drops his laptop bag by the door and engages the safety lock.

"You look cozy," he remarks before loosening his tie and grabbing onto the molding of the bathroom door to lean in toward me.

Does he know how sexy that is?

But more than sex, I want Josh to hold me tonight. I want to cuddle my man and, for a night, forget about the stress that is my family and what Manny's offer to Josh might mean. Sure, a few orgasms could accomplish that, but I'm desperate for a deeper connection with him.

"Want to join me?" I offer. This tub is much smaller than his, but it's deep enough that I can have my legs and tits in it at the same time, and that's really the bar for a quality tub.

"Not tonight, treasure. I'm content to just look for now."

"Why don't you go lie down in bed, and I'll be there in a few minutes?" I offer, trying to keep the smirk from my face.

"And miss you getting out of the tub in all your dripping glory? I don't think so."

"Would you just do as you're told and get into bed?" I order.

"Yes, ma'am." His voice goes deliciously dark, and okay, yeah, we can cuddle after we have a few orgasms.

He leaves the bathroom, and once I hear him settled on the bed, I reach over to the wall beside the tub and flip the switch. I'm a little sad I'll miss his face, but the screen that blocks off the bathroom from the bedroom rises, and when Josh's face is exposed, his eyebrows are lifted in surprise.

"Aren't you glad you listened?" I ask, standing only once the curtain is all the way up.

"Why don't you come over here with that smart mouth so I can put it to work?"

Now is my turn to sass him. "Yes, sir."

I don't bother with a towel, even if it means leaving water trailing me all the way to the bed. My hair is still dry and up in a clip when I reach Josh. He grabs my upper arms and tosses me onto the bed, and I land with a giggle.

"You think it's funny to be such a cocktease? Did you enjoy when Manny found your panties in my couch? I wonder how on earth those got there." He reaches into his pocket and pulls them out.

"How long have you been carrying those around with you?" I ask. I try to close my legs to rub them together, but Josh grips my knees and forces my legs apart.

"Since Manny gave them to me a few days ago. The satin felt so nice as I jerked my cock with them. Don't worry, I didn't get my cum on them... this time." He tosses them at me, and I laugh, grabbing them only to discard them on the other side of the bed.

"I put them there over the weekend and forgot to mention it."

"'Forgot?'" He uses air quotes, but I can see his amusement.

"Yes, I forgot."

"We have a lot to talk about, but it's been a week since I was in that tight pussy, and I'm feeling like I want something else. Roll over."

I don't hesitate to do as I'm told, but I stay flat on my stomach. He swats my ass.

"Yow!" I complain, but it's halfhearted.

"Don't let me forget I still owe you a punishment for coming into my office while I was on a call with no panties on. Is that where they went? Were you hoping I would find them in my couch one day and think of you? On your knees."

I comply, pushing onto my knees, leaving me vulnerable. "Did you miss me?" I ask breathily, daring to glance at him over my shoulder.

"Like you wouldn't believe."

He nips and kisses all along my spine down to my ass before he grabs my cheeks, spreading them.

"What are you...?"

It's fairly obvious what he's doing. He's leaving me exposed for his perusal. It's hard not to squirm, knowing that he's staring down parts of me that even I've never looked at. He must be remembering what I said about what I wanted and how I was left unsatisfied previously. His mouth covers the bud before licking it and pulling away. A rim job was never something I ever considered wanting, but I want him to do it again.

"Oh, fuck," I moan, fisting the sheets and burying my face into the comforter.

"Did you like that treasure? I wanted to mark you there in a way I bet no other has before. If I can't be the first person to lay claim to your ass, I'm going to be the last one for sure."

He releases me, and it leaves me on edge, wondering what he's going to do next. The sounds of him moving are confusing to me, and I know that I could just lift my head to see what he's doing, but I like the mystery. I like wondering what's going to happen next.

"You would tell me if you didn't like something, I hope." He's being sincere, so I nod.

"Of course. You haven't done anything I haven't wanted."

"Good." I can hear the sound of a cap opening, and I don't have to wonder what it is. It's lube. My filthy mind imagines him jerking himself to lather it over his cock before spreading some on my ass.

"Do you want me to tell you what I'm going to do?" he asks.

"No." The word escapes in a rush, and he gives a dark chuckle.

Heeding my request, he doesn't prepare me as he presses a wet, blunt object to my cunt. I tense up and pull away from him reflexively.

"It's just a toy. A small one, but I want you to feel full everywhere."

I nod and try to relax my body as the small toy is pressed inside me. He wasn't kidding; it really is small. It takes no time at all to adjust to it being there, but I nearly jump out of my skin when another part of it that I presumed was holding it inside me starts to vibrate over my clit.

"Oh, Jesus, *fuck*," I cry out, rolling my hips, trying to chase the vibration.

Another laugh from Josh. There's a cold wetness that I can feel along my crack, and I clench my body in anticipation. Behind me, I can hear the sound of a condom wrapper being opened, and I appreciate the added protection, even if we haven't used them before now. I had a feeling I knew where this was going, and my whole body feels electric with the possibilities.

He chuckles again. "You need to let your body relax," he instructs as his fingers circle my asshole. Taking a deep breath, I try to do as he instructed, but the toy vibrating against me is making it impossible.

"Can you turn off the toy, just until you're inside me? I can't... I can't help it," I pant, trying to keep the whine out of my voice.

"Of course," he rushes to say, and I feel him move away from me, and then the vibration stops abruptly. "When you're ready, you're in control; just turn it back on." Josh presses the toy remote into my hand, and I have to fight the urge to cry because he's being so attentive and caring.

His hands go back to my ass, and I feel him start to work a finger slowly in, stretching me as he goes. Reaching to the side, I grab a pillow and shove it under my face so I can bite into that. That one finger slowly pumps inside me, and I moan.

"Treasure, I want you to scream when I make you come." He's still slowly pumping one finger until I feel the second digit enter me, and I'm panting through some indistinguishable noise that escapes me. I've been fucked better in the ass by Josh and his two fingers than any guy previously with his cock, and damnit, if that isn't the best feeling in the world, knowing that I'm with a man who truly treasures me and my pleasure. I press the button for the toy, and it comes to life again, making me squirm.

"Okay," I respond, but it's barely coherent because all I'm thinking about are his fingers slowly working in and out of me while the toy buzzes against my clit.

Josh plays with me like this, and I don't even know for how long, but I know I just want him to fuck me at this point. I'm desperate to be filled and fucked.

His fingers pull away, and I tense, which I know is the opposite of what I'm supposed to do. I should be relaxing and letting him slide easily into me without hurting either of us, but I can't help it.

"Shh," his lube-free hand strokes down my spine. "If it's too much, I can stop. I trust you'll tell me if it is too much?"

"Of course."

"Then relax and let me take care of you."

I do, and when I feel the tip of his cock press against my rosebud, I remember to breathe through it as he enters me. The intrusion feels wrong for so many reasons at first, and I want to squirm and fight against it, but I know that relaxing into the feeling will be worth it. I really let myself give in to the feeling, and I can hear him grunting as he slowly works himself inside me. I stop the vibrator so I can hear him better because his sounds are making me hotter. I push myself back, further impaling myself on his dick. When I turn the toy back on, he must feel it too, because he moans before pressing a kiss to my spine.

"God, you take my cock so well."

And then he starts to fuck me. Each stroke is slow to start as my body adjusts to this fullness, but I'm pressing back on each stroke, trying to feel him deeper. The toy was a good call because the vibration against my clit has me getting lost in every sensation.

"Take it, Taryn, take my cock like it was made for you."

His words ignite in me, and I let my orgasm roll through me. It feels different having something in my pussy and my ass while my clit is stimulated by the toy. It feels incredible, and not just that, but thoughtful too. Not only did Josh hear me when I told him this was something I wanted, but he made sure that I had anything I needed for an orgasm while doing it.

Behind me, Josh groans and, without warning, withdraws. He must pull off the condom because I can feel his cum coating my back in hot lashes. Feeling over-stimulated, I quickly pull the toy away from my body, dropping it off to the side.

"What have you done to me?" I moan into the pillow as my legs slide out so I can lie flat on the bed.

"Ruined you for any other man. It's the best way I know to keep you." His voice sounds like it's on my other side, so I open my eyes and turn to face him. He looks just as sated and satisfied as me.

"I need a shower."

"Me too. I also need to brush my teeth after rinsing with mouthwash."

"You did lick my asshole," I point out with a laugh. Then I realize he's still dressed, and I can't help but smile at the raunchiness. He needed me so badly that he couldn't even spare time to take his clothes off.

"I did. Did you like that? I know it was unexpected, but I had this burning possessiveness, and maybe it was a little wrong, but it felt right. I would kiss you, but I don't feel great about that yet."

With a loud groan, he pushes off the bed and pulls me with him toward the bathroom. My legs feel weak from the orgasm, but having him take care of me like this feels perfect.

Josh attends to his oral care and cleaning the toy before joining me in the shower, where we make out while scrubbing each other down. When we're fresh and clean, he's careful about bundling me up in a bathrobe and carrying me to the bed.

Tomorrow. Tomorrow, we can talk about Manny and Darren and work. Tonight, I'm going to luxuriate in his embrace and the feel of our bodies touching as we both fall asleep.

There are things I want to say to him, feelings that are gripping me tightly that I don't know how to feel about, but with surprising clarity, I realize that if it comes down to my job or Josh, I'll pick him every time. It's with that thought that I let the sound of his gentle snores and heartbeat drag me into dreamless oblivion.

Sixteen

WE'RE SITTING near the frog pond in Boston Common, eating ice cream, when someone says Josh's name. We're both in our thirties and acting like teenagers with my legs thrown over his, and it's like we're teenagers again. I'm leaning in to fake a kiss to get another lick of his birthday cake ice cream cone when the voice calls again.

"Josh? Josh Bartlett? Is that you?"

I stiffen as I lower my legs back to the ground and look over my shoulder at the man. I feel cold all over. I highly doubt he remembers interviewing me, but I remember him because he was the only one in the room I *didn't* catch checking out my boobs. Lorcan Bristol. He's somewhere above me but below Josh in the organization, and I feel like I'm white as a sheet. I hope he doesn't take notice of me whatsoever.

"Lorcan, how have you been? I feel like you haven't been in the office in ages," Josh says, getting to his feet and shaking the man's hand. For now, neither of them has acknowledged me, and that's totally fine.

"Ah, I don't know. I must have pissed someone off because they have me traveling the country for recruiting events. But I guess that's what happens when you're caught knocking boots with an intern." Lorcan laughs it off dismissively, but I have to wonder what happened to that poor intern after they got caught.

I see the smile slip from Josh's face at the admission. "And you see them sending you to colleges where you can prey on other young women as punishment?" Josh's face is dead serious, and I think I might swoon for him standing up for this faceless girl.

Lorcan clenches his teeth. "*He* is my boyfriend and has been for the last five years. He was working in the accounting arm as an intern, not in my department, and we got caught fucking at the year-end party for the interns, not that it's any of your business." Loran casts a look in my direction before giving Josh a pointed glare. Josh opens his mouth to speak, but Lorcan holds up his hand to stop him. "I can't say it's not almost sweet how protective you are of the women in the office given your father's...history... but maybe don't assume someone's sexuality, and maybe don't cast stones. You know what they say about those in glass houses."

Josh lowers his head for a second and nods. "No, you're right. I'm sorry. It was wrong of me to make assumptions like that." Josh offers his hand again in apology.

Lorcan looks at it a second before taking it. "I can't say I didn't deserve the scolding after how I presented the information. Sometimes, I get sucked into pretending I'm a douchebag to fit in that I forget that not everyone is like that. I'll leave you to enjoy the day. Maybe catch one of those touristy duck tours or something." Lorcan turns to look at me. "Have a good rest of the day, you two. Nice to see you again, Taryn."

He walks off, and both Josh and I let the tension in our bodies slowly slip away. But knowing that there are at least two people in the office who know Josh and I are a thing makes me feel uneasy. It's not even concern about my own career for the moment. It's clear that Josh having a relationship with a subordinate, even if I'm not in the same line of business, would affect his reputation, which is already tarnished by the actions of his father.

What were the chances that we would run into someone from the same firm in a totally different city in a different state? When we head back to our room after that, we come to the unspoken agreement to just stay in for the rest of the trip.

We spent the rest of the weekend wrapped around each other, watching some international house-hunting show, bemoaning the poor decision-making of some people when it comes to buying a house. It felt safer than running the risk of stumbling across anyone else.

All too soon, our weekend is over, and when we have to check out, I whine about it all morning.

"I don't want to go back to work. I have the Sunday scaries."

"I know you do, and I don't want to either, but when we get home, we have to talk about what Manny said."

I don't know if "when we get home" means New York in general or his place specifically, but I want it. I want my home to be with him. This weekend only proved it as we laid about and did normal couple things.

"About Quincey basically being a hot piece of ass?"

"That too, but about him trying to transfer you to my team. You and I work because we don't work closely together. I think you would be a great fit for my team. If what he said about the numbers is right, then I know you would be an asset. But what concerns me more is his sexist undertones that you wouldn't be as good at your job by virtue of you being a woman and this insinuation that you are having problems with the males on your team."

"To be fair, I *am* having problems with the guys on my team." This is my chance to tell Josh that Darren made a pass at me and that Eric seems incapable of understanding the word no. I don't think I'm this ultra-desirable woman who has all the men in her life falling all over themselves to get with me. I do think that I've thrown the gauntlet by saying no to Eric, and now Darren has to see if he can break my icy exterior. If only they knew I wouldn't be an ice bitch if they were decent fucking people.

Josh pauses, setting our bags aside to face me on the bed. "Do you want to switch to my team?" The rest of his statement hangs in the air. He's questioning if he was wrong about what I would have wanted.

"No." I wave my hand, dropping my face onto the pillow I was resting on in a dramatic fashion before looking back at him. "No, I don't want to switch to your team. I think it would be seen as a huge hit to my career that I can't play well with others."

Some tension leaves his shoulders. "Let me handle putting Manny off about this idea. Is there anything I should know about your team?"

He's holding the door open for me to tell him about Darren, but he'll insist I go to HR. Human resources is a department that's not there to help employees but to protect the company. All these micro-aggressions will become he said/she said moments where Eric will back Darren up without question, and it will get out that I made complaints at a second company about how a male coworker treated me. I'll be blacklisted.

"Just that they're sexist goons who think that by virtue of having breasts, I must have no brains. They keep making mistakes, and I keep fixing them." It's a half-truth, really a lie by omission. If I told Josh that Darren made a pass at me, I would also have to face the possibility that he could make a complaint and turn it into a bigger mess where I get a reputation for having my boyfriend getting people fired for "being mean to me." It's an oversimplification, but it's a worry all the same.

"Okay, I'll take care of this situation with Manny. Now, my lady, your chariot awaits."

The train ride home is long, and since we can't have sex on the four-hour trip, I manage to grab some of the sleep I didn't nab during the weekend. It's relaxing to sit with his arm around me while he works, using one hand to tab around like he's a magician.

"You're good with your fingers," I tell him after spending five minutes just watching his hand fly across the keyboard.

"So you've said," he teases before dropping a kiss on my forehead. "I'd like you to come spend the night, but I'm also supposed to do family dinner tonight. I can respect that you may not want to meet all of my sisters in one go, but what do you think? You've already met my mother."

"Don't forget Bex and Han," I point out, mulling over the idea. It's a huge step, but the fact that he wants to take it makes me nestle closer to his side. In the few weeks we've been doing this, I've seen what a patient partner he is. He gets it when I have late nights, or I can't manage to give him any attention when I have to survive a soul-crushing project.

"They might be there. I can text Bex to make sure she is in attendance if that works for you."

Abruptly, I sit up so I can look at him. The urge to crawl into his lap and kiss him silly for such a small consideration rides me until I give him a deep kiss that is not nearly as long as I want.

"Should I take that as a yes?"

"Yes," I whisper against his lips. His face is cradled in my hands, and he doesn't seem to mind in the least. The contented smile he sends my way sends my insides melting.

Filled with the buzzing anxiety of knowing that we're going to be seeing his family tonight keeps me from resting for the rest of the trip.

Before going back to his place, we drop by my apartment so I can pack a fresh overnight bag along with clothes for work. Josh looks so out of place sitting on my bed in a pair of shorts and a baseball tee. He doesn't look like the suave businessman that I've started to fall in love with. Instead, he looks more like an everyday guy. The kind of guy I could see helping my dad around the house.

"Which is the real you?" I ask as I shove my personal laptop into my bag.

"I'm sorry?"

"There's the scary guy in the office who always has his door closed, and then there's..." I gesture at him. "This guy, who looks casual as can be and who gives his woman everything she needs. The same guy who cooks like he was born to work over a stove."

He gets to his feet, a dark look on his face, and I wonder if I've misstepped. He stops in front of me and peels my jean shorts down. I don't know where this is going, but I'm very interested in seeing where he's going to take it.

"They can be the same man. The same man who can take an order as well as give it. You need to decide right now: are you the woman who can take an order?"

I think I'm nodding my head, but I can't be sure. I feel like prey caught in the sights of a dangerous predator. One wrong move, and it's all over.

"I want you to say it, treasure."

"Yes, I can."

"Good girl." He pushes me backward on my bed before undoing his pants and dropping them around his ankles. "How thin are these walls?" He glances around my room with my college pennants hanging on the wall alongside pictures of my friends and the same posters I had in my dorm in college.

"Thin enough that I could shine a flashlight against one and see the glow on the other side."

"No point in staying quiet then."

He gets to his knees and devours my pussy until I'm writhing below him. There is no finesse. There is just the gift of pleasure as I lay spread out on my bed. In the other room, I can hear the sound of the video game my roommate was playing slowly turn up, and I laugh through the body-shattering orgasm Josh gives me.

He doesn't even let the tremors stop before he's sliding his cock into me, pounding another orgasm from me. If my moaning wasn't loud enough to tell my roommate what we were up to, the rhythmic squeak of the mattress and banging of the frame against the wall would give it away. It's the first time I've brought a guy home, and he's going to be the last because everywhere in this room is going to be a reminder of what we've just done. It's a reminder of Josh's impact on my heart.

I thought I was always going to be too busy to find someone to settle down with me, but today, Josh has shown me that I can find a way to make it work. And while I've learned I *could* make it work with someone, I only want it to be him. We both understand what our jobs require of us. He hasn't made complaints about my role as a woman or even a word that I need to work less. If I say I have work to get done, Josh just kisses me and pulls out his laptop too. There are moments it feels too good to be true, like when I "five more minutes" him for an hour until I get that last thing done before I can give him my attention. Fear pricks at me that this is just the honeymoon phase, and he's eventually going to want more. But I know that's just my deeper insecurities. Josh has always shown me that my career matters to him too.

"Relax, Taryn," Josh murmurs before kissing the top of my head. At my insistence, we picked up flowers on our way out to Long Island so I would have something for his mother. It was at the flower shop that I caught sight of the hickey he managed to give me on the car ride from the city, leaving me with no way to cover it up. I want to beat him with the flowers until the petals fall off.

"Because having your mother meet me for the first time while still dressed in last night's clothes wasn't bad enough. Now I'm showing up to her house with a hickey the size of Texas."

"You like it when I mark you," he teases as we head up the walkway to the mansion that Josh calls his childhood home.

"Yeah, in places people can't see, like my breasts or on my thighs or my hips. *Not* my neck on the night that I'm meeting your sisters without any makeup to cover it up. You, sir, are in a sex timeout."

One of his sisters chooses that moment to open the door. She looks young, like a baby, and I assume she must be Gigi. She has black hair that's piled in a bun on top of her head and a white crop top paired with short black high-rise shorts. She's got a full body and enough confidence to have me wanting to stagger back. It's the winged eyeliner similar to Bex's that has me wondering who taught whom.

"Mom!" she calls over her shoulder. "Josh is in a sex timeout. You should set him a seat at the kids' table." Gigi turns and gives me a smile. "And you are?"

"My girlfriend, Taryn. This is Gigi, the baby," Josh says with a scowl, pushing past her, no doubt annoyed by her very loud announcement.

Another tall woman walks over with a baby on her hip, and she smacks Gigi on the back of the head. "You get to explain to Ana what sex is you little degenerate." The woman says it with such deep affection that I feel like I'm missing the joke. When she turns to look at me, her eyes study me, and I feel like I should have picked something else to wear, maybe. But it's hot out, and I needed to wear shorts because I don't trust Josh to not hoist me up on a bathroom counter and have his filthy way with me while his family is in the house. Mostly, I couldn't promise myself I wouldn't give into the temptation if it came to that, so shorts were the best way to not get myself into a compromising position.

"I'm Taryn," I say, offering my hand.

The woman hands me her baby instead. "I'm Connie, Josh's big sister. I don't normally hand my babies to strangers, but I need to take Gigi out back and strangle her to death, and to do that, I need both hands. Lovely to meet you."

A child, maybe six or seven years old with pale blonde hair, comes running into the room. "SEX! SEX! SEX!" she shouts on repeat with a streamer in her hand.

"Well, shit, I didn't realize she was *listening*," Gigi explains as Connie grabs her ear.

"SHIT! SHIT! SHIT!" This child seems to know which words she's not supposed to repeat but also when she can get away with saying them, so she starts to repeat both words back and forth as she runs.

I readjust the baby in my arms and realize that this will be some good practice for when Ainsley has her baby, not that I even know how to hold this one right.

"That's Nolita. Do you want me to take her from you?" Josh offers, holding his hands out, but I curl protectively around the baby. She's large enough that she's basically able to sit on my hip while also being young enough to not squirm and run from the stranger who has her.

"No, I don't. I want to cuddle the baby for just a little while before she starts screaming or tries to escape my hold."

Josh leans forward and kisses the little one in my arms. I may be ambivalent about if I want children, but seeing such a caring and paternal act definitely does something to my ovaries. Like they're calling out for attention before being labeled geriatric at the ripe old age of 35. I'm still a few years away from that, but it makes me stop and think.

Josh leads me further into the house, where there is a lot of activity. There are two children, the aforementioned little girl and a bigger boy, who is more interested in the video game in his hands than acknowledging anyone in the room. There are two guys sitting in the living room with glasses of amber liquid in their hands, but the women are obviously running the roost.

I recognize Josh's mom, along with Gigi and Connie. There are three other women also in the kitchen, but one of them is just standing in the way, scrolling on her phone.

"For fuck's sake, Imogen, would you get the fuck out of the way?" Connie snarls, shoving the woman.

Gigi lifts her head from where she is leaning over to grab something from the oven, and I freeze when I see shrimp on the oven tray. "Oh, so you can curse in front of your precious crotch goblins, but I can't?"

"Yes, because they are *my* crotch goblins to corrupt, and also, you know I hate that term."

One woman in a yellow sun dress who is stirring a literal pot turns and glares at everyone. "All this stress is *not* good for the baby. So, could you assholes please stop fighting?"

"Everleigh, what did I *just* say about cursing."

"You are all ruthless," Josh says, shaking his head.

Imogen looks up from her phone, Everleigh turns to face Josh, and the last woman I still don't have a name for, pauses where she's placing biscuit dough on a tray.

"*Jessica!*" two of them shout in unison, running over to him, but biscuit girl looks unsure.

I can feel Josh's eye roll from where he's standing, but as his sisters swarm him for a hug, he smiles and embraces them both.

"You know I hate that nickname," he grumbles but kisses them each in turn.

Biscuit girl walks over tentatively, and he gives her the biggest smile when she hugs him. She turns to look at me where I'm standing and still holding Nolita, almost using the baby as a shield. This family is so much more than I expected. They're loud and vicious, but I can tell their love for each other runs deep. Their barbs aren't meant to cut or sting; they're intended to convey that caring as much as you can in a family of women.

"I know it's been a while since we saw you, Josh, but to get a girl knocked up and roll up with a five-month-old? Even that's got to be a record of some kind."

He gives the girl a gentle shove on her shoulder. "Kayleigh, this is Taryn. Taryn, if you want to walk out now, I wouldn't blame you."

"None of us would," Connie calls from where she's cutting up the shrimp, dumping them into the pot that Everleigh was stirring.

I have to take a second to really pinpoint their differences and commit their names to memory. Everleigh is the shortest of the group and more rotund thanks to the protrusion of her very pregnant belly. At least, I'm going on a hunch that she's pregnant, as she keeps rubbing soothing circles over it. Her chestnut brown hair is pulled up and away from her face, and she seems to be glowing despite the tired look in her eyes. I may know fuck all about babies, but I know that exhaustion is only going to get worse.

Kayleigh, formerly known as biscuit girl, has the darkest hair of them all and is taller than the rest. It occurs to me that this could be his half-sister, but I wouldn't dare voice that question. If Josh isn't going to make that distinction, then who am I to do that? She definitely seems more timid than the rest, but that doesn't stop her from being warm with those she does interact with.

Last up is Imogen, who, after greeting Josh, went right back to her phone. From what I remember Josh telling me, there are only a few years between them all, except for Gigi, who has the largest age gap as the baby. Imogen has light brown hair that's cut into a short bob, and just seeing that tells me a lot about her–not everyone can rock a bob. They're high maintenance and require regular cutting if you want to hold on to it. I can appreciate someone with that level of care.

"Sorry to say, you're all stuck with me, at least for the night." I bite back my comment that it might be my last night if I eat any of the food they put out.

"If you lot make a good impression on her, she might stick it out. Otherwise, this will be the last time you see her." Josh glances around. "Is Bex coming?"

Imogen finally looks up to shake her head. "No, they found out that this round didn't stick, so she and Han are going to just spend some time together."

"Damn it," Josh curses, shaking his head.

Connie doesn't even correct him, showing just how deeply this hurt goes for the whole family. My heart breaks for Bex and Han, knowing how hard it must be what they're going through.

His mother jumps in with a topic change before everyone can get too in their heads about Bex and Han. "Well, for dinner, we have some cheddar bay biscuits. I made a twist on shrimp scampi pasta, and we also have some fresh asparagus and a Caesar salad."

I watch as the same spatula that was used to pull the shrimp from the tray is also used on the asparagus, and my heart sinks. I'll have to take very little of the food so as to not waste it when I don't eat it. I'm thankful that my allergy isn't bad enough that I can't be in the same room as shellfish, but honestly, just being in this kitchen surrounded by shrimp makes me feel itchy.

"Mom, I told you that Taryn *can't* eat shellfish."

She stops what she's doing and immediately turns around. "No, you said, 'Please make something with shellfish.' I remember because I had a nice rack of lamb in my cart, and I put it back."

Josh takes a deep breath in like he's going to let out a long-suffering sigh, but instead he kisses his mom's cheek. "I said please *don't* make something with shellfish because the next text was that Taryn is allergic."

"Well, you should have put that all in one text. Okay, that's fine. I have some pork chop and cauliflower that we can make for you. I'm sorry, dear. I promise this was not intentional."

"That's a lie," Connie pipes up. "I told you that Thad hates salmon, and the first meal you cooked for him was salmon."

"That *was* intentional. But who wants the father of their grandchildren to be named Thad?" His mom whispers to Josh and me before rubbing her hand over the baby's bald head.

"It's okay. I can just eat when we get home. I don't want to put you out," I assure her.

"Nonsense. It was my cock up. I'll fix it."

Canada chooses that moment to run through the room, screaming the word "cock" as she goes. Connie grabs my upper arms.

"Under no circumstances should you have children. As a loving mother of three, I am telling you right now, they are a trap and a prison sentence. I wouldn't change it for the world, but they are a very adorable trap." Connie kisses her baby's head before chasing after Canada.

Josh takes me out of the kitchen to introduce me to who I assume are his brothers-in-law and Tennessee. The little boy lights up when he sees his uncle for about three seconds before going back to his game.

Connie seems to have given up on chasing Canada because she's picked up a plastic toy golf club that she's now swinging around, screaming, "I'm a SITH," before smashing things as she twirls around the room. The child nearly takes out her father and uncle's drinks, but they both lift them at the exact right moment without breaking their conversation. It comes at the expense of a lamp in the room.

"Is it always like this?" I ask. If this isn't the best form of birth control there is, I don't know what is.

"Yep," Josh confirms as Connie comes running into the room.

"Thad, I told you to watch Canada," she scolds, vacuum in one hand and a broom in the other.

"Oh, sorry," he says sheepishly before looking at his daughter. "You need to keep your hips squared for golf swings, honey."

"I swear to God, if your dick wasn't perfect, I would leave you tomorrow," she growls at him before handing him the cleaning supplies and disappearing again.

Josh winces. "Things I Never Wanted to Know for $800, Alex."

I turn and look up at him with hearts in my eyes. "Oh, you're a Jeopardy nerd? Could you be any more perfect?"

The words come out before I can stop them. While the situation around us is so chaotic, it's also perfect in a way. I love the constant bustle of people in the room and the overwhelming sense of love coming from all of them.

"No, it's not possible," Josh teases.

He introduces me to Thad and Kip. Both seem disinterested in talking to me, which I try not to take offense to.

Sitting down at the table a little while later is just as chaotic, and I'm grateful when Kayleigh sits next to me.

"I get it. They're overwhelming but honestly good people."

"I think Josh mentioned you're taking a trip soon?"

She bites into her biscuit just as I say this, and I find I'm the one blushing at putting her on the spot while she's eating. I know I would hate that.

"Yes, we're headed to Tahiti for our high school reunion. It was a bit of a last-minute decision because of work bullshit."

"*Kay*," Connie scolds.

An evil grin spreads across Canada's face, and I'm more than a little scared of the self-declared Sith as she says 'bullshit' over and over as Connie tries to breathe through it. I catch the strife on her face as she tries to feed Nolita while Thad still talks to Kip.

"Are you going to help at all with any of your children?" she asks.

Thad turns and looks at his wife, seeming oblivious to anything going on around them.

"The older ones are fine." Thad drops a whole shrimp on the baby's plate before looking back to Kip.

Connie is quick to snatch it from the baby, who has a handful of asparagus she is ready to abandon in favor of some new food. "We said we were going to wait until Nolita was a year before giving her shrimp."

"Sorry, I must have forgotten."

Beside me, I can feel Josh getting tense as he watches this exchange. Connie looks at Josh and just shakes her head before looking at me.

"If he ever says he got a vasectomy, call the doctor's office to verify or drive him there yourself."

"For fuck's sake, Connie, I forgot. It was a mistake and I didn't think it mattered."

The strangled noise that escapes her captures the attention of the rest of the table. Meanwhile, I have been unable to look away since they started arguing.

"Didn't think it mattered that we were raw dogging it while I was off birth control? We were done having kids. You *agreed* that you would get snipped."

"You agreed, Con, not me. You *told* me what to do like you do with everything. Maybe I *want* more kids."

"Because you pay *so* much attention to the three you have now? No, your male ego is just too fragile to handle the thought of being emasculated by having your balls snipped like the dog you are. Or was it that you didn't want me to go back to work and earn more money than you? Which is it?"

"Neither. I don't really care. God, Connie, I can't do this anymore." Thad pushes to his feet. "I'm leaving you. Suzette is pregnant, and I'm leaving you."

Connie flinches back. "Suzette? You mean your secretary?"

Beside me, Kayleigh has gone totally still, and it doesn't take a genius to figure out why. I know we hardly know each other, but I grab her hand anyway. I glance at Josh beside me, and he's gone sheet-white.

"Jesus, and you all thought *I* was the problem," Gigi snarks before taking a bite of her pasta.

"Shut up, Gigi. My asshole husband is leaving me right now. That's what you said?" Connie asks, turning back to him. She doesn't seem overly upset. In fact, I can see a shrewd look in her eye.

"Yes, I'm leaving you. What is so hard to understand?"

"For your secretary, whom you're having an affair with?"

Thad seems to sense danger but doesn't know what to do about it. He opens his mouth, but Josh gets to his feet.

"I think you should go. You've done enough damage, don't you think?" Josh's gaze flicks to where Canada and Tennessee have gone quiet. Both children seem confused and uncertain, and it hurts my heart that Josh is the first one to actually consider this whole disagreement's impact on them.

"I didn't mean–God, I didn't want to do this in front of them, but I'm so tired of–" Thad runs a hand through his thinning hair, looking at his children, sympathy flashing in his eyes.

"If you want more children, I would first consider the impact it's going to have on the children you already have," Josh says.

"This is none of your business, Josh," Thad shouts, getting in Josh's face. My boyfriend moves to stand in front of Thad. They're roughly the same height, but it's obvious to everyone in the room that Thad is at a disadvantage. This is Josh's home turf, and he's protecting his family.

"That's where you're wrong. That's my sister you cheated on. That's my nieces and nephew that you're abandoning. This is entirely my business, and don't think that this is going to be the last you see of me, either."

Thad's face hardens like he has a leg to stand on. "Your family should be used to this. They do say girls pick their fathers to marry."

Josh steps closer and leans in to whisper in Thad's ear. It's too quiet for anyone to hear, but we all watch as the color drains from his face. Josh steps back and crosses his arms with his chest puffed out, the ultimate protector. It's obvious that after his father left, Josh stepped into that role in his family, trying to protect the women he loved.

"Get out of my house," Janet orders, also getting to her feet. Canada, seated next to her grandmother, starts to cry, no doubt confused by all the emotional turmoil working its way through the room. Josh's mom picks the child up and hugs her to her chest.

Thad doesn't spare a second glance as he storms out the door.

"I hope all of you are willing to sign affidavits to what Thad said tonight." Connie gets to her feet to take Canada into her arms.

"What just happened? Do I need to go out there and beat his ass?" Imogen asks.

"Ass," Canada chirps between tears.

"No, please, *don't*. I have him tied up six ways to Sunday in the prenup. If dad taught me anything, it's that men think with their dicks. He was my roommate that I had sex with. Sure, losing that is a major bummer, but now I can hire a nanny and finally go back to work."

"And why couldn't you do that before?" I ask, well aware that it's none of my business.

"Because Thad didn't want to hire one, but he has a trust that he only got access to with marriage. I read the trust documents when he first came to me with this twisted marriage of convenience. I liked him enough. I knew he had a great dick and was good in bed, so I didn't see the problem with it."

Imogen has the presence of mind to cover Tennessee's ears, but he's gone back to his video game under the table.

"The trust wasn't totally protected in marriage. It actually specifically became marital property as part of the trust because the intent was to encourage the continuation of the family name. So, now, because he violated the prenup by A. leaving me and B. having an affair, I get 75% of that trust. Which I will use for the nanny that Thad never wanted. I think he was too afraid of getting caught banging a live-in nanny, so he removed the temptation. Instead, he screwed his twenty-one-year-old secretary."

Josh drops into the seat next to his nephew, but Tennessee is focused on his game. I can see the movement of his lips as he talks to the kid, but Tennessee doesn't bother to look at him.

Everleigh turns to Kip and whacks him with the back of her arm around his middle.

He winces and rubs his chest. "What was that for?"

"Don't you *ever* cheat on me. My daddy did it to my mother, and now Thad's done it to Connie. I will have your balls removed painfully and turned into earrings if you even think about it."

"Noted, cupcake, but I have everything I need right here." He kisses his wife and rubs her belly with a tender smile.

Josh is up and moving back to his original seat, messing up Everleigh's hair as he goes.

"At least one of my children is in a normal relationship." Janet scowls while sitting down.

There is an uproar from Josh, Imogen, and Gigi at this. While they all argue about being in a relationship, I squeeze Kayleigh's hand under the table.

"Talk about awkward when you're the kid of that extramarital affair," she says nervously.

"It seems like, for the most part, everyone has accepted you for you, though," I say.

Josh's hand slides to my thigh, and he gives it the same reassuring squeeze I just gave Kayleigh.

"They have, even Janet, which has been incredible. But what happened with our dad and mom is why I think Josh has been so reticent about getting into a relationship before now. I'm glad that he met you. I don't get to see him often because you know how his work can be, but we text, and he's seemed happier, that's for sure."

"I'm glad you think so. He definitely makes me happy."

"We may not have grown up together, but he's a great big brother and fiercely protective. I think the only reason Thad *walked* out of here is because Josh didn't want to upset the kids."

"I think you're probably right." I turn my head to look at Josh, who is now in a heated debate over how Imogen's last relationship doesn't qualify as normal because her last girlfriend was a pole dance instructor turned nun.

"I know I probably don't have to say this, but if you hurt my brother, I'm going to hurt you, "Kayleigh says. "I work as an accountant, but I'm more of a Ben Affleck The Accountant than a normal accountant."

"I didn't think anyone actually saw that movie," I say, appreciating her willingness to go to bat for her brother. "I don't think anyone did," Kayleigh says, "but you knew enough to understand what I meant. And if I can't do it, I'm sure one of my sisters knows someone who could."

"Fact," Imogen says, nodding. "I once dated a sniper. He could pick you off over two thousand meters away. Not even fucking me broke this man's concentration. He could nut and take the shot at the same time, and when I tell you that was the hottest fucking thing I've ever done in my life, I'm not kidding. So a little thing like you, you would just be his morning snack."

"She did not date a sniper," Josh tells me with a laugh, finally sitting back down beside me.

"You wouldn't know. You remember Jeff?"

Josh laughs and leans back in his chair, putting his hand on the back of my neck so he can rub circles on my skin. It's such a possessive move that I have to press my thighs together. He's making goosebumps break out all along my arms at the simple touch.

"That man was *not* a sniper."

"He totally was. He even took me to a gun range and taught me how to shoot."

I rest my chin on my hand as I lean onto the table to look at her. "You mean to tell me you dated a sniper and a pole dancing instructor turned nun?"

"I also dated a cop, a tightrope walker, and a mafia don. There might have been some overlap with the cop and the don."

"Bullshit." Josh takes a sip of his wine.

"Vedremo chi riderà per ultimo, fratello." She lifts her glass and waggles her eyebrows at her brother. Lucky for me, she offers a translation. "We'll see who has the last laugh, brother."

Watching the banter around the room, it's reassuring to me that he has people in his life who are just as protective of him. More often than not, I feel like guys don't get that same level of attention or protection, so knowing that Josh is so well-loved by the women in his life just reaffirms for me that he's not just a great guy; he's *my* great guy.

And maybe we're moving too fast. Maybe I shouldn't be ready to say my "I do's" to this guy, but there's an intimacy between us that goes past sex and rim jobs and giving head. It's in the ways we've come to know little quirks about each other, like how we take our coffee or that neither of us likes to be on our phones within thirty minutes of going to bed. It's learning that he has a specific routine in the shower that he doesn't even interrupt while I'm blowing him.

Seventeen

THE NIGHT MOVES on as we drink wine and the drama of Thad lessens in our minds. Before it gets too late, Josh sweeps us out the door, and thankfully, no one protests too strongly. Janet apologizes again for the mix-up with dinner and promises to make it up to me.

When I tell her I would like that very much, it's not an exaggeration. I love how close the family is, both physically and emotionally. It's the kind of bond my parents and I had before all of these money issues.

The thought turns my stomach sour, and I go quiet as I retreat into my head. As surreptitiously as I can, I check my phone to see just how bad my finances are looking. I can try to refinance my loans and maybe their mortgage, but that's like slapping duct tape on the hull of the Titanic; it's ineffectual and a waste.

Before I can think any more about it, I'm startled by Han and Bex walking up the front steps.

"Are we too late?" Han asks, her eyes a little watery. She's dressed down in a pair of faded black capris and an old race shirt, while Bex is similarly dressed in a pair of leggings and an old t-shirt.

"Depends on what you think you're late for. You don't want

to go in there, trust me," Josh tells them, approaching each of them in turn for a hug.

"But we drove all the way out here from Morningside Heights," Bex whines.

I hang back, too afraid of overstepping, but Han gives me a look and then beckons me forward. "You too, Taryn. I know what it is to be indoctrinated by this family."

"Indoctrinated? You make it sound like a cult," Josh objects.

"It is," Han and I say at the same time with a smile.

"How about the four of us go out for drinks, and then I'll drive us back into the city?" Josh offers. He slides his hand into mine so easily that I can't help but let it wash away all my worries.

"I think that sounds like a remarkable idea," Han says cheerfully.

"I can drive my *own* car," Bex objects but then stops. "Actually, that means you two are on your own for getting home. We drove the coup down here. Only two seats."

Josh rolls his eyes, pulling out his phone. "I'll order a Pick-MeUp! and we'll meet you at McGuffins."

They agree and head back to their car, leaving Josh and I on the street while we wait. I look up at Josh and give him a small smile.

"Where did your mind go earlier, treasure?" Josh asks, poking my thigh. The PickMeUp! rolls up much faster than expected, and I hope he'll drop it as I climb into the car with him, but when he turns to face me expectantly, it's clear I'm not off the hook.

"Just money stuff. Nothing too bad."

"You mentioned there were troubles, but you failed to give me details of just how bad it is."

"It's... It's bad." I'm torn about telling him the exact details, not because I don't want to share these things with my partner, but because tonight has already been full of so much emotional turmoil. I really want to turn the conversation on him and see how he's feeling about this mess with his sister and Thad, but the look on his face tells me that he's not going to let it go, and maybe being mired in my troubles will help him forget, albeit briefly, about his own. So, I finally unload just how bad the situation is, down to the car breaking down just before the opera.

I can see his eyes moving side to side as he does the mental math. There's no point in giving him vague information. If I'm going to completely block him out of what is going on at work, the least I can do is be open about this.

"I can pay off the mortgage; that's not a problem."

"*No!*" I shout at him and then realize just how loud I was. He actually flinches back but waits for me to say something else. "No, sorry. Thank you, that's incredibly generous, but I'm not going to take your money. Not for this."

"Why not?"

"Because it's not your problem, and while I appreciate your generosity, and I know that you're coming from a good place, I'll just always feel indebted to you. I'll always be wondering if you feel like you're seeing a return on your investment while we're making love, and I'll constantly be wondering if you regret it."

"Taryn, that's not even a third of what I took home *after* taxes from my bonus last year. If I can help, I want to."

"Josh, leave it. I don't want your money or involvement in this. You asked what was bothering me, and I'm telling you. I was looking to vent, not for a solution."

He puffs out an annoyed breath. "You're being stubborn about this for no reason. Is it pride?"

"No, Josh, it's because money changes things. It will change our dynamic, which I'm *already* at a disadvantage in. Please, Josh, leave it."

"Fine, if you won't let me write a check, then you should move in with me."

That just spikes my anger further, and I shake my head, looking away from him and pulling out my phone again. I should be a big girl and explain to him why I'm so mad, but I'm afraid if I open my mouth, angry words I can't take back will come spewing out, so I just clench my teeth instead.

Taryn: Someone send me something happy. Something like a puppy saved a kitten from drowning or a chimpanzee acting as a crossing guard. Please. I need something.

Ainsley: I caught Ken jerking off in the shower, and when I asked him why he chose to do that instead of just fucking one of my three available holes, he told me it was because he didn't want to wake me up because I look...and I'm fucking quoting here guys...tired. He said I looked tired. So if anyone knows a guy that's into fucking hot pregnant chicks, I'm in search of new dick because Ken is now dead.

Elia: Mr. FBI agent reading our text messages, she didn't mean it.

Ainsley: Oh yes, I fucking did. His body is going to be discovered by some jogger in Central Park tomorrow morning. This is why I won't run. Joggers are always getting murdered or finding bodies.

Vivian: I can dust off my criminal defense books. I got you, boo.

Ainsley: As if there is a jury out there that would actually convict me. I just need three mothers on my jury, and I promise they find in my favor. Tired. JFC.

Elia: Since you asked for a bit of good news or something happy, I saw a video of a kitten pulling keys out of a hole that a kid dropped them into, so that was fun.

Ainsley: You and your cat videos. Was the cat your cat?

Elia: You know my cats are indoor-only cats.

"Would you please talk to me?" Josh says, and I lift my head to look at him. He plucks my phone from my hands and slides it into his pocket.

I scowl at him. "You have my attention," I say, unable to keep the bite from my tone.

"Please help me understand what I did wrong because I obviously did something."

"If you can't figure out why I have a problem with what you just said, then I don't know if I know you as well as I think I do."

Josh flinches. "What do you mean what I just said? The mortgage?"

"No."

"Moving in with me?"

I huff and twist to face him. "Yes, Josh. Moving in with you. I want you to want me in your space all the time. I want you to want me to move in. I don't want you to move me in because I can't handle making ends meet, and you think saving me a few hundred books a month is going to make a difference. Don't move me in for pity."

"I'm not moving you in for pity."

My raised eyebrows and scowl disagree with him.

"Honestly, it's not pity. It's that I want to help you."

"I don't need you to come in and play white knight in my life."

"If I can, why shouldn't I? Why should I watch you suffer? Yes, your apartment is decently closer to the office, but if you're staying with me most nights anyway, why bother wasting money on rent?"

"And what if this doesn't work out? What am I supposed to do? I have quite possibly the cheapest rent in the city that doesn't involve having my shower in the kitchen. Sure, my roommate sucks, but I have my own bedroom, and for the most part, Zelda lets me live my life. I can't give that up."

"You're already planning an exit strategy?" Josh asks. I can see the fight on his face to keep the hurt out of it.

"No, Jesus Christ on a cracker. You're not this dense, so I don't get why you're acting like it now. You have five sisters. Would you honestly be okay with them moving in with a guy they've been dating for–generously–a month? No, you wouldn't. I'm invested in this as much as I can be. I spend almost every waking not-work moment with you. I don't know what more I can do."

Josh slams his head back against the seat, closing his eyes. "Fuck, Taryn, you're right. I'm being a dickhead about this situation. But what else am I supposed to do? You have financial troubles, and I have a lot of two things–sisters and money. I want to help."

I grab his hand and thread my fingers through it. "You're wrong. You also have a lot of love to give. I cannot even begin to tell you how much it means to me that you want to help and take care of me, but I want our relationship to be a partnership, not you acting like a walking/talking bank. I'm trying to not guilt myself over the dress, and the shoes, and the train tickets, but it's not easy for me. We're never going to be on equal footing because you're old and shit, but I want to try to get there if we can. So, all I'm asking is that you listen to me when I need to vent and not to try to fix it. I can survive on ramen and minimum student loan payments for a few years while I work down my parents' mortgage, but I can't do that if I'm going to feel like I'm a failure for even trying. Our industry pays really fucking well. I just have to survive a few years like this."

"And I'll be there to celebrate each final payment with you. You have a point about how I wouldn't want my sisters to put themselves in such a vulnerable position, but it's because I have five amazing sisters that I want to take care of you the best way that

I can. I'm not going anywhere. I'm going to be there for whatever you need."

"I can think of a few better ways you can take care of me."

Josh casts a surreptitious glance toward the driver and then back at me. "Later," he mouths before kissing me.

I'm going to hold him to that promise. I'm going to hold him to all of them.

Our mood is decidedly less settled by the time we pull up in front of McGuffins. It's closer to the city, which I appreciate, and it's surprisingly lively for a Sunday evening. A baseball game is playing on several of the TVs hanging over the bar, but I can't see which New York team is playing. My feet stick to the floor as we walk to a round booth where Han and Bex are each chugging a dark beer.

Han slams her drink down a half-second before Bex, and she blenches loudly, wiping her mouth with the back of her hand.

"Still got it!" she cheers as Bex gives her own burp.

"What are you doing?" Josh asks, sliding in after me. It sits me right next to Han, intentionally, I think. Being on the inside keeps me a part of the conversations going on at the table.

"Car bombs. We haven't gone drinking since we started trying to get pregnant as part of a solidarity thing. A glass of something in a social setting is a different story. But tonight, we're letting loose." Han practically stands up, gesturing for a round.

Josh is quick to intercept the waitress. I'm not sure what he says, but I sure hope it's not to order us car bombs. I could do with a drink, but not something that heavy.

We fill them in on what they missed at dinner, namely, that Thad seemed to think that cheating on his wife would put Josh on his side.

"This is why I eat pussy," Han says after her third car bomb.

"I mean, same, but Josh is a good guy," Bex points out, placing a water in front of Han, who drinks it down greedily.

Han covers her mouth. "I'm sorry, this is not the impression that I wanted to give you, Taryn, of some sort of drunk mess. I thought you were so cool at the opera, and I just wanted to be friends, and I'm making the worst sort of impression."

I cover her hand that's gripping her water with mine. "You're not even close to making a bad impression on me. We've all had nights that are less fun than others. I'm not going to hold it against you."

"I don't know what I was thinking," she whispers to me while Bex and Josh try to have their own conversation noisily, letting Han and I talk.

"What do you mean?" I nudge her water at her, and she takes a few more sips. I know that hangovers over thirty are nothing to be fucked with.

"I mean, I left business school determined to strike it out on my own, and then I said we should have a baby at the same time, and I just can't devote my whole self to my business-baby and a baby-baby. I want them both, and I don't want either of them to suffer because of the other."

The age-old question that ambitious women all around the world have to answer–to follow ambition and do the thing they feel driven toward or follow the path of motherhood? They're not mutually exclusive, but Han is right. Eventually, something suffers. Be it work, the baby, or the mom herself. There are the lucky ones who can have it all, and something tells me that when the time is right, that will be Han and Bex too.

"There isn't a right answer for me to give you, but I do think that as you and Bex try for a baby, you don't have to write off growing My Way Consulting."

"That's what I keep telling her," Bex pipes up. "We want it all, and we will have it all, but until we get there, there is no reason for her to give up work."

"It's hard," Han says, turning to her wife. "And I've told you this so many times: I can't just hire someone. It needs to be the right person because they're effectively going to become the second in command."

"You started when we graduated?" I ask, picking at the label on my beer.

"Yeah," she says slowly, unsure where I'm going.

"And you have how many clients?"

"Well, just the one because I'm only one person, but..."

"But what?" I press.

"But I want to grow it."

"You're also billing them six grand a day for work." Bex's comment is poorly timed because I've just taken a sip of my drink, which I spit out. "I know. She's sitting at home in her jammies working all day, making more in a month than I do in a year."

From the look Josh gives me, it's not lost on him that that's as much as my parents' car repair was.

"My point is," I continue, "you graduated in May. It's only your first summer after school. Give yourself a break, and I don't mean, like, take it easy with work. I mean, stop being so hard on yourself. You have so much time to grow in all ways."

Han turns to Josh and points an angry finger at him. "Keep her. I like her. She might actually be able to survive your family."

With bright eyes, he looks at me. "I plan on it."

Eighteen

"TARYN, I'm going to step out and get lunch for everyone. Want to come with me and stretch your legs?"

I lift my head and glance at Eric, who looks perfectly genuine in his offer. I planned to take advantage of the brief Tweedless lunch to pop into Josh's office for a mid-day blow job. There is something about thinking about feeling his piercing against the back of my throat that makes me have to cross my legs from arousal.

But it would be good to actually try with my team and let Manny know that I am not the problem. I know Josh and Manny had their conversation about me, but I hardly know the contents. I trust Josh not to have said anything that's going to get me fired or anything, but it still makes me antsy. Whenever I ask him about it, he just assures me that he took care of it.

"Sure, I could use some fresh air." I rise to my feet and stretch my arms over my head. I feel my shirt come untucked from my skirt, but my back muscles are on the verge of spasm, so I don't do anything about it until I'm comfortable enough to lower my arms again. The first thing I do is tuck in my shirt again and scribble a note to myself to talk to Josh about taking some yoga classes together. He spends just as much time bent over a computer as I do, and besides being bendy, it could be fun for us both.

Darren waves us off, his face in his computer, double checking the numbers that I already ran twice. But fine, if he wants to be a killjoy, I'm not going to complain.

"So, I heard Manny is trying to transfer you to another line of business," Eric says just as the elevator doors close.

"Where did you hear that?" I ask, twisting to face Eric.

"Manny told us, but apparently, that Josh Bartlett guy is a huge dick and said he doesn't want you on his team. I told Manny that we didn't have any problems. I don't get why he wants you transferred."

"Really? You can't think of any reasons?" I cross my arms defensively.

"Look, Taryn, I'm not trying to start a fight. I just thought you would want to know before you got blindsided by it. I know Manny and Darren are close. You're a cool chick. That's why I've been trying to get you to agree to go on a date with me. It's not like there's ample opportunity to date outside the company for our first few years as an associate. We've all been living in the office."

I relax a little. His explanation doesn't excuse away how relentless and spineless he's been, but it is hard to meet people and make friends when you're stuck with the same faces for twenty hours a day, seven days a week. It also doesn't give me the ego boost he probably thinks it does. So, I'm just what's convenient? Saying no to him just gets easier and easier.

"I get it, but if you're about to lead into asking me out again, my answer is still no, and I'm actually seeing someone now."

"Is that where you were this weekend?" Eric doesn't sound mad, and I can almost feel bad about looping him in with Darren, but not quite.

"Actually, yes. He also works insane hours, so it was good for us to get some space, even if it meant doing some work."

"Does he work in the office?" Eric asks as we get off the elevator, and I think I can hear a bit of betrayal in his voice, but it's really none of his business who I'm fucking. "Sorry, that was invasive. We're just starting this tentative truce, and I'm about to ruin it by running my mouth."

I don't give him an answer since he retracted his question, and it's frankly none of his business. Part of me wants to fold, to try to fill the silence that has fallen between us, but I also refuse to give him that satisfaction. If he wants to make shit awkward, then he can deal with the consequences.

We walk into the salad bar, and Eric orders for both him and Darren while I order for myself. Eric pays before I even get up there, and I'm a little annoyed. I barely let my boyfriend pay for me, let alone some jackass from the office with a hard time understanding the word no. Instead of getting angry and becoming some overly emotional female, I reign my temper in and just say thanks.

Before checking out, I grab three cookies and tuck them into my purse. They are most definitely not for Eric and Darren.

Eric tries to strike up another conversation, this time about college, and I play it safe and give him simple answers as we walk back. Normally, a walk in heels, even just a few blocks, would be killing my feet, but there is something about these red soles that really make it feel like I'm walking on a cloud.

"New shoes?" Eric asks, noticing them. The only reason I think he would is because he was looking at my legs, and that makes me just...a lot furious.

"Yes," I answer tightly.

"Aren't those like a thousand a pair?"

His question only serves to twist my annoyance higher like I'm a wind-up toy, and with each stupid comment and question, he's pushing me closer to letting my temper go.

Again, he's saved by the elevator. "We have the same paycheck. I'll meet you back at the desks. I'm going to run the cookies over to my friend."

"Aw, I was hoping that they were meant for Darren and me as a symbol of our truce."

"Nope, sorry." My words are terse, but if I don't walk away, I might hit him.

I power-walk toward Josh's office, motioning to ask Quincey if I can go in. She gestures me through, and I'm grateful that Josh is alone.

He brightens when I close the door behind me, and he sees it's me.

"Hello there, gorgeous. How is your day going?"

"I need you to fuck me right now," I say, still holding on to my temper.

Josh does a double take and leans back in his chair. "What happened to–"

"Josh." I just repeat his name, trying to get my emotions back in check. I get why he's confused. This is a total 180 on every stance I've made, but if I don't release some dopamine, I might quit. And I can't quit this job. "If you're not okay with fucking me right now, that's fine, but don't throw my words back in my face."

He gets to his feet and smooths his hands down my arms. "Do you want to talk about it?"

"If I wanted to talk about it, I would have come in here and said, 'I want to talk.' Josh, please. If you don't want to, I totally understand, but just tell me so I can go to the bathroom and practice breathing exercises instead."

Josh seems to consider what I'm asking before he walks back behind his desk, and I think he's saying no, which I can completely respect. He picks up the phone, and I watch him because I still want a kiss. I have to give him his cookie, although I might just rage-eat all three cookies instead of sharing like I planned.

"Quincey, take lunch."

He hangs up the phone and walks over to me. His eyes search my face, and I don't know what he's looking for. Gingerly, he cups my face.

"Just one last question. Are you okay?"

Why does something that simple cause tears to prick my eyes? "Yes," I choke out. I don't even know why I'm being such a drama queen about this. It's not like anything happened, but it's the way Eric made me feel. It's a culmination of all these little microaggressions that have built up under my skin. I hate how it's made me feel, and I just want it all to go away, even if it's just for a quickie.

Josh opens his mouth as if to refute me, but instead, he kisses me and walks backward, dragging me with him until I'm pressed against his desk, and it's like that first time when he ate me out.

"Don't move," he orders. He walks away from me, and I do as I'm told, staying perfectly still, listening to him engage the lock before he's back in front of me. It's like he can read exactly what I need because he's not soft or gentle. I think that would break me even more.

His kisses are bruising as his big hands push my skirt up until it's around my waist. With one finger, he strokes me over my underwear, and I keep fighting to choke on my moans as he teases me just enough that I'm wet and desperate for him. With his other hand, he undoes two buttons on my blouse so he can get to my breasts. He gives me a rather hard lovebite on one of them that makes me want to whine with need.

I grip the lapels of his jacket to stop from running my hands through his hair. He kisses my jaw, nipping at my ear as he unbuckles his pants. It's just Josh and I and the sound of our panting as he frees his cock, spitting on it, and shit. It's so dirty and wrong to be doing this in the full office, and yet, I would do this again tomorrow. I think I might.

Pulling my panties to the side, he pushes into me slowly, not out of a desire to tempt and tease, but because I'm still wound too tight everywhere, and I doubt I'm as wet as I usually would be when we play these games. Once he's seated in me completely, he groans.

"You feel too good, Taryn. You feel like temptation, and I want to give in. I want to give everything to you. But right now, I'm just going to give you my cock until you come around it like a good girl, and you're going to have to walk back to your desk with my cum dripping down your legs. Oh fuck, baby, I felt you clench at that idea. Does that turn you on?"

His words are whispered and hot before the frenzied fucking begins. I whimper once as he begins, and it causes Josh to come to a complete stop. The look he gives me could wither a plant, but it has me clenching around his cock so hard I'm afraid I'm about to come, and it will be over before it even starts.

"Not a fucking sound," Josh whispers almost sweetly against my lips. Slowly, he starts to move his hips again before he's pounding into me, rattling his desk. It's a low sound, enough that it's obvious to the two of us exactly what he's doing as each movement shakes what's there. Our heavy breathing is louder than the pens, and the illicitness spurs my orgasm. My body explodes, pulsing around him, coming harder than a freight train. He has to actually cover my mouth with his hand because my orgasm kicked off his own. I bring my hand up to his mouth, and his own eyes widen. I think both of us are more than a little into the edge of exhibitionism.

We take a second, breathing heavily into the quiet of the room before he pulls out. Josh gives me the softest kiss on my lips and then my forehead before helping me off his desk. I'm about to set myself to rights when he guides my panties off my hips.

"We'll talk later about what that was about, but I hope I helped." He pockets the underwear. He's trying to be playful and mischievous, but I can see the hint of worry in his eyes.

I squeeze his bicep. "I'm okay. I mean, stealing my panties was rude because I have no time to go to the bathroom. Do I look like you've just been fucking me senseless?"

"No, I'm actually irritated by how un-fucked you look. We should try again."

I swat at him, grabbing a few tissues to stick between my legs.

It's honestly gross and wrong, but I need to do something so I don't leave a wet stain on my skirt until I can get to the bathroom.

"I promise to tell you later. It's not even a big deal," I say, already downplaying my feelings and the whole interaction.

"Okay."

I turn to walk away from Josh, but he grabs my wrist and spins me to face him so he can plant one on me, and it's incredible. I mean, fireworks, leg-popping, weak-in-the-knees good, and then it ends, and he lets me go. "Just remember–"

"I know. I promise to tell you."

"Not what I was going to say, smartass. Remember that I'll always be here for you when you need me, if that's a quick fuck or to talk. Remember that you're incredible. Remember that you're bright and clever and that you are capable of amazing things."

The gooey knees are back at those words, but I can't help it. "But not pretty?"

"Nope."

My jaw drops in faux outrage.

"You're stunning. You're more than I ever dreamed of having in my life. Now, go. I have a call in ten minutes I have to prepare for."

I love you. The words are on the tip of my tongue, but I hold them back. This isn't the right moment to say it, not when I'm on the verge of such big emotional feelings.

Instead of returning to my desk, I go to the bathroom, only after leaving a note on Quincey's desk with both cookies that were intended for her and Josh. Josh can have some nookie–I mean cookies–when we get home.

Shit, at what point did I start thinking of his home as my home? I know I should come into the office this weekend, but I need brunch with my friends. I'm hoping I can talk them into meeting me in the financial district for brunch Sunday. We usually go to Claudia Jean's but haven't been in what feels like forever.

"Where have you been?" Darren asks, looking up from his

salad with a scowl. I guess I can't really blame him; eating salad doesn't exactly inspire happy feelings the way that cookies or bread do.

"Gossiping," I answer, crossing my legs as I feel just a little bit of wetness. I did a rush clean-up job, and going sans panties means that I'm going to be feeling Josh in me for the rest of the day. And yes, it's a little bit gross, but I also weirdly don't hate it the way I would have with past partners.

Manny comes over and rests his hands on my shoulders while he looks over at my blank computer screen. I tense up as he squeezes them before pulling his hands away. That gross feeling is back, but before I can say anything, Manny speaks.

"I was wondering where you were, Tara. I wanted to let you know the result of my meeting with Josh. We both agreed it would be best for you to stay on my team since this project is almost over. I have been reaching out to other managing directors to see if they would be interested in the level of skill you've been displaying."

I can read between the lines–he doesn't want to work with me because of whatever shit Darren has been whispering in his ear while they've gone to strip clubs and done who knows what else while I was actually doing the work for this client.

"I would appreciate it if you didn't–"

Darren cuts me off, and my rage spikes again. "Manny, I just want to make sure you're considering all angles. Taryn has been a delight to have on the team. Her skills with PowerPoint have been great, and her attention to *some* details is great." Darren makes eye contact with me, and then he rubs his chest and taps the center of it, which feels almost like a signal.

As surreptitiously as I can, I readjust in my seat and glance down to see that one of the buttons on my blouse popped open, and while, yes, I'm showing a little more cleavage than I ordinarily would, it's the bite mark on the curve of my breast that is the detail that Darren is referencing. I thought I was all put together. It's mortifying, causing tears of shame to prick my eyes.

"Manny, I'm not feeling great. I'll email the team what I've been working on, but I have to go."

"Again?" Manny asks, but I don't care. I leave my salad on my desk, suddenly too nauseated to eat, and pack up my stuff as quickly as I can. I feel like I can't breathe in this office, and it isn't until I'm out from under the shadow of my building that I feel like I can finally fill my lungs.

I send an SOS to my friends and tell them where to meet me.

I'm stressed to an unbelievable level when Elia, Ainsley, and Vivian walk through the door of Claudia Jean's. It's unreal luck that I used to work here, so when I walked to the back and just grabbed a bottle of wine without saying anything, they let it go. Really, it isn't luck. I came here because I knew that if anyone was going to be understanding, it was going to be this place.

Elia is the first to arrive, which isn't a huge surprise since she works from home doing graphic design. She's closely followed by Ainsley and Vivian, who sit right down. Vivian signals the waitress for drinks all around, except for me. I'm still drinking from my own bottle. Other patrons are glancing our way curiously, but I don't care.

"Do I need to be filing a wrongful termination claim?" Vivian asks when I fail to say anything right away.

"No, no, I just. God, I've had an absolute shit day and shit week, and I hate my shit job, and I'm trying really hard to, like, remind myself that I knew finance was shitty like this when I wanted to get this job, but it was too good to turn down. The money is great, and who cares if sometimes there are some dick-heads who don't care what they're doing. God, Josh must think

I'm insane. I walked into his office and demanded he fuck me and then walked out of the building."

I wish, God, I wish I could have just gone into my boyfriend's office and asked him to just comfort me. I wish that I didn't have to hide our relationship behind closed doors. I want to be able to go to him when I need comfort.

"Let's start from the top, hun," Ainsley says. That's how I know I must look bad. Ainsley is many things, but never in the almost fifteen years that I've known her has she ever tried to treat me with kid gloves.

So, I go right back to the beginning. How bad my parents' finances are to explain why I stay at my job. Ainsley knew some of that already, but it's new to Elia and Vivian, who keep neutral expressions on their faces. They only break when I tell them about my internship drama, which earns a curious nod from Vivian, who mutters something about the psychic we saw in Vegas. I tell them about how work has been brutal, and Eric keeps asking me out. I tell them about the Pictogram photo on Darren's computer and how Darren made a move on me. When I get to today, I feel stupid all over again as I convince myself I'm making a big deal out of nothing.

"Listen to me," Ainsley demands, and I snap my head in her direction. "You're going to hold your head up and go back into that office tomorrow with your head held high. You're going to start copying Manny on *every* email you send to Darren and Eric from now on so he can see the exact tone of every email you send, in addition to demonstrating everything that is said and done. You are going to tell your boyfriend about everything that has been going on, and you are going to start a list of everything they do and say, including witnesses."

"I feel like I'm making a big deal out of nothing," I whisper the words, looking away from them. Some part of me, the smarter, stronger voice in my head, tells me that this is just what I've been conditioned to think growing up as a woman. I'm just thinking that because I've been having to explain away comments and innocent touches my whole life. That voice *insists* that this is not nothing and that I need to stay strong and defend myself. I almost said something today too, and then fucking Darren.

"That's what they're expecting you to do, Taryn," Vivian says. "They're expecting you to stay quiet because individually, these things feel small, except for hand on the knee and what shit-for-brains Darren said. But I promise you, Taryn, this isn't small. It's a pattern. You were brave when you stood up for yourself at your internship, and just because this sexual harassment isn't taking the form of a blatant demand for a blow job doesn't make it any less important or serious." Vivian is fierce when she says this, taking my hands.

"You never have to bear this burden alone," Elia adds, placing her hand on my shoulder. "I know I'm a little late to the pep talk speech, but Ains and Vivian are right. Just because you feel like it's a small transgression doesn't mean your feelings about it are small. You felt uncomfortable, and you don't deserve to. You're working in a very hostile environment without even taking into account what has been going on with your parents. Work has been crazy, I get it, but we're your friends. Lean on us."

"And for fucks sake, move in with one of us," Ainsley says, shaking her head as she sips her water. "You have no excuse. Vivian is still single. Or better yet, take Josh up on his offer."

"I need to do some of this myself. I thought you would understand, Little Miss I'm Going to Have a Baby by Any Means Necessary."

"Sure, sure, but I also reached out for help when I was ready. Eventually, it will be too late to throw you a life preserver. Your credit is taking a hit, and sure, you're making Scrooge McDuck money now, but at a certain point, you may not want to be working 140 hours a week. You also need to protect your financial future."

"I hate you all for being right," I tell them.

Vivian wraps her arms around me and tugs me close. "False, it's why you called us. You needed someone to read you the riot act, and I think you got it. Sometimes, you just need to hear the truth from someone else to act on it."

I feel guilty when I do it, but I text Josh that I'm not coming to his apartment tonight. Instead, we all go to Elia's place for a midweek sleepover. Charlie is kind enough to keep us stocked with drinks and snacks while giving us our space. We're all too old for it, but it's the exact right balm I need before I tell Josh everything that's been happening in the office.

Nineteen

THE FIRST THING I do the next morning is go to Josh's office. Quincey is picking at a sad little breakfast tray with a fully loaded omelet. When she sees me, she brightens.

"He's in meetings *all* day today. When he's out, I can let him know you stopped by?"

"Thanks, Quincey."

"Of course, and thanks for the cookies!"

I give her a wave before I head to my desk. I'm a little hungover and green, but I have to hold my head high. I have just two weeks left with Darren and Eric, and I completely agree with Manny that I should find another team to work with. I'm going to ask Josh if he happens to know anyone who's looking for someone who doesn't mind doing the long hours as long as they're treated with even a small modicum of respect.

"Manny is piiiiiiiisssed," Darren greets, his eyes roving over me.

"I've already emailed Manny." Twice, I don't say. Once to tell him I'm feeling better and I'll be in the office today. I wanted to email and apologize, but Vivian and Ainsley both told me that would be an awful idea. I'll trust the lawyers on this one. The other time was to "catch him up" on what I had been working on in case Darren and Eric needed it during the day.

Passive aggressive? Yes.

Effective? Also yes.

"Feeling better?" Eric asks as he takes his crossbody bag off and sets it on his desk. He reaches for me and grabs my bicep like Josh would in a loving way of showing care. I pull back and out of his grip, and a hurt look flashes across his face.

"I am, thank you. I would also appreciate not being touched without my permission in the future." Clear, direct, and to the point. My whole body feels like it's shaking, but I'm glad I set the boundary, one that should have been obvious from the get-go, but clearly, I was remiss in not stating it.

We stop fucking around from there and get to work.

Things are actually calm until I point out an error that Darren has been making for weeks. I've been trying to correct him as we go with simple notes like, "You should double-check that." But instead, he hasn't, and I've just been going back in and making the right calculation.

Today though, New Leaf Taryn has had it. This time when I point it out, he throws his pen down and swivels in his chair to face me.

"Why don't you just blow me, fire crotch?"

I flinch at the vehemence in his voice and take a glance around to see who else might have heard him. Ainsley did say to get witnesses, after all.

"What did you just say?" a deep male voice demands, and I turn to find Josh standing tall with his arms crossed.

For a second, Darren looks like he's going to try to walk it back, pretend like he didn't say it, but there really isn't any room to say that he didn't.

"I was just frustrated. I was wrong to say it. I'm sorry, Taryn." He sounds almost reasonable, and if I didn't really know who Darren was, maybe I would believe him, but I've seen through him this whole time, and I don't feel like dealing with it.

"No, that's not acceptable," Josh says. "I'm going to write you up for that comment. You should know better than to say shit like that, ever, let alone in an office setting. I'll also be telling your managing director what I witnessed today."

Fury lights in Darren's eyes, but it's no match to the anger riding Josh. "What are you even doing over here?"

"None of your business." Josh doesn't even look in my direction.

Before Darren can shoot back, Manny approaches us with a broad smile. "Tara, I'm glad to see you're feeling better. Josh, can I do anything for you?"

"Let's go talk in your office, Manny," he says, not even glancing in my direction.

For a second, a brief flash of insecurity tries to rear its head and tell me that maybe he's actually mad at me, but common sense prevails, and I shake my head. He's not mad at me; he's furious about what he overheard, and he's just focused on that right now. I still have time to tell him about yesterday and all the other shit before.

"It was just a joke," Darren calls, like it's going to make a difference. His anger turns to me. "Why was Josh over here anyway? Seems like you two have been spending an awful lot of time together for someone who doesn't want to date coworkers."

His insinuation, while it might be the truth, cuts a little too close to home for comfort. How closely has Darren been watching me to notice that?

"It's none of your fucking business, Darren. Maybe if you were half as good at your job as you were kissing ass, you wouldn't be getting reprimanded for sexual harassment. I wonder, when you apply for a new job, is it like a mark on your permanent record, and they tell your new employer when they call for a reference?"

"*Bitch.*"

I look over at Eric to see if he's got *anything* to say, but he's already got his headphones back in, and he's not paying attention to us anymore.

What a sad sack of balls both of them make.

I anxiously wait to see Josh again, but he never stops by. I do get a ping on the company messaging app to wait for him tonight to go home. I'm notoriously bad at checking my phone during the day, so while I hate sending personal messages on it, it's good for exactly this.

As stressed as it makes me having to wait to talk to him, I do it. It's only karma for how I ditched him yesterday after having him fuck me in his office.

Fuck, what was I thinking?

Josh is waiting for me outside when I leave at two in the morning. I probably didn't need to stay that long, but I did feel guilty about leaving yesterday. While I can understand that it's not ultimately my fault, I still want to do a good job and do my job right. I take pride in providing a good work product.

Jost slowly uncurls from where he's leaning against the car so he can walk over to me. He pulls me into a tight embrace, his lips meeting mine in the kind of kiss that carves out a part of your soul for the other person. Forever, Josh will be walking around with a piece of me, and I can't even find it in me to be mad.

"So what–" I start, but Josh cuts me off.

"Later, please, treasure. I'm fucking beat and just want to get us home and into bed. I missed you last night."

"I'm sorry. I just...yesterday sucked except for you. And I couldn't do it anymore. I couldn't be there for a second longer."

"When we get home, we're going to have a talk about what

happened yesterday and today, but I need the drive home to just close my eyes. I barely slept last night without you by my side."

"I would say the same, but Ainsley is this tiny heat-seeking missile. She turned herself into a backpack and clung to me all night long."

"Hmmm, that's my job."

We both manage to drift off in the car, only to be woken up just as we pull up to our townhouse. A manic giggle escapes me at thinking of it as *our* townhouse when it is still very much just Josh's. Maybe someday, it will be ours. He did ask me to move in with him. Does that still count?

Once the front door is closed, Josh watches as I take my shoes off.

"Yesterday, I was tired of being objectified and being made to feel like less than because of my sex. I was tired of being made to feel like I'm just office ornamentation when I do so much of the work, and I just wanted to feel in control of something. I could control you fucking me while the assholes that want me, while the assholes that treat me like less than were still in the office. And it was wrong of me to use you like that. Honestly, this conversation is much heavier than I think either of us really counted on for two in the morning. But I want off Manny's team. I want away from Darren and Eric as soon as this project is over. And before you say that it must not be that bad if I'm willing to stick it out, that's because I'm not a quitter. I will see this through as long as I can."

"Treasure, I would never, *never* say that. I am always, always going to be there for you and be on *your* side. Has this been going on this whole time? Has that little shit Darren been making comments like that since you started working together?"

"Well, yeah."

"And does Manny know? Have you told anyone?"

"My friends, and now you. I don't think Manny knows. He's either obvious or willfully turning a blind eye. I mean, even he is a little inappropriate. Again, not a big deal, but yesterday he put his hands on my shoulders, and it was just one of those final straw things."

I hear the deep breath that Josh takes in through his nose. When I look up at him, I can see that he's barely holding back his anger. I can't say I blame him. There is a reason that I straight up walked out of the office after it happened. It was either snap or walk away and keep my job and sanity.

He's silent for several moments, and I start to worry that maybe he's mad at me and maybe I was wrong about who I thought Josh was. His tongue darts out to wet his lips before he takes another one of those deep, deep breaths. Yeah, yoga would be good for us both.

"He put his hands on you?"

Right away, I jump into the thing I've been raised to do my whole life, minimize my experience, and make it seem like it wasn't as bad as it was. It could have been so much worse, and shouldn't I be thankful that it wasn't? Hell, I've been in worse situations before.

"I mean, it wasn't an overtly sexual touch. It was more like–"

"Stop, Taryn. Stop right there. You didn't want to be touched, correct?"

I can feel my head bob a nod, but it feels awkward and tight. "Right."

Another one of those breaths, and I'm worried he might pass out from all this extra oxygen. "Have you spoken with HR?"

"No, I literally walked out of the office. I couldn't... I couldn't deal with it, okay?"

"I'm going to give you a hug now. Is that okay?"

"Of course, it is. It's always okay for you to touch me."

He steps forward and wraps me in a big hug. As much as my friends were able to comfort me yesterday, they weren't able to give me this reassurance. I needed their girl power yesterday, but tonight, I need my lover to remind me that I'm safe and that I can get past this.

"What happened to the girl who told me she wasn't going to blow me?" he asks when I tip my head back to look at him.

"Don't blame me," I start to struggle out of his grip, a new wave of anger rising.

He won't let me go, though. "I think you misunderstand me. I'm not blaming you for your actions. I'm just surprised that Manny is walking around with his hands still attached to his body. They probably won't be when I get through with him. I just mean, a few weeks ago you wouldn't have stood for this. You would have told Manny where he could stuff it. So, what changed?"

"What changed, Josh?"

This time, he lets me go when I pull from his grip. I start walking back to the kitchen to get a glass of water. I want so badly to go to bed, but I know neither of us are going to sleep while we're still hashing this out. "What changed is that Manny walked into your office threatening to throw my entire career off just because Darren and Eric don't know how to deal with their little boy feelings. I already have something of a reputation for getting men fired for propositioning me. Eventually, people will stop believing me and think of me as the girl who cried wolf. It just is mindblowing that if I was a man, *none* of this would be happening."

"How often does Darren speak to you like that?" Josh wisely grabs an open bottle of red from the wine rack and pours me a glass.

"All the damn time. A few weeks ago, I told him to fuck off, and Manny heard me and sent me home because he heard me and *not* Darren asking about my period."

"Okay. Tomorrow, we're going to go *together* to talk to HR about this. I witnessed what he said to you today, and I already told Manny I was going to be reporting that to HR, but this has been going on long enough."

"No. I mean, yes, I will go to HR, but my lawyers told me to start a list with witnesses to each comment. I need a stronger case because, at this point, it's he said versus she said, and Darren has Manny and Eric to back him up."

"Ah, but you have me."

I melt into his hold as he wraps me in another hug. "I do, but we're fucking, and that's going to count against us."

"Who are these lawyers you're talking to?"

"Vivian and Ainsley are both attorneys. Neither of them does employment law, but they said they know people if it comes down to it. They're just coaching me through how to handle the situation."

"Fine, but you have one week, and then we're reporting this. I'm going to be putting the paperwork in for what Darren said regardless, and that's going to start an entire investigation. So, be ready for that."

"In the morning. I'll be ready in the morning. Right now, I want to go to sleep. I was able to sleep some last night, but somehow I'm already getting used to sleeping by your side."

"I feel the same way, baby."

I keep waiting for the other shoe to drop, but Darren ignores me for the rest of the week. Manny not so subtly told him to take the weekend off because of the talk that he and Josh had. I'm torn between being pleasantly surprised by it and worried. He's been too quiet.

Darren now copies Manny on all email correspondence. I got an email from HR looking for time to discuss what happened the following week because they're attending mandatory training all week. It certainly feels like things are looking up, even if both Josh and I are just working with our heads down, trying to get everything that we can done before everything blows up with the allegations.

I'm almost a little frustrated now that Darren has gone quiet. If he's not making comments, I have less sturdy facts to back up my case. I can't pinpoint exact dates and times that he's called me fire crotch, commented that I must be on my period, or asked if the curtains matched the drapes before offering to do a thorough inspection. These comments all just faded into the background. It's awful, but I actually got desensitized to them.

It's another quiet Saturday in the office when I walk into Josh's office. I told him I would meet him there because I needed to get a change of clothes from my apartment. My annoyance at having him ask me to move in stemmed more from me being mad about it being for the wrong reasons. If he asked me because he cared about me and wanted me to move in because he wanted me close, I would say yes in half a heartbeat. I would say yes before the question was even out. But because I'm financially strapped? It might make sense, but it doesn't exactly give me the warm fuzzies. It's practically a marriage of convenience, and I don't want that.

Josh is so wrapped up in his work that he doesn't even notice me for a few minutes. It's refreshing to watch him work with his brow furrowed. His fingers fly over his keyboard, and I can't stop myself.

"I love you," I blurt out, the words springing from my mouth.

It's the honest truth. It's not grand gestures that make you fall in love with someone. It's a collection of the quiet moments, making each other coffee and doing little things that make your partner's life easier. I know that my parents have this incredible love story, and I know that I want that for myself. I think I found it too, in the form of Josh, and while I may have only just realized how deeply in love with him I am, I know that I don't want to lose him. I don't want him to walk away from us, the same way I don't want to walk away from him.

Once the words are out, my whole body relaxes because it's not something I would even want to take back if I could. Maybe in another life, I would have wanted to create a "moment" for me to say it, but our love isn't about big moments. It's about being there for each other through it all. It feels right to have said the words, even if the realization has only just hit me. I would be worried about his reaction if I wasn't confident he felt the same.

His head lifts, and he looks at where I'm leaning against the doorframe in a green sundress. He's quiet, and I worry I read the room wrong. Not that it would change how I feel about him at all, but it does make things hella awkward.

"Come here, treasure." There is a softness to his voice as he beckons me toward him, and I comply easily, closing the door behind me. The sound of my heels is muted by the carpet.

"I'm sorry, was that too much?" I ask. I know that people move at their own pace, and I don't want him to feel pressured in any way.

When I reach him, he pulls me onto his lap for a long kiss, and I don't hold back. Our bodies mold together, and I'm glad I had the presence of mind to close the door because his hand is creeping up my dress, along the inside of my thigh.

"It wasn't too much. God, it was perfect." He nuzzles his nose with mine. "I love you, too, treasure." He reaches the apex of my thigh, kissing me as he starts to drag a knuckle over my panties.

Dropping one leg to the floor, I open up for him. Josh wastes no time, stroking me just hard enough that I start to buck my hips, but it's only a teasing touch. He's going to make me beg him for it, and I'm not even a little bit mad about it. I want to give him everything I have. I want to let him in and take care of me in every way, not just with orgasms.

"What do you want?" I ask him, but the question is more of a whine. I want to get closer. I want to fucking explode around his cock, but I'm handing the reigns over to him for now. I've been pushing him away since we had dinner with his family. Opening up about what has been happening in the office was a step in the right direction, but today, this is *the* step. The confirmation that I'm in this with him, whatever form that takes.

Even if it means going public with our relationship in the office. Which I'll have to do before my meeting with HR. I don't like the idea of Josh feeling like a dirty little secret any longer, even if it means having people believe I'm sleeping my way up. Declaring that I love him changes things. This thing between us no longer feels like fog, an intangible thing about to slip through my fingers. This all feels very real, and I want to be able to come talk to him without worrying about whispers as I walk past in the hall. People are going to talk anyway, and going public feels like the best way to show Josh that I choose him.

Josh pulls my panties to the side and slides one long finger inside me, completely obliterating all thoughts outside of his touch.

"I want to bend you over this desk and fuck you."

I moan, and he covers his mouth with mine. "Hush, treasure, there are people in the office. I would be mad to know they could hear you as you came around my cock." He chuckles when my body clenches involuntarily around his finger. "Do you want that too? To come around my dick while you know there are people walking past the door? You're a little exhibitionist minx, aren't you? You like just enough risk."

"Shut up, Josh, and make good on your promises."

He helps me to my feet, spinning me around so I'm facing his desk. Fuck, if I don't love this position, the feeling of being utterly dominated by him. I plant my hands on his desk, leaning over so my ass is right there for the taking.

He clucks his tongue and confusion hits me as he pulls me upright with a hand wrapped around my hair. When he releases me, his hands go to the zipper on my dress, sliding it down my body so it pools at my feet.

"No bra, treasure?" He reaches around me to cup my breasts for just a second, rolling both nipples between his fingers.

My body hums with excitement, and desire has me clenching my pussy again. There is something so decadently dirty about being naked while he's still fully clothed. Lifting one foot, I start to step out of my heels, but he clucks again, and I stay perfectly still while he pulls my underwear down my legs, nipping at my ass as he does it.

I'm completely fucking naked except for my heels, and I might come on the spot just from this.

"Like what you see?" I ask saucily, looking at him over my shoulder. He's pulled his cock out while he looks at me.

"It's hard not to when you have a body like this." He crowds around me so I can feel his hardness pressing into my ass. The fabric of his shirt is rough as he reaches around to pluck at my nipple.

I push back into him, desperate for some friction between my legs. "Are you going to show me who's boss, or am I going to have to put my dress on and walk out of here unsatisfied?"

He pulls away from me, and a dark part of me enjoys the not knowing. His foot between my legs nudges my feet apart, still being careful not to knock me over in my heels.

As he insists, I spread my legs and wait and wait. I can hear the sound of his hand working over his flesh, and I might die of anticipation.

In one brutal move, he spears me on his cock, his hand coming around my mouth just in time to stop my cry from escaping. We're both panting as he doesn't move. It's a punishment for my attempt to top from the bottom, and I know it. I know that I also wouldn't have it any other way with his zipper roughly rubbing against my bottom with each little micro-thrust he's making, just keeping me on the edge.

"God, you take my cock so well. This pussy was made for me."

Josh places one hand on the back of my head, pushing me down, down, down until my cheek is pressed onto the hardwood. I'm facing his bookcase, looking at all his achievements as he works his body with mine. It's so degrading to be used for his pleasure, and I fucking love it. I want him to use me every day to get what he needs because I know he would do the same in a heartbeat.

And that's why we work, because we have a firm grasp on each other's needs.

"Touch yourself, treasure," he orders as he holds me there. I could easily push back up if this wasn't working for me or tell him to stop, and he would, but I want this, so I reach between my legs and play with my clit as he continues to torture me with his cock.

The expectation was that he was going to take me fast and hard and fuck me, but I think this is just a rougher way of making love, and the thought almost brings a tear to my eye. It's the realization of just how deep my love for him goes that sends me hurdling into my orgasm. I bring my other hand up to my mouth to stifle my moans.

Josh follows me over the edge almost immediately, his hips breaking their steady teasing to pounding into me hard enough that my hip bones connect with the desk on each thrust until he stills inside me.

He bends over, kissing my shoulder, then across my back to the other side before he can look me in the face.

"You good?" he asks, concern in his voice.

"I'm so much better than good, but I need a minute. Holy shit."

He gives me that time, pulling out of me and tending to the cum slipping down my thighs as I stay there, face down, ass up on his desk. I'm still panting, trying to catch my breath as he pulls my panties back up and then my dress, holding it around my waist.

"Do you have a lot more work?" he asks as I finally straighten up, pulling my dress with me. I slide my arm back into my straps before turning to face him, even with the back gaping open.

"Excellent segue," I scoff.

"I'm asking because I want to take you home and ravish you some more, or is that a problem for my darling treasure?"

Josh moves so he's behind me again, zipping my dress up.

"I do actually have a few more hours of work to get done, so maybe we can take tomorrow off and do brunch with my friends?"

I don't know where the idea comes from, but I want them to meet Josh, and I want them to like him. I know he already knows Charlie, and he's met Elia, but now that I've decided I'm keeping him, I want them to meet him and approve.

"I thought you would never ask. Of course. Why don't you just bring your laptop in here, and you can work right there so I can see you?"

"Wow, say the "L" word and some guys get so possessive. No, if I do that, I know I'll wind up on my knees sucking your dick. There is no time for that."

Josh strokes his hand down his crotch, and I see that all the fucking we're doing has boosted his refractory period because he's already sporting a little woody.

"You don't have to do anything with that."

Okay, maybe being a good employee can wait till later. I drop to my knees, pulling his half-hard cock out of his pants. It takes a few strokes before I can wrap my mouth around him and suck.

He drops into his chair, so I'm just bobbing on his cock while he sits over me like a king. One glance at him through my lashes makes me want to do this regularly, maybe set up a nice little spot under his desk so I can suck him off whenever I feel like it.

It doesn't take Josh long before he's thrusting up into my mouth and exploding down my throat. Sinking back onto my ass, I look up at him, a contented smile on my lips.

"Be a good girl and get your ass on this desk so I can eat that pussy for lunch," he orders, but I dismiss him.

"Why don't you go get us lunch, and I'll get to work? You can eat this pussy for dinner and dessert, but I have work to do."

"Yes, ma'am."

Josh takes my order for lunch. He walks me back toward my desk, swatting my ass once he's sure no one else will see.

I'm shocked to see Darren standing there. I want to wipe my lips, which I'm sure are swollen and bruised not just from the blow job but from the kisses that came before and after.

"Don't mind me. I just needed to get a file from my desk." He's dismissive as he looks back at his desk.

"Why not send Eric then?" I don't know why I need to needle him about it, but Eric mentioned on Friday that they were going to spend the weekend working together. He said it like he felt bad he couldn't invite me, but Darren's treatment of me was the reason he was told *not* to work from the office today.

"Because I know where my shit is. I see you're being productive today." His gaze flits down to the black screen of my computer.

"I was talking to Josh about lunch. He offered to go get some when he saw I was working."

"Sure, that's what that smell is."

I stand up straighter. Josh is right; a few months ago, I wouldn't have stood for this, but now Darren is in just as much jeopardy as I am. "Excuse you?" I demand, crossing my arms.

Darren moves from his desk across the aisle to right next to me. He doesn't touch me, but I lean away from him as he gets in my space. He takes a deep whiff, starting at my shoulder and working up to my ear. "Smells like desperate office whore."

If he thought I was going to back down, he was sorely mistaken. "Fuck off, Darren. If anyone here is desperate, it's you. There's a reason you've been put in time-out."

He steps back and laughs. "Oh, I'm not worried. I'm sure Manny will see the truth of who you are soon enough."

Darren grabs a file from his desk before shaking his head and walking out to the elevators. The entire confrontation couldn't have taken more than ten minutes at most, but it left me feeling just a little shaken.

Refusing to let Darren get under my skin, I focus back on my work and doing it as quickly as I can. There are plenty of people on the floor, but everyone is so focused on what they're doing that I don't know that anyone even noticed our exchange of words. Still, I make a note of them all. At the very least, Darren's check-in with his keycard will confirm he was here when he was told not to come into the office.

I need every bit of ammo I can get.

Twenty

CLAUDIA JEAN'S IS BUSY, which is why it pays to have friends in high places. The new girl managing the hostess stand is someone I hooked up with the job, so she sets me up at the best table in the place. We have a view of the street, and we don't have to wait for our whole party to arrive to be seated. Other patrons waiting for a table eye us enviously, but I take my time getting settled while I wait for everyone else to show up. It's summertime, and the city is *packed* with tourists.

Predictively, Josh exploded when I told him about what happened with Darren while he was getting lunch. Although he didn't have to, he reassured me that I'm not some harlot strolling around the office with nothing on, though he teased he wouldn't mind that in our home office.

When he said our home office, it made me realize I wanted him to ask me to move in again, but I'm afraid I did too good a job of shutting him down the first time he asked that he might wait for me to make that move.

That decision can wait until after I'm done with this project and paying off the car repairs, something I prioritized. After finding the apartment without AC on, I told Zelda I'm not paying rent until she deals with the electricity issue caused by her nonpayment. I put that money into the credit card payment. It's a temporary stopgap measure, but I needed to do something.

"Are *you* nervous?" Josh asks, grabbing my hand where it rests on my lap. My knee is bouncing like crazy, but he doesn't try to make me stop, recognizing the nervous tic for just what it is: a self-soothing gesture for my nerves.

"Yes, because I like you; no, I love you, and if my friends don't like you, then I don't know what I'll do."

"Am I that much of a beast?" he asks with a loud laugh.

"No, but they're also my best friends."

"Okay, tell me a little about them so I know how to impress them."

I give him a little glare as if it's going to be that easy. "Well, you know Charlie and Elia. They've been married for about a year and a half now. They met when Charlie's cab hit Elia while she was on a bike."

"Jesus, and she's alright?"

"Mostly perfectly fine, but that's a whole other story. Then there is Vivian."

"She's one of the attorneys."

"Yes! Very good. And last but not least are Ainsley and Ken. They're also a relatively new thing." I could mention she's pregnant, but I think she's still playing that one close to the chest until she's out of her first trimester, which should be soon if she isn't already.

"I'm here. I'm here!" Ainsley says as she bounds up the two stairs from the hostess stand to our table. Ken trails behind her, running a hand through his hair that looks like it's already greying from living with Ainsley in her apartment. It's by no means small, but it certainly isn't enough space for the two of them.

"You're not late," I assure her, getting up to meet her with a hug and a kiss on the cheek.

"Yes, but Ken told me I was late, so now I've rushed, and it's *so hot* outside."

I greet Ken with a hug too, and introduce them while we wait.

"So, you're the boss Taryn is banging. You certainly could have done worse. I know I've fucked some sad-looking finance bros."

Ken rubs his mouth with a laugh as they settle in, but when he looks at my friend, it's clear that she hung the moon in his eyes.

"You're an attorney?" Josh asks, settling his hand on my knee.

"Yes, I do divorce and family. That's how I met Ken." She wastes no time grabbing a roll and shoving a broken-off piece into her mouth without apology.

"And I own a bar," Ken adds. "It's Peculiar Tastes down in the East Village."

"Oh, I've heard of it," Josh says. "You use mason jars as the glassware. I thought that was different."

"See? Even Josh here thinks that is stupid." Ainsley takes a sip of water before another bite of bread.

"I never–" Josh starts.

"You don't have to. If you liked it, you wouldn't have described it as 'different.' You would have said 'clever' or 'cool' or even 'interesting,' but you said 'different,' which tells me that the words were out of your mouth before you really thought it through, and oh good! Chuck and Elia are here with Viv." Ainsley dusts her hands off as she pushes to her feet to greet them.

Ken looks at Josh. "It's not worth it. Let her have this one."

"You say that a lot, don't you?" Josh asks.

"More than I used to, that's for sure," Ken confirms with a laugh, getting to his feet.

"I'm just saying, I would like to see a Mr. Eligible whose personality isn't just lifting heavy things," Vivian is saying as she follows the couple.

"I think the franchise as a whole needs to move on to more mature leads," Elia confirms.

"If we get one more influencer as a contestant, *I* might scream," Charlie adds as they reach us.

Vivian smacks his arm. "See? I knew you watched with us."

We make another round of introductions, but Josh already knows Charlie and Elia, so it's not long before all of us are sitting around the table.

"So, how's that work situation going?" Vivian asks me vaguely.

"Work situation?" Charlie asks, looking at me. He would want to get into it since he's in the industry too.

"Knox Benedict says he knows someone in that area of law," Vivian says, which prompts Ainsley to act like a twelve-year-old with a low "ooooohhh." Vivian cuts her off with a glare.

Charlie clears his throat and looks like he's reaching to smooth a tie down his chest, but since he's dressed down, there is no tie for him to fidget with. "I repeat, work situation?"

I'm thankful for Josh's hand on my back.

"She clearly doesn't want to talk about it, Charlie," Elia murmurs to her husband.

"I'm actually a little surprised you didn't tell him," I say, appreciating her discretion.

"I told Ken," Ainsley confesses. "But that's just because I needed to make sure he would be willing to bail me out after I cut some asshole's balls off."

"And I confirmed I would be ready to bail her out," Ken says. He's more reserved in the group setting than I think he is with just Ainsley, but I can't blame him for that. We can be a little much. Even Josh is on the quieter side.

"I'm having problems with a guy at work who seems to think that because I'm a woman, he can say shit. I'm officially not standing for it."

"It also helps that he said something in front of me so I can be a witness to HR. I also reported him for his comment."

"Is that going to be a problem, though? You two being together?" Ken asks, stretching for more bread and putting it on Ainsley's plate before she even has to ask. She looks up at him with hearts in her eyes as she tears into it.

"I'll have to come clean to HR about it when I finally talk to them, but they've been out of the office at a conference," I say.

We pause briefly to order drinks and food before returning to the subject.

"I actually already told them," Josh says, sipping his water.

This makes me freeze, and I look up at him. "What?"

The rest of the table goes quiet. Josh glances at everyone before looking at me. "As soon as we started dating, I let human resources know that I started a relationship with you, even though you aren't *my* subordinate."

"Why would you do that?" I demand, lowering my voice.

"So, how about those Giants?" Ainsley asks loudly across the table. I'm grateful for her attempt at giving us some privacy because I think I'm a little mad. No, I know I'm a little mad that he did that.

"Wrong sports season, hun," Ken tells her, patting her knee.

"I already told you what happened with my father. I wanted to ensure we were both protected if something happened to our relationship. I wasn't going to leave you vulnerable to a situation that could call into question your character."

"No, instead you just alerted them to the fact that I'm a ladder-climbing whore."

Josh flinches. My words are just an echo of what Darren said to me yesterday, but I can't help it. There is no way that the situation with Darren will land on my side. They know that Josh and I have been fucking for weeks, and now my boyfriend is suddenly making accusations against the guy I've been working with who already has a record with me because Manny heard me tell him to fuck off.

"You know that's not true, Taryn."

My voice shakes when I answer him. "Do I? Because all you had to do was crook your finger, and I was on my knees for you."

Josh is silent for a second. I keep waiting for him to lash out or say something. "We can either leave and have this conversation somewhere not in front of your friends, or wait to talk about this later. I don't appreciate you using that language to talk about the woman that I love. Because I do love you, Taryn, and you're so much more than that."

A smaller hand on my other knee distracts me, and I shift my head just enough to catch a glimpse of Ainsley out of the corner of my eye. She's giving me this small amount of support, and I can't even begin to think about how much I appreciate this.

"Later. We can talk later," I assure him. My instinct is to run, to go back to my apartment, where I don't have to really face him and talk about how much of a betrayal it feels like. He was trying to protect me, and some common sense part of my brain knows as much, but I also wish he had talked to me about it first. He knew I didn't want people in the office to know about us.

I want to control the narrative about our relationship as much as I can because I know there are going to be people who look at me and see exactly that, a ladder-climbing whore looking to find some guy I can take for everything he has after the ink has dried on the marriage license.

My friends try to draw me out, but I'm too deep in my head to enjoy this brunch as much as I want to. It's clear that Josh is winning them all over. He had Charlie in his corner already, but when he gives Ainsley half his French toast after she gets order envy, I know the rest of my friends are just as in love with him as I am.

When we all get up to leave, Charlie pulls me to the side. "I know you want to fight tooth and nail to do this on your own, but you will always have a job waiting for you at my company. I don't know exactly what is going on, but I've been in this industry long enough to know that I wouldn't like it. You probably won't make as much as you would, but I can help you. Stop being so stubborn."

"What does that mean?" I ask, getting hung up on the last part of his statement.

Charlie snorts. "It means ever since freshman year at college, you have been stubborn to a fault. You walked back to your dorm on a broken ankle in the snow because you said you could do it yourself. No one denied that, but you were injured, and we just wanted to help you. Not every helping hand means you're weak. It's okay to accept it once in a while. No one will *ever* think less of you for you."

"That's easy for you to say, Charlie."

He crosses his arms and looks down at me. I can see Josh watching us in my peripheral vision, but I want to know what Charlie means about me being stubborn.

"Easy how?"

"You were born shitting bricks of gold."

"Don't do that, Taryn. Don't act like financial standing means you can't accept help. You don't know everything. I don't know everything. Did you know that I asked for Knox's help to change the ownership of my condo because Vivian and Ainsley didn't know how to help? It's okay to need help. It's okay to reach out, and when someone extends a hand to you, it's okay to take it."

"Charlie," Elia warns, coming up to his side. She focuses her gaze on me. "We'll catch up with you later. But no more hiding behind work as an excuse. If anything, we should be your excuse to get away from work."

When Vivian hugs me, she whispers in my ear. "It's also possible Knox offered to knock some teeth in on your behalf, and since that comes with the potential for jail time, I think you should consider it."

"Why would he do that?" I ask with a giggle.

"Because I was vague and told him I knew someone was being sexually harassed at work, and despite the man's many flaws, apparently he won't stand for that. So, please, take him up on it. A few nights in jail will get him off my case."

"I thought your project was over?"

"You and me both."

With the final goodbyes said, Josh offers me his hand, and I take it while Charlie's words echo in my head.

As much as I want to, I don't run from Josh and stay at my apartment. I stick it out and go home with him after brunch. He seems nervous about broaching the subject with me again, but he holds strong to his promise to talk about it. I'm still mad about it. I told him in no uncertain terms that I wanted to keep our relationship under wraps, and he told human resources about it.

"You're not a whore."

"Your situation with me is different than your father's," I counter almost immediately.

"I know that you aren't, but do you?" Josh asks. "Our relationship is exactly that, an actual relationship. I wanted us to be public in the office from the get-go–you're the one who wanted to hide from everyone and everything. I'm not ashamed of you, Taryn, so you can't pretend like I'm treating you like my office whore when I'm just following your lead."

I flinch. "But can you understand why I would be upset that you decided to talk to HR about me and our relationship without me?"

"If I didn't tell them, then I couldn't defend you from how Manny keeps trying to pawn you off because you're a woman. If I didn't tell them in advance that we were dating, then I wouldn't be able to protect you from the accusation that you're sleeping with me to advance your career like Darren keeps trying to insist."

My brow furrows, and I stare at Josh intently before wrapping my arms around my waist, hugging myself.

"What does that mean?"

Josh closes his eyes and curses. "It means that Darren is already trying to spin the narrative that you're sleeping with me to advance your career. When I had my sit down with Manny regarding Darren's comments, he mentioned it. I pointed out to Manny that he was the one who wanted you transferred to my team and that I am specifically *not* getting involved in your career."

"Except when you happen to overhear my shit-for-brains coworker calling me something nasty."

"Obviously, but I would have done that even if we weren't dating. That's unacceptable language."

He has me there. As much as I want to believe that most men are scum, Josh has done everything in his power to show me just the opposite, and looping him in with almost every other man I know in finance would be doing him a huge disservice.

My phone vibrates in my hand, and I silence it without looking.

"Taryn, talk to me."

"I don't know what to say, Josh. I just don't. I'm annoyed because I feel like our private business has been aired out without me even knowing, and I don't like that. Our bed isn't big enough for me, you, and the whole of human resources."

A smile is pulling at his lips, but he's fighting it with everything he has.

"What? What is it?"

"You said our bed."

I blush. It had to have been a Freudian slip or whatever. I'm trying to be brave for Josh, so I put it all on the line. "Well, yeah. I spend more time here, anyway. Why wouldn't I think it's our bed? But if you don't like that..."

"Treasure, I *love* that. I love that you think of it as yours and your space. And maybe I was rushing you when I asked you to move in, because you were right, we've barely been together, but I know how you take your coffee, and I know that it takes you three snoozes in the morning to get up and the exact right temperature of your shower. I want you to move in because I like having you in arm's reach when I wake up, even if it isn't for sex. I like being able to feel the warmth of your body beside me."

"That's the reason you want me to move in?" I have to put extra effort into my words to make them stay firm.

Before he can answer, my phone goes off in my hand again, and I look down and see that it's my mom and that my missed call is from her already.

"Answer it," he tells me, sitting on the back of his couch and watching me.

"Mom, now isn't really a good–"

"Baby, I got the job!"

I stand up taller. "What?"

Josh gets up from where he just settled to move close to me, concern on his features, and I shake my head.

"I got the job. I mean, it's nothing like I used to be doing. It's low-level admin work, but it's a paycheck, and it's enough that I can take some of the pressure off you. I wanted to tell you in person, but you're always so busy with work. They even said I could start tomorrow."

I walk past Josh into the kitchen and pull out a glass to fill with water. I need to finish my conversation with Josh, but this is a call I've been waiting months for. I sit on the stool at the island.

"Will you tell me about your new job, mom?" I say it so Josh has a better idea of what's going on.

His features change immediately. His eyes widen and brighten as he realizes what this means for me. Is this the financial lift I really need? No. But it's enough that I can breathe again. Not everyone gets as lucky, and my parents are by no means out of the woods yet, but it's a firm step that means that hopefully soon we can return to a normal parent/child relationship instead of one where I'm holding all the purse strings.

I listen to my mom talk for an hour. Eventually, Josh abandons me to my call, giving me the space I need to hear her and share in her excitement. Throughout the call, even though I'm delighted by the news, the thought that Josh acted in what he thinks is my best interest without talking to me still nags at me. I can understand where he was coming from, but it doesn't mean I have to like it. I understand his constant need to protect the ones he loves, especially after what his father put them through, but I was dead serious when I said I wanted our relationship to be a partnership.

When I hang up, I find him sitting in the living room with a video game controller in his hand. My entrance into the room has him pausing and looking up at me.

"Good news?"

"Great news," I confirm.

He sets the controller on the table and pulls me onto his lap. "I'm so glad to hear that things are looking up for your parents."

"Yeah, it's nice. I mean, it's not everything that they need to get out from under all the debt they have, but it's a great start, and having them cover even just half of the mortgage means that I'll be able to actually breathe when I get a credit card bill."

"I still want to talk to you about your living situation."

I loop my arms around his neck. "Like a dog with a bone."

He thrusts up just enough for me to feel his growing erection. "More like a dog with a boner."

"Joshua," I scold but lean into him.

"You don't sound that mad."

"I'm not, but I'm also trying to be realistic here. This is like Anna from *Frozen* level–I'm going to marry a man I just met."

"Wow, getting a little ahead of ourselves, are we?" Josh tickles my side to show me he's only teasing. "I want you to move in. I don't like where you live, and besides that, it just makes sense. You stay here all the time. I can make sure you get where you're going safely."

"Why do men always go there? The safety point. I mean. It's not like we're mobsters. Unless you have something you need to tell me, in which case, I'll need to make it abundantly clear that I really have no money and that you will never be able to extract a ransom from my family."

Josh stands up abruptly, holding me in his strong arms until he tries to dump me on his couch. "In that case, I'm out."

I fake outrage and poke at his sides until he leans over me, tickling me in retaliation. It's only once I'm breathless on the floor, with aching sides, that I cry mercy.

"You're serious?" I ask.

"Dead serious. I like knowing you're safe because I love you, and you matter to me. You don't have to say yes and move in tonight, but I'd like you to think about it. Maybe asking you after meeting my insane family wasn't the right call."

"More like asking me as a solution to my financial issues wasn't the right call. I love your sisters. They all seem lovely and so terribly clever. But saying, 'Ah, yes, save on your rent by moving in,' doesn't exactly scream, 'I need you like oxygen.'"

"Was that the reason for the cold shoulder?"

I sit up and lean against the coffee table, avoiding eye contact for just a moment. I've been mature enough to have this conversation with him, even with the teasing in the middle; I should be mature enough to see it through.

"Yes, it absolutely was. It hurt me to think that you wanted me to move in because you wanted to solve my problems."

"Think of solving your rent problem and shitty roommate issue as a fringe benefit. That was just a bonus to me having you and being able to *have* you at any time I wanted."

"You think I'm that easy?" I challenge, but we both know that I am.

A dark look crosses his face, and fuck, if I don't get turned on just by the look he gives me. He shifts from lying on the couch to sitting up.

His gaze drops to my lips, and I'm a total hussy because I lick them, my eyes flicking down to where I knew he was hard for me before our conversation and our tickle fight.

"I know you are, baby. And I'm going to reward that mouth for being so forthcoming tonight."

Hmm, maybe I should try this communication thing more often. Josh unzips his pants, freeing his cock. He doesn't even need to give the command, I fall on his cock with my mouth like it's my salvation, and maybe that's exactly what Josh is for me.

He's the salvation for what I didn't know I was missing in my life.

When he gets too impatient from not being able to control the speed in this position, he tries to force me on my back, but I'm enjoying it too much, the teasing as I lick him from base to tip, playing with his piercing, the way I've started to recognize when he's getting close, and I can pull back at the right moment. And maybe it's a little shitty of me to edge him like this, but I know he's going to devastate me once he gets me on my back.

Tears are filling my eyes as he hits the back of my throat, but his hand in my hair has me pulling off as he tugs at it.

"Come here, Taryn."

I withdraw and climb onto his lap, straddling him. I want to keep up the torture. I want to wear down his resistance until he gives in to the urge to fuck me senseless.

It never comes.

He shifts my panties aside so I can sink down on him, and even though it's driving us both mad, I take it slow as I use him for my pleasure the way I like him to do to me.

I moan low as my orgasm flays me. Our foreheads are pressed together when his orgasm rips through him. Josh holds my hips as he bucks up into me, stilling only once he's spent.

His arms band around my back in an iron embrace as he holds me close to him. We stay there, still joined, with my head nestled into the crook of his neck until our hearts beat in sync, the way I think they were always meant to.

Twenty-One

MONDAY MORNING IS AN OPTIMISTIC DAY. My mom has a new job and is on her way out from under financial ruin, and I've tentatively agreed to move in with Josh. At the very least, I can't stay with Zelda. As much as I appreciate having my own space, I'm tired of constantly worrying about the utilities and rent being paid.

I would also love it if my stuff stopped smelling like weed.

Darren and Eric are already at their desks for the morning, and for the first time since I started seeing Josh, I don't care who sees us walk into the office together. I'm not brave enough to kiss Josh when we get to our floor, but I do hold his hand until we have to go our separate ways.

"Ah, Tara, you're here. Those numbers you sent last night look good," Manny says as I set my stuff down. After we had our post-sex clean-up, we both sat down to work at the dining room table. We played footsie while we worked, and while we weren't the most productive, we also didn't care.

"I'm glad. I also managed to finish up those last two slides we weren't sure about, if you wanted to take a look at that."

"Maybe after our meeting. Our client is coming in at nine to look at what we have so far."

Darren, Eric, and I all straighten. I'm thankful that Josh had the wherewithal to have my clothes sent to the dry cleaner so I had something fresh to wear. My red dress might be a little more ostentatious than I usually wear, but I feel powerful in it because it matches so well with my hair.

"I'll be ready," I chirp, taking a sip from the coffee Josh and I grabbed on our way in.

Feeling like Josh and I can be out there without concern has really taken a weight off my shoulders that I didn't realize was there. I think HR could tell me they're letting Darren off without even a slap on the wrist, and I would be fine. Well, I wouldn't actually be fine, but it wouldn't wreck me the way I would have thought.

We keep our heads down, focused on work for the next two hours until we meet in the conference room with our client. They're a few minutes early, so I plug my laptop in for the presentation. Manny, Darren, and Eric all have their laptops open in front of them, and Darren doesn't even snipe at me when I ask to take lead with the presentation. This morning is smooth sailing.

Until nine.

I'm confused at first because my back is to the presentation as I look into the faces our four clients. They look engaged with my PowerPoint, and I'm bursting with pride until I glance down at my computer to click to the next slide.

My stomach flips over and sinks, pulling my heart with it. On the screen is a video that's playing, and in my haste to turn it off, I hit the volume button with shaking hands.

The sounds of heavy breathing and the wet sounds of sex echo in the once-silent room. It's not possible to see the man's face because there is a flare of light over it, but it's impossible to miss how mine is pressed into the wood of a desk. My hair is a clear identifier.

My breasts are hanging as Josh pounds into me from behind. I can hear the sounds of my moans and how I beg him for more, for harder, and he complies.

"God, you take my cock so well. This pussy was made for me." Josh's words echo through the room.

I can hear an excited murmur outside the conference room, and I have to wonder if I'm not the only one getting this. I'm completely frozen in horror.

Eric gets to his feet and slams my laptop shut, but it's still connected to the projector so it keeps playing until both Josh and I finish. Eric rips the cord from my laptop just as Josh drops his head back in ecstasy.

It's an out-of-body experience to see what you thought was a private moment broadcast in a room with your boss and colleagues.

"Tara, what was that?" Manny asks.

I can't find any words. I don't think there are any, so I don't say anything.

"We'll reschedule," the only other woman in the room says. When I lift my gaze to her, I can see the sympathy clear as day.

Where did they get this fucking tape?

"Taryn?" Eric asks but wisely doesn't touch me.

I barely hear the words because white static has filled my head. Or is that just my heart pounding away in my chest?

"God, you take my cock so well. This pussy was made for me." I hear the words echoing just outside this room. *"I want you to remember who owns this pussy."*

People must be watching it again.

"I have to go." They're the first words that I can manage, and my feet start to lead me woodenly toward the door.

"Tara, I think we need to have a conversation about this."

Before I can leave, the conference room door is thrown open and Quincey is standing on the other side of it.

"Oh, thank God. Come with me," she orders, holding her hand out like a lifeline.

"Miss Adams, I believe it's in Tara's best interest to stay here."

Just beyond the open door, I can hear the laughter and the comments about how they had no idea I had such a tight body under that dress, and that's not even the worst of it. I wish I could go back to my mind being static.

"Her name is fucking Taryn, you misogynistic prick," Quincey barks, but a comment over her shoulder catches her attention, and she steps into the room and closes the door behind her. She ignores the look of outrage on Manny's face. I try to appreciate her, but she has one hand extended toward me, and I know if she touches me, I'll break down. The only thing keeping me standing up is the absolute lack of comforting physical support I've gotten. I wouldn't want it from anyone in this room, but all the same.

"That's out of line," Manny complains.

Quincey turns her attention to him, ready to lay into him.

I take a step back, then another, and bump into a solid form behind me. It's too big to be Eric, and I realize it when he speaks. "You're just some cum dumpster slut who dreams higher up the food chain, and now everyone knows it," Darren whispers while holding my laptop out to me as if trying to hasten my getaway.

Tears prick my eyes, and I'm about to crumble. But if I do that, I'll be completely ruined. Not that I'm not already. Who knows how this video was disseminated and saved? I could be a meme at this point.

The conference door opens, and I recognize the human resources woman I had been emailing with from her profile picture on our company site. From the look on her tanned skin, she is not having the best day, and she's really mastered the Tommy Lee Jones "I really don't want to be here" face.

I want to tell her to fuck off even though she hasn't said anything to me yet, because I can promise my day is going *so* much worse.

"Taryn, I'm going to need you to come with me."

I would greet her, Miranda, if I could, but I know if I open my mouth again, I'll just be screaming.

"Come with you where?" Quincey demands.

Miranda focuses on my fearless protector. "To a less centrally-located conference room so we can talk about this...incident."

"I'm coming with her," Quincey demands.

"Josh needs you," I tell her, but it comes out as more of a croak.

Quincey spins, one of her braids nearly hitting me in the face. "I know what Josh needs, and Josh will need me to stay with you."

Miranda doubles down. "I need Taryn to come with me so we can sort this whole situation out away from prying eyes."

"Where is Josh?" I ask Quincey, finally starting to get my head on straight.

"I want you to remember who owns this pussy."

"He was asked to meet with a client uptown for a breakfast meeting at their hotel before they flew out. I think his phone might be off."

"Miss Robins," Miranda insists.

"God, you take my cock so well. This pussy was made for me."

I need a goddamned minute to think without hearing Josh's words said in a moment of intimacy, echoing through the office. Without Darren breathing down my neck, getting what he believes are my just desserts.

"We're coming," Quincey snaps, threading her arm through mine, but I flinch away. That kind of comfort will tear away the wall I need to erect, the wall that places me on an island all my own.

"Keep trying to reach Josh. Tell him where to find me." I snatch my laptop from Darren's hands and finally look up into his expression of smug satisfaction. I don't know how, but he had something to do with this.

I tuck my laptop under my arm as I follow Miranda, but I

focus on pulling my phone out of my pocket instead of the hushed whispers around me.

"Who knew she was hiding a rack like that?"

"Think she'd give me a go?"

"I wish I made enough money to fuck her like that."

"Like what you see?"

"So condescending."

"You know the type."

"I want you to remember who owns this pussy."

"Another whore just looking for a rich husband."

"Didn't look like he wrapped it."

"Think she's trying to trap him with a baby?"

"God, you take my cock so well. This pussy was made for me."

I want to keep my head held high, but I need to look and see what I'm doing. I send out two different texts.

Taryn: 911. Things just got so much worse.

Taryn: I need you. I need your help. I'm in a lot of trouble. Please.

Twenty-Two

I'M SEATED in a conference room on the floor that human resources occupies. Better for them to have plausible deniability from all the sexist comments that occur on the higher floors. Even down here, I can hear the sounds of my sex tape echoing, or maybe that's just my imagination. That video being broadcast to the entire company sort of makes it hard to deny.

Miranda took my laptop when we passed her office, and now I'm sitting in an empty conference room, too afraid to look at my phone. I texted my friends but almost immediately wished I hadn't because I don't even know what to say to them. The other text I sent was to Josh, but I wish I hadn't. I want to keep him out of this mess. With any luck, no one knows that it's him in the video, even if that's not hard to figure out. I put my phone on silent and left it face down on the table.

I turn my attention to something that I know won't make me cry. I focus on doing my multiplication tables until the door behind me opens and five people walk in, only one of them female.

A quick glance at my watch tells me it's been forty-five minutes of sitting here waiting, waiting for someone to come in and tell me what the hell is going on. Josh should be here by now, right?

"Miss Robins," one of the men says sternly. He's giving this air of disappointment that makes me sit up straighter.

I've had forty-five minutes to stew in my feelings. I'm trying to process that this moment, which was meant to be a private one, has been broadcast so my peers could watch it again and again.

I have no doubt become spank bank material, whether through memory or saving of the actual video, I don't know. I'd rather never know because the whole act makes me feel just...gross. It makes me feel less than, and while I enjoy the moments when I'm with Josh and I become an object for which he can achieve his pleasure, I don't relish the idea of other people being able to do the same.

Down the line they all introduce themselves, ending with Miranda.

"This most unfortunate situation is, uhm, unfortunate," the man named Taylor says, shifting uncomfortably in his seat. It's impossible to miss how he's straightening his pants, and the feeling of disgust just intensifies.

"You're going to let me in there, or there is going to be a lawsuit so big they're going to have to demolish this building," an unfamiliar male voice says from outside the conference room. Just what I want, another man in there to witness my ruin.

Maybe this one will have a scarlet letter just for me.

The door is pushed open, and a man walks in. He has dark brown hair and a clean-shaven face. It's not hard to miss his gorgeous jawline or perfect teeth as he strides into the room. He fills out his suit well, but until I know whose side he's on, I'll reserve final judgment. His brown eyes are assessing the room as he walks in before they alight on me, and I hate the flash of sympathy that rises in them.

"Knox Benedict, ladies and gentlemen. I'm going to need you to give me the room so I can have a few moments with my client if you don't mind."

"And who are you?" the first man that spoke, Calvin, says.

"Knox Benedict," he repeats, but slower this time. His gaze travels back to me with a "Are these guys serious?" look on his face before back in its place is the hardass attorney Vivian's been complaining about for months. He looks like he's built like a linebacker, thick and stocky. It makes me wonder what he's hiding under that suit.

"We got that the first time. Who are you in relation to Miss Robins?" Calvin asks.

"Oh, that's right. I'm representing her in her workplace harassment lawsuit that I'll be filing against your company for what I assume is about to be a wrongful termination. But I would like a few minutes to confer with my client to see if that's still the issue at hand. If you'd rather, I'll sit here and just take notes."

Miranda rises. "We can give you five minutes."

The rest of them rise as well, grumbling again before they leave. Knox doesn't say anything but looks down at his phone. I wait for him, unsure where this is going, when the sound of static fills the room.

"Sorry, I don't think it's totally necessary, but I don't know if they have someone waiting outside listening. It's just my fan app. I need white noise to sleep. Unimportant. I'm Knox Benedict. Vivian sent me. Want to catch me up?"

"You want me to believe that Vivian sent you?"

"We can talk about the complicated dynamic between your best friend and me, or I can find out what happened that was so bad that she actually asked me for help. Your choice."

I choose to tell him the whole sordid situation, starting with Eric's repeated come-ons and my rebuffs, Darren's comments, dating Josh, and Manny's inability to remember my name.

"When you had sex in Josh's office, was it during normal business hours?"

"No, but–"

"I'm going to stop you right there. There is no 'but' in what is going to happen. Give yes or no answers. Don't elaborate unless you have to. I don't intend to let you have any reason to speak, though. What do you want out of this situation?"

"What do you mean what do I want?" I start to pick at my cuticles in search of something, anything, to do.

"I mean, I need to know what you want from this situation. Do you want to leave here with your job? Do you want to work on a different team? A different line of business? What is your goal in this room? I may not do employment law, but I am *very* good at getting people to cave to what I want. So, I need to know if you want to keep your job. I want to know if you want to walk out of here ready to sue their pants off, which, from what you've told me, you could. But unless I know what you want, I can't do it."

"I want Josh," I whisper.

"I know, and I wish I could find him for you. Have you checked your phone? I know Vivian was looking for you."

"No, honestly, I've been too afraid." I reach for my phone and stare at it like it's going to attack me.

"Do you want me to check it for you?"

"How much is this going to cost me?" I ask, unlocking my phone and handing it over to Knox.

"Not a damn cent because having Vivian Abernathy owe me a favor is worth its weight in gold." Knox looks at my phone, but before tapping my messages, he looks up at me. "I'm not going to find dick pics if I check your chat with him?"

"No, no you won't."

"Good. Not that I mind a good-looking dick, but I do like to be prepared." He scrolls for a few seconds before handing my phone back. "Nothing. I'm sorry."

There is a knock at the door before I answer Knox, but I don't even know how I would have answered him. I don't know if I can walk back in here tomorrow with my head held high because what would I do? How could I face this company of people, of men who know what I sound like when I come? Men who have seen me naked?

"Stay silent and trust me," Knox murmurs before the friendly face that had been reassuring me fades into a blank stare that honestly terrifies me. He turns the noise app off and looks at the army of human resources officers that have walked into the room.

"I really don't think that Miss Robins needs representation here," Taylor says, directing his statement to Knox. I'm not sure if it's because he's representing himself as my attorney or just because he's a man.

"I disagree, so proceed. Let's hear what you have to say."

"This is an internal company matter," Calvin blusters, and Knox turns his attention to him.

"That's cute you think that, but my client has been verbally and sexually harassed since coming to this company, to the point that she had a meeting this week to discuss this with Miranda."

"She's also claimed this at her previous job. Eventually, you have to question where the fault lies."

Knox laughs, and it's dark and honestly a little scary. I don't want him to fight this battle for me, but I know when it comes to a situation like this, it's best to trust the lawyer. "I know you didn't let your misogyny show during a human resources meeting where my client was subjected to revenge porn in the workplace for daring to turn down a male coworker."

"We have no evidence as to where this originated," Calvin says.

"You have to have some idea. I imagine you left my client in here for forty-five minutes not to make her sweat but to terminate the video that was playing through *your* company server."

"Of course," Miranda rushes to add. "Of course, that was exactly what we were doing, but it doesn't change the fact that there is video evidence of your client having sex on company property."

She's not even a little wrong, and everyone in the room knows it.

"The fact is, we don't know who sent this video out, and

having Miss Robins return to the office in the same capacity would be more than a little...disruptive."

"Disruptive," Knox deadpans. "Please, continue to dig your grave even deeper. I'm looking forward to the tidy sum I'll make from this lawsuit."

Calvin does the only thing he can–he blusters. "I'm certain I don't understand what you mean."

"It means you're punishing my client for something that involved two to three people, given that someone had to spread the video." Under the table, I kick Knox. The last thing I want is for them to fire Josh. I don't think his career matters more than mine, but the fact is, I love him, and I don't want to see him hurt.

The realization that the whole reason the tape was made after I told Josh I love him isn't lost on me, and it has me rubbing the spot on my chest over my heart. I don't understand how things could have fallen apart so fast.

"It's unclear who the man in the video is," Taylor asserts, tapping his pen on a pad in front of him.

Knox takes a moment to look at each person in the room before steepling his fingers and leaning back like he's the one with all the power in this room. I don't understand how he has that impression. We're in this room because they're about to fire me, and it's suddenly too much.

"Have you determined if you're going to look for the perpetrator of this crime? Or how someone was able to get access to your systems to send out a company-wide video like that? I trust you haven't erased all the footage. I have my college roommate on speed dial. He's actually a detective for New York's Finest. I'm sure he would be willing to come up here and take a statement and interview *every* employee who was sent the video. Plus, tech geeks will need to see who recorded the video while it was playing to save to their hard drive. I'm sure they will be able to play around and find who sent the video if your own tech team can't handle that level of sophistication."

"Absolutely not," Calvin shouts, slamming his hands down on the table. Miranda casts her glance at him, disgust on her face before she clears it and dons her bored affect. "There is proprietary and confidential information on our systems, and we cannot just allow anyone to come in and poke around our system."

"Seems to me you already have a problem with your internet security. It's clear you're about to fire my client for what you believe is cause. You're going to do it while *not* investigating how exactly someone was able to broadcast a sex tape to your entire company and *not* investigating who did that in addition to, based on your previous comments, *not* punishing the man who my client had intercourse with. I think that about sums it up, right? Right."

Knox doesn't even breathe as he barrels forward. I'm trying to stay on track with him, but my mind is fumbling over the getting fired for cause part. I can't get fired for cause. I don't want to be fired. I can't afford it, and honestly, I like what I do even if I hate who I do it with.

Knox continues, "We can leave this room one of two ways: happy with the outcome or with both parties deeply dissatisfied. I don't want that. You don't want that. Come up with a *very* reasonable severance offer for my client, considering she's possibly going to be out of work for the next several months, or I'll call my friend, and we can start looking for the instigator and bring this to trial criminally and civilly while dragging your company through the media mud for *years* because, let's be honest, you'll fight it and you'll lose because one female juror will ensure my client is paid out the ass for this disgusting show of misogyny and carelessness. I'll be sure to name the man in the room with my client in addition to each and every one of you in the lawsuit just to make sure that this lingers until you're paying ten to twenty times the number you could have paid today." Knox leans forward. "You can have five minutes before I call my detective friend."

How they're not shitting bricks walking out of the room, I

don't know. Calvin is the last to leave the room, and Knox lifts his wrist, showing off his nice watch, and he taps it. "Tick Tock."

Once the door closes, I sag in my seat. "I thought you didn't do employment law."

Knox smiles. "I don't, but I did, once. My old firm made me a jack of all trades, so I've dabbled just about everywhere."

I slide my phone to Knox. "Can you check for Josh again?"

"Of course." He's silent as he scrolls through. "Nothing, but your friends are worried. I can drop Vivian a text if that's easier."

"I thought you two hated each other. Why are you here?"

A funny look crosses Knox's face. "Because Vivian Abernathy bends to no one, and she was ready to bend herself into a pretzel to get me here to you. You've done something to inspire an incredible show of loyalty from the ice queen, which makes me think you're a damsel worth saving."

"She's not an ice queen," I object because it's the only thing I can say.

Knox lets out a small sigh, and I barely catch the words he says under his breath. "I know." He keeps an eye on his watch before looking at me again. "What number will you feel okay walking out of here with? I have them by the balls, and they're going to cave. I can feel it. Josh is more valuable to them not being named. I also need to know if you want to pursue a legal case against who did this. My guess is they're going to cover this up as best they can, so we may not find out who it is."

"I think I know who it is, but I don't want Josh dragged through this if we can avoid it. His only mistake was falling in love with me."

Knox violently spins my chair so I have to face him dead on instead of the mess I've made of my cuticles. "Taryn, I want to make one thing *abundantly* clear. I may not know this Josh guy, but I'm willing to bet that he wouldn't consider falling in love with you a mistake. And if he did? If he took one look at this situation and wrote you off for it, then he's a fucking monster, and you don't want him in your life. I'm honestly peeved he's not here. He's in a position of power, and regardless that you're not on the same team, fucking you in the office is an abuse of that power."

"You can ask the receptionist to find Quincey."

"Quincey, what?"

"Quincey Adams. She's his assistant."

"You're shitting me, but okay." Knox rises and pokes his head out to talk to a woman on the other side of the door before he comes back in and sits down. "Think about the criminal charges. You don't have to do anything immediately, but we need them to hunt who did this in their system. There is no way that I think they agree to let the NYPD into their systems without a warrant, and as awful as I think this entire situation is, I don't think I can actually get the NYPD to throw their resources behind finding who did this to you."

I'm not surprised. I know that there are revenge porn laws out there, but I have no idea what kind of penalties they carry, and honestly, I never expected to be in this position. Tears spring to my eyes, and I quickly press my fingers to the corners of them to stem the tide. If I start, I don't think I'll stop.

There is a light knock on the door. "Taryn? It's me." I recognize Quincey's voice and open the door to her. She reaches toward me, but I step back again, and she nods as if in understanding. With the door closed behind her, she gives us an update. "I still can't reach Josh, and his phone has been going straight to voicemail. I think he turned it off because this investor has been so cagey to tie down. He probably wanted no interruptions."

"No," I wave her off, trying to keep my voice from cracking. "Of course, it's not like he went to this meeting knowing this would happen." The idea slips from my mind just as quickly as the intrusive thought made itself known. There is *no way* Josh knew.

"Of course not, honey. I'm sure as soon as he turns on his phone, he'll be here in a flash." She sits on my other side, reaching past me to introduce herself to Knox. She gives him a once-over, but he doesn't even acknowledge it. "What I do know is that this is classified as revenge porn, which New York State and City have a statute on, but the penalty is pretty low, and the jail time is also minimal."

I blow out a shaky breath and close my eyes. "Naturally. I don't want to go forward with criminal charges. They'll just find a way to get swept under the rug."

"I did take screenshots and confirm that it's made its rounds on every computer, including Josh's, which he left here for the meeting. Whoever did this has a strong technical know-how."

"You said you have your suspicions about who did this?" Knox asks, looking up from his notepad, which he's filled with information.

"I mean, I would think Darren, but honestly, he and Eric have one functioning brain cell between the two of them."

Quincey pipes up, "Didn't they go to MIT, though? I'm sure they have friends who could help. *Also.*" She reaches into her pocket and sets something on the table. In a plastic ziplock bag are three pieces of equipment. There's a back cover, a battery, and a small fucking camera.

"Is that what I think it is?"

Quincey nods. "I went into Josh's office to look and see if it was still there, and it was. I took pictures of where it was before grabbing a ziplock bag and grabbing it. Obviously, I took the battery out once it was in the bag in case they needed to dust for prints."

This at least gets a smile from Knox, and he finally looks up at the knockout assistant, who apparently doubles as a crime scene investigator. "Obviously," he repeats.

She blushes under his attention. "I watch a lot of procedurals when Josh doesn't need me."

"Smart and beautiful. A lethal combination, for sure." Knox gets to his feet and opens the door. "Tell your bosses time's up. I'm waiting on a return call from my detective friends and I happen to know a plucky female reporter for the New York TattleTale paper. They're always looking for stories of financiers doing wrong."

He closes the door before turning to face us. "I need that number, Taryn, and then I want you to double it for the price of them making you wait."

Knox sits back in his chair, swiveling it as he taps a pen against the palm of his hand while we wait. When I look at my watch, I feel the blood drain from my face. It's not even noon yet, and I feel like I've been pushed through a meat grinder.

What amount of money is my career worth? It's not easy to put a figure on the six years of education, the countless hours studying in school and out of school, and for entrance exams. The amount of frustration and stress that went into preparing to be my best, choosing to work hard instead of going to parties. How do I account for the late phone calls on birthdays and anniversaries? To being three hours late to my friend's engagement party because of my internship and missing being there for Vivian when she left her fiancé because I had interviews?

It feels wrong to take the money. I didn't take it last time, but this is a totally different problem than last time. There are people here who I could possibly work with again who know the sounds I make when I come. They know how my breasts bounce and what flavor of dirty talk I enjoy.

I feel dirtier at the thought of having to walk back up there than I do taking the money. The money that my family desperately needs. I pick an outrageous number. This is going to be a negotiation, so the least I can do is make sure we get closer to what I actually need. An eight-figure settlement feels like too much, but for what I've gone through today, it might not be enough. I rub my arms, trying to soothe the persistent chill in my bones away.

It takes another twenty minutes before it's just Calvin, Miranda, and two new people. Knox leans over to whisper in my ear. "Lawyers. It takes one to know one."

Knox pushes to his feet, smoothing down his tie as he holds his hand out to one of the men. He has a wide smile on his face, charm, and confidence oozing out of his pores. I wish I could hold on to some of it for myself. "Jeremiah, it's been a while."

"Knox Benedict," Jeremiah says, sounding decidedly less excited to see Knox.

"You've made my client wait far over the five minutes I asked for. Might I remind you five minutes was all the time you initially allowed me to confer with my client?"

"Knox," Jeremiah says, sounding exhausted already. "This isn't a courtroom or an interrogation room. You don't have an inane right to be here. We're letting you stay as a courtesy."

"You're right, Jeremiah. This is a conference room, a board room, and as they say in your industry, time is money. This is the number my client *was* willing to accept." He looks down at his legal pad and scrawls a number on it that's double what I said. Knox sets it down hard on the table so everyone can see before he rips the page out and tears it into tiny pieces. "I would tell her she needs to ask for four times that number since you made her wait four times as long, but because Taryn is a decent human being, she's only asking for double."

The number he flashed them is obvious hush money, and I think I should be offended. I should have a greater sense of worth than taking what money they're going to give me for firing me. That sum wouldn't be enough to clear all the debts, not after taxes get their claws in it, but it would help ease the weight of my financial responsibilities. I just don't know if it's worth the weight on my soul. Knox writes down a new number and turns it toward them, giving their attorney a chance to look at the figure.

I feel like I should be doing better, doing more, but I don't know how. I don't know why my emotions are such a quagmire, and maybe if I had been talking it through with Knox instead of just sitting here waiting for this company to make their decision, I would be going into this with a clearer head.

But the honest truth is, it's not Knox I want to be talking this through with, even if he is playing the part of my lawyer. I want, no, I need Josh. I need to talk this through with him and see any of the potential pitfalls hiding in this conversation, but he's still missing in action, and I get the feeling that this offer is only going to be on the table for so long.

"I think it would be best if Miss Adams were to step out of the room," Miranda suggests.

"I agree," Knox says, glancing at Quincey and tapping his phone. She gives him a scowl but steps out anyway.

"This is extortion," Jeremiah uses his pen to point at the legal pad with the new number on it.

I feel like a passive observer in the room while Knox goes to bat for me. Whatever is going on between him and Vivian, I can't help but notice he's like a bulldog, relentless in getting what he wants. Heaven help Vivian if she's it.

"Hardly. Due to a breach in your company's security, someone, most likely one of your own employees, utilized that opening to bomb revenge porn on the whole company, not just embarrassing my client by exposing a private moment, but also doing it so even your *clients* could see it, no doubt embarrassing the company as a whole. And to top it off, now you want to *fire* my client. Tell me, Jeremiah, how is your sister doing after that fiasco with her ex-boyfriend?"

Jeremiah grinds his teeth together. "Do *not* bring my sister into this."

"It's the same thing, and you know it, Jeremiah. The only difference is those pictures that were disseminated of your sister were ones she consensually took. My client had no say in that tape being made and shared. The video, by my client's own admission, was taken on a weekend. She came in to get extra work done."

"She got extra, that's for sure," Calvin murmurs as if none of us can hear him.

"Respectfully, sir, shut the fuck up," Jeremiah snaps.

"Do you see this, Jeremiah? This is your company. These are

the people you're working for. My client understands the issue of her having sex in the office was wrong, but we wouldn't be here if someone hadn't taped it and shared it, and that, Jeremiah, is the crux of the issue. Even if they had been caught just by a colleague, this would have resulted in a slap on the wrist and a note in her file because her boyfriend is high enough up at this company that you don't want to piss him off. But because this person who filmed it..." Knox picks up the camera from its bag, "sent the video to everyone, you have to do something about it. What I can't figure out is why your company doesn't want to find the person who did this. They're illegally placing video cameras in offices and sharing those videos. What privileged conversations did this person record?" Knox studies the faces before him, and he must come to a realization before I do because he sits up abruptly. "Unless you already know who did it, and you're taking steps to deal with them separately."

"That has no bearing on this conversation."

"Well, that's not fucking true," I finally snap. I've been sitting down, letting them kick me like a dog that knows she did wrong because yes, it was wrong of me to have sex in the office. I can admit that. The fear of what my future is going to look like has kept me quiet for far too long, but if I'm getting fired, anyway. I'm going to bring the whole house of cards down with me.

"Miss Robins," Miranda warns.

I only glare at her. "Do not 'Miss Robins' me. I've been sitting here quiet as a church mouse this entire time. If you know who did this, you have a duty, a responsibility, not just to me, but to the company and my colleagues, to ensure that he's fired, if not having charges filed. It is extremely fucking relevant to this conversation."

Knox tugs on my elbow, and I realize I'm now standing. At some point while screaming, I got to my feet and planted my hands on the table. Sure, I'll get labeled an emotional or hysterical woman, but things can't get very much worse.

"What my client means is that while you may feel that it's an internal matter for you to handle the hacker, by using those abilities to damage my client's reputation, this individual has made it her business."

Trust a lawyer to say what you mean in twice as many words.

"Knox, I can appreciate the tough position that your client is in; however, through her actions, she's put my client in a very tricky spot."

Knox and Jeremiah stare each other down while I stay silent like Knox wanted me to in the first place.

"Like I told your judgmental team of HR crackpots, you can either make a reasonable severance offer that includes the termination of and charges filed for cyber crimes against the responsible individual, as well as any individuals who found it appropriate to record the offending video, or I can take this to trial and have a very good time indeed calling Kandi at the New York Tattletale and letting her know about the civil filing I'll be making shortly for your company's inability to defend a victim of sexual harassment. Why have your company stand with all the other financial giants accused of sexual harassment when they can stand as a leader in taking the right steps? You're on the precipice of being able to make a huge change that could potentially make your company a magnet for smart, capable women, or you can send the message that women in your company are not safe and you would rather protect the aggressor."

Knox waits and lets his words sink in. The way he speaks, you would think I was someone close to him and not just a woman that he met less than an hour ago. God, I can't believe this has been going on for only a few hours. It feels like it's taken days off my life.

Jeremiah looks at Calvin and then Miranda, then back at Knox. His Adam's apple bobs as he swallows. "Let me see that number again and tell me your *exact* demands."

Knox rips another page off his legal pad that I see has the number at the top along with a list below it. I don't even know what is on the list, but I have to trust that Knox has my best interests at heart. He hasn't steered me wrong yet.

Jeremiah reads them, but Knox explains for the others in the room. "Like I said, we would also like to have the responsible party fired and charged for his crime of hacking the company. My client has no interest in pursuing a revenge porn charge against this individual, given how public those proceedings can be. And I think we can agree that your company would also rather not have their name dragged into it. Anyone who thought to download the video should also be terminated at this time. Miss Robins also has no interest in having her partner named, so to the extent possible, she would like him to be left out of this, which I'm sure you agree is the best course of action. She requests that the balance of the salary due to the responsible party be donated to the charity against workplace sexual harassment of her choosing. And also, that figure is the post-tax number. I trust your company is good for it."

"And I trust your client is amenable to signing an NDA?" Jeremiah asks.

My anger comes back hot at that. Everything Knox has asked for so far, I'm on board with, but a non-disclosure agreement? They can eat rocks if they think I'm going to stay silent about this. I open my mouth, but Knox squeezes my wrist and shakes his head.

"Of course, my client will gladly do so, as long as every single person who saw the video today is given a similar agreement to sign with the financial penalties being paid to my client, half of which will be donated to the same aforementioned charity. Wouldn't want the bad guys to get the tax break, would we, Jeremiah?"

"So that's a nonstarter then," Jeremiah grumbles, and then he gets to a different line on the paper in front of him. "Wait, you seriously want everyone to sign a document?"

"I absolutely do. This hinders my client's ability to obtain future employment if it gets out. Given that it's a little late to put the toothpaste back in the tube, I suggest you not put a gag order on my client, and you handle your own shit in-house."

"There needs to be some sort of document that will silence your client on this matter."

"No. She needs to be able to answer future employers truthfully. In addition to the therapy she will no doubt need to seek after having all of her peers see a video of her having sex. I'll permit Miss Robins to sign an agreement that she won't go to the press, and you'll get all fifty thousand of your employees to sign an agreement that they won't ever discuss the video, and if it's found that they have, they'll be fired and subject to financial penalties. Seems fair to me."

Jeremiah stares Knox down, and there's a heated moment between them. "You understand I have to go talk this through with my superiors, correct?"

"I wouldn't expect any less. If possible, I would like to get my client out of here. There is no reason for her to be subjected to the toxicity that is this office."

Miranda sits up. "First, I need to do an exit interview."

Knox scoffs and stands as well. "Respectfully, Miranda, no, you don't. Everything you need to know about my client's experience here can be summed up in two words: misogynistic bullshit. While you work on the final paperwork, I'll be having a meeting with my client detailing every moment of harassment she experienced working here, including your own human resources insinuating that she was crying wolf. If we're not happy with the documents and settlement amount, I'll be ready to file in New York Superior Court the next day." Knox grips my elbow and motions me up.

I look at him, alarmed. "My stuff?"

"Miss Adams has already boxed it up for you. She also turned over your work phone."

It feels so final standing there, looking into the faces of strangers as my life is turned upside down. I feel like I've been cast adrift with no real hope for the future. I still want to know where the hell Josh is.

"Miss Robins," Jeremiah says softly. "For what it's worth, I'm sorry about what happened today." He holds his hand out to me, but I just stare at it before looking at him.

"Not bad enough if you continue to protect the person that did this to me."

I walk out of the conference room, and while I don't have to go up and face everyone that I worked closely with, I can still see people who are averting their gaze. It's all over their faces that they watched the video.

I will hold my head up as I walk out of the building for the last time.

Twenty-Three

I'M grateful as Knox and I ride the elevator that we don't see anyone from my company. He's doing the gentlemanly thing of carrying my box of belongings while I have my purse slung over my shoulder. It's strange to think this is the same elevator where Josh and I really got started, and he missed this whole disaster.

When we step outside, I lift my face to the sun, hoping it will do something to warm the chill in my bones. I still feel cold everywhere, and I appreciate more than words can say how Knox isn't pushing me.

"Taryn!" I hear my name called, and I open my eyes to see a frantic Josh hopping out of a cab. "What the fuck happened? What is going on?"

"Where were you?" I can't help the hurt in my tone. He promised he would always be there. It's not his fault for not being in the office when this happened at nine, but a glance at my watch tells me it's noon now.

"What?"

"I asked where you were. Where have you been?" Beside me, Knox shifts uncomfortably.

"I had a meeting in Midtown. I've been trying to get this

investor on board, but he's been weasley. This was my first chance to lock him down. He gave me a short window, but after his flight was delayed, I was able to continue the meeting." He runs his hands through his hair, and the already abused strands stand on edge. It's like he spent the entire cab ride here repeating the motion over and over again. Josh takes my arms and pulls me in for a hug, but I'm still not ready for affection so I resist.

I resist even more so that it's him. Josh should have been the one to swoop in and save the day. It should have been Josh fighting to defend me. Instead, I was on my own, left to leave my career in shambles. It took two of us to make that video, but only one of us gets to walk out of this with their dignity. I'm sure there are people who recognized Josh's office or his voice. I'm sure when he goes up to the office and or runs into those people who know, he'll get handshakes and congratulations instead of being treated to a scarlet letter. The double standard nearly knocks me on my feet when I realize that while I want to protect him, he's really going to walk away from this entire situation scott-free, and that just doesn't seem fair at all.

If our roles were reversed and he was the subordinate getting railed by a female superior in her office, he would probably *still* get off without any damage to his career, and that just only drives the fury I'm feeling up a notch or two, even if she's this hypothetical woman who doesn't exist.

As much as Josh is this feminist ally who agrees that it's unfair how men take advantage in the workplace or that men generally have an unfair advantage in life, it doesn't change that I'm the only one left with nothing at the end of today. Because it's clear that I don't even really have him if he couldn't even be there when I needed him the most. It's easy to throw your money around, but right now, I need more than dollars. I *needed* him.

And he wasn't there.

When I really look at him, I can see the bloodshot look in his eyes and smell hints of whiskey on his breath. While my life was getting turned upside down, he was having a morning cocktail.

"I think I'll go," Knox says, trying to hand me my box. Josh turns and seems to take notice of him for the first time before looking back at me.

"Who is this?"

"Knox Benedict, my knight in shining armor while you were off getting day drunk on a Monday."

"I had two drinks with a client who insisted. What happened? What did I miss? I have a thousand missed calls from Quincey."

I turn to Knox. "Can I buy you a cab back to your office? I'm going up to Central Park East."

"I was just going to take the Four up to 59th," Knox says slowly.

"Great, I'm going to take the Six to 103rd. Do you mind if I ride with you?"

Knox stands up taller, seeming to catch on that I'm not in the mood to deal with Josh right now. I'm angry. No, I'm more than just angry. I'm livid and furious. I'm hurt and disappointed, and crushed at how the day has gone. I feel like I hardly know the man I've been sharing a bed with.

"Of course," Knox says.

I really should go home, but I don't want to. I want to go to Elia's place and curl up on her couch with her cats. All that comfort I've been rejecting all day, I'm suddenly craving.

"Taryn, don't run away from me. What happened? Why are you so upset right now?" Josh sounds desperate as he reaches for my arm, holding me so gently. I tear out of his grip again, and Knox moves to position himself between us. Josh looks at Knox like he's seeing him for the first time before looking back to me for my explanation.

"What happened was I needed you, and your phone was off for three hours. I needed to have you in there on my side, arguing for me. And instead, I've been fired, and you weren't there." I start to walk away but turn back to face him. "I would have understood, too. Work happens. I'm just as career-driven. I understood for the first hour, but you never checked in. I needed you, and you let me down. I can't talk to you right now because I'm just...I can't talk to you. I can't even look at you."

He can get the full report from his friends in the office, but I have no interest in filling him in, not right now.

I need to look away from the absolute devastation on his face. He opens his mouth, but I glare at him, and I don't know if he can see the same hurt reflected on my face or if it's from years of experience with all the women in his life that he knows to give me my space, but it's space I don't think I actually want.

It's stupid and contradictory, but I want him to fight me on this. I need that show of love right now because I feel like I have nothing. I give him the chance to make things right, to stop me, to call out to me, but he doesn't.

He just lets me walk away.

Knox keeps up a steady stream of small talk. He mentions his cousin's kid and talks about the various ways he's been keeping Vivian busy with nonsense just for the hell of it. He gives me a chance to text my friends. I know they have their own jobs, and they can't drop everything and come to my rescue, but I have to let Elia know I'm using the spare key she gave me to hide out in her apartment until we can all get together, and I can tell them how bad it got.

When we get to Knox's stop, he looks me over. "Are you sure you're okay?"

"Not even a little bit, but I know that Elia has a pint of ice cream hidden in the back of her freezer for emergencies. I would also appreciate you not mentioning this to Vivian until I've had a chance to tell her."

"I wasn't kidding when I said I was *your* lawyer. It might be Vivian who has to pay the piper, but privilege still exists."

"Thanks, Knox," I say as I step onto the local train I need. "You're not as bad as Vivian said you were."

If he were a dog, his ears would perk up. "Wait, she talks about me?"

I balance the box on my hip, the first hint of a smile hitting my face since my world detonated at nine a.m. I give him a saucy finger wave as the doors close.

The walk to Elia's place helps to clear my head, and I'm mostly okay until I think about having to tell my parents that I also lost my job. I can't count on the money that Knox is trying to get me. The idea of having to tell them fills me with such deep dread. They were so proud of me for the schools I got into and the jobs I landed. When I think about the financial cost, not just the actual spending, but the opportunity loss so they could get me to where I was, the crushing guilt threatens to suffocate me. My family is on the brink of financial ruin because of all they gave me. I was the only one holding us up, and I just took that security away.

What are they going to think when they realize that I ruined it all because of a guy and some orgasms?

But that thought isn't fair to Josh. He's not just some guy. He's *the* guy. *The* guy I left standing in front of our office building about to walk into a completely different kind of shit storm. Only, where I was made a pariah, I'm sure he'll be lauded as a hero for banging someone on his desk.

When I walk into the building, the doorman, Benji, rushes to get the elevator since my hands are full of this stupid box. I should have just tossed it out. All that's in it is some stupid promotional swag and my phone charger.

At least with each telling of the story, it will get easier to rehash, and maybe eventually, I'll get okay enough with the words to tell my parents. I will never tell them it's because Josh was debasing me on his desk.

I don't even have a chance to find the keys in my bag before Elia is whipping the door open, her brown hair and green eyes wild.

"There you are! We've been worried sick!" When I look past her, I see Charlie with his hands on his hips. Vivian, Ainsley, and Ken are all there too.

Charlie rubs his hands over his mouth before looking away, and something makes me think he might already know.

"I didn't know anyone was waiting on me. I thought that...I don't know, that it would just be you, and maybe Charlie, here." My tears have started, and when Elia hugs me, I let loose the torrent of tears I've been holding back.

It isn't until Vivian and Ainsley both have their arms around me as well that I let the grief and shame I've been feeling over the situation free. In my heart, I know I shouldn't feel shame, but it's hard to argue with that ingrained mentality.

We move slowly to the couch, where the four of us huddle until I've gotten through that initial crying jag. Tissues come from somewhere, and I go through about four of them, apologizing to Elia for all the tears and snot.

"Why are you all here?" I ask, my voice a raspy croak.

"Because you texted 9-1-1. We all just waited for something, and once you said you were headed to Elia's, the rest of us converged," Vivian explains, squeezing my forearm.

Ainsley wipes at a tear before taking a tissue for herself. "Are you ready to tell us what happened? You don't have to, but Taryn, I don't think I've ever seen you cry, and that gives the impression that I need to cut balls off."

I glance at Charlie and Ken, unsure if I really want them to hear, but the anger burning in Charlie's eyes all but confirms he knows.

"Someone took a tape of Josh and I having sex in his office and blasted it to the entire company."

Charlie hisses out a breath before walking into the kitchen. No, not walking, stomping.

"You've got to be fucking kidding me." Ainsley struggles to her feet, marching toward her bag.

"Where are you going?" Vivian asks, an eyebrow raised.

"I am going to call my father because he has a cousin who is very good at making people disappear, and I want to put him on retainer until I find out what fuckturd did this."

"I know who did this," I confirm as Charlie swoops in with wine for each of us, except for Ainsley, who gets a glass of orange juice.

"Okay, well, that makes this so much easier. Who is this asshole?"

"Darren Williams. I'm at least mostly sure. The camera he used is in the box. Knox said I should hold on to it as evidence. Thank you for sending him, Viv."

"Of course. I was arguing with him when your text came through. I don't think he even stopped to tell anyone where he was going."

Ainsley, having already been warned that comments about Knox were a boundary, makes an overdramatic show of biting her tongue. "I'm glad he was good for something."

"He was honestly...amazing. He's negotiating a massive severance package for me. I mean, he's extorting them, but I don't even care."

"I'm sorry that this trash thing happened to you. You don't deserve it," Elia tells me before grabbing one of her cats and dropping it on my lap.

"No. I was stupid to have sex in his office."

"That's bullshit," Ken says from where he's slouching in one of the chairs. He rubs his eyes, likely exhaustion from a late night at the bar. "It's bullshit. There's no way you and Josh are the first ones to have sex in an office during business hours. You just happened to be guilty of being the victim of a targeted attack. Someone knew you were having sex with each other, and they just hoped to get lucky with you doing it in his office. It was just a matter of this evil fucker biding his time."

"Right, Darren Williams. I think I'll have his kneecaps removed first, right? Or no?" Ainsley asks.

"No knee caps, no hits. I want him fired too, and to put the whole thing behind me. But for now, I have to figure out how I'm going to break it to my parents."

"You're an adult. You don't have to tell them," Elia says.

"I do when I'm paying their mortgage."

Charlie drops onto the far side of the couch, displacing Bonsai. "We'll get to that later. What I want to know is where the fuck Josh is in all this? He sure as fuck isn't here."

I have to take in a deep breath. "He was at some meeting in Midtown. He got back to the office just as I was leaving. Honestly, I just left. He had clearly been drinking during this meeting, and he wasn't there. I needed him, and he wasn't there. His assistant, Quincey, kept calling him and just...nothing. His phone was off or on silent."

"Has he called?" Elia asks, biting on a nail.

I glance at my phone to see ten missed calls and numerous texts. I flash the screen at her.

"How are you feeling about that decision?" Vivian asks gently.

"What decision?"

"The decision to tell him to fuck right off," Ainsley elaborates.

"I did not."

Vivian, ever the diplomat, places her hand on my arm, "But you did. You left him on the sidewalk by your own admission. So... how do you feel about that?"

"So I get it, he wasn't there, and you needed him, but it sounds like as soon as he knew, he came to be at your side," Ainsley explains, going to sit on Ken's lap. He tugs her close with his hand resting protectively on her belly.

"Whose side are you on?" I demand, grabbing a fresh tissue.

"Yours, every day, babe, but..." Vivian hesitates. "We're not trying to tell you what you need right now, but what I *think* you need is Josh. He's your person, and you're hurting right now, and that makes sense, but you were *both* victims today. And yes, that is a super strong word, but you were both sexually harassed in the workplace. And while I understand that it is harder on you as the woman in that scenario, he's also probably hurting and confused." Vivian's explanation makes sense, but I don't know if I'm ready to really hear it.

"You know they didn't even want to know who was in the video with me? Josh's face is obscured by light, but they never even asked who it was. They know I'm dating Josh, but it's like they're planning to willfully ignore the fact that I wasn't fucking myself on his desk."

"There are a lot of feelings right now, but maybe you should think about it. I doubt he meant to hurt you or even wants you to be hurt," Elia tries to reason.

"Tell me to fuck off, but do you want my alpha male two cents?" Charlie asks.

"Shut the fuck up, Chucky," Ainsley says with a laugh. "You are *not* an alpha male. You are a cinnamon-bun, golden retriever who stumbled into the finance field. *Alpha* you are not, my friend."

I can't help but smile and lean into Elia's embrace by resting my head on her shoulder. "You may proceed with your gooey cinnamon bun feels."

Charlie glares first at Ainsley and then me before he finally speaks. "Josh cares about you. A lot. He wants to see you succeed, and I don't think that shutting him out is going to do either of you any good. If you want to be mad at him, be mad at him, but he just walked into an office where his colleagues have also seen him having sex with his girlfriend. He's going to, and I hate to say what we all know, but he's going to be hearing all of the stupid bullshit male locker room talk about you before he even knows what happened. Give the guy a half a break, and just let him know that while you may not be totally okay, you're with people who are going to leave their jobs in the middle of a Monday to be by your side and help you through this."

"How *are* you all here?" I ask, hating that Charlie's words are getting me choked up again. They're right. I know they're right. When I walked out of that building, I lashed out at the first person I could hurt, and that was Josh. It was unfair to him in the way that everything that happened all day has been unfair to us both.

I open my phone to let him know I'm safe at Elia's before I focus on my friends and their explanations for being hooky from work.

"I told my bosses I had to go have a meeting with Knox," Vivian says.

"I told Sean to fuck off and that he's not my real dad," Ainsley says. "I don't have any clients today, though, so Eloise is going to let me know if something urgent comes up."

"I work from home," Elia says with a shrug.

"I go where my baby momma wants me," Ken mumbles from where I bet he's trying not to fall asleep.

"I live here and happened to be working from home," Charlie says.

"You don't all need to be here. I just needed some friendly faces, and Zelda and her weed apartment are not it."

"Stay here as long as you need," Elia reassures me.

"You should all go back to work. You don't need to comfort me when you have actual shit that needs doing," I tell them, speaking into my glass of wine.

"Oh, shut up," Ainsley snaps. "You're allowed to wallow, but don't use that tone like you're some worthless loser who doesn't have a job. You were forced out by something that wasn't your fault. I love you, and I'll let you be bummed you don't have a job anymore, but the blame for this doesn't sit on your shoulders. It also doesn't sit on Josh's shoulders, but more on that when you're ready to actually hear that."

I stick my tongue out at her beyond words, annoyed at the truth that she's forcing down my throat.

"Distract me then. What is new? Tell me something," I beg, looking for anything to distract me from my sorry state of affairs.

"Ainsley and I are buying a townhouse on the other side of Central Park," Ken volunteers.

I let the conversation carry over in excited chatter about that, but as soon as he says it, I have a pang in my chest. They're going to be so close to Josh.

Josh, who I owe an explanation to.

And an apology.

I want to wallow in my hurt, but he doesn't deserve to be the target of my anger. That anger should be directed squarely at my former employer. It should be directed at Darren, who did this.

But I can't see clearly past my hurt, not just for Josh not being there during the worst moments of my life, but for not fighting for me and letting me walk away when I told him I wanted space. The contradiction isn't lost on me, but it doesn't change the hurt that keeps me rooted to the couch, not responding to any of the texts he sends me.

It's an awful sort of agony that the one person I want to comfort me most in this moment is the one that I'm ignoring right now. That push/pull of needing him but of not wanting to see him might be the thing that's hurting me the most at this moment. I'm endlessly thankful for my friends who dropped everything to come to my aid when I needed them most, but who I really need isn't here, and that's my own damn fault.

Twenty-Four

"LET'S DO SOMETHING TONIGHT," Ainsley suggests as day melts into dusk. My friends have talked about everything from new coffee shops to the actual weather and how hot it's been lately.

Elia's brow furrows, and so does mine. The last thing I want to do is leave the safety of the apartment we're in. The outside world has proven itself too cruel. In a city of over eight million people, I'm very familiar with how easy it is to run into someone you know. Who knows how many times the video was recorded and shared? I could be all over that porn site Prism, owned by Rhys King.

Vivian pokes me. "We're going out tonight. Whatever thought that just put that look on your face is exactly why we should."

"I think it's a good idea," Charlie chirps, barely looking up from his phone.

Ken is snoring from his spot on the chair, and Ainsley pokes his middle, causing him to wake up. "Who looks tired now?" she asks, smirking at the rest of us.

"I have nothing to wear," I point out. They may be right. After spending the day wallowing, fresh air might do me some good. But

I also want to keep wallowing in this negative feedback of emotions.

"Easy," Elia says, getting to her feet and dragging me up.

Somehow, we wind up back in her closet, pulling out glamorous dresses.

"These are all practically ball gowns," I say as Ainsley thrusts a slinky black dress at me.

"Then we will just look really good while we get margaritas. I know this excellent place up by Lincoln Center. They have one of those guac stations that they mix at your table." Ainsley rubs her belly. "And the baby wants some guac."

It's how we all wind up getting dressed up. Elia chooses to wear a foxy red number, while Vivian dons a green dress, and Ainsley picks white.

Charlie and Ken look up from where they have their heads bent over a phone, and I narrow my eyes at them suspiciously.

"You girls have fun. Enjoy your drinks, and don't do anything I wouldn't do," Charlie says, practically pushing us out the door.

"That's a very short list," Ainsley points out as she closes the door behind us.

I try to keep up with their excited chatter, but each buzz of my phone from an email or anything else sets me on edge. I'm constantly worried that it's something that's going to show that my life is just blowing up, but for the most part it's been Knox making sure I have his number, Zelda telling me she's having people over, Han asking if I'm going to attend some Columbia alumni thing, and coupons for some stupid website I signed up for.

It's at least distracting me enough from thinking about the last time I was at Lincoln Center dressed to kill. It was with Josh, and it was my first time seeing the opera. I never expected to understand Violetta's heartbreak so well. At least, I'm not dying of tuberculosis.

When we pull up in front of Lincoln Center, my heart cracks, and I struggle with finding the strength to even get out of the Pick-MeUp! because of the reminder of the last time I was here. As much as I've spent the afternoon freezing Josh out, I need the comfort that he can give me. I need him to heal from the pain we're no doubt both experiencing from having our private lives shared so widely.

"Miss?" the driver asks, turning to face me. I'm alone in the car. My friends all are standing on the curb looking at me.

Vivian breaks ranks and leans into the car. "You don't have to get out of the car, but for what it's worth, I really think you should."

"Come on, Taryn. We're going to take some cute photos and then eat some guac, and I'll watch you drink margaritas with my mocktail," Ainsley calls.

"Ignore her, but if you want, I'll get right back in this car. This driver is already probably going to give me a bad rating, and I'm okay with that, but I promise that getting out of this car will heal your heart."

"I will not give you a bad rating if your friend gets out of my car," the driver says from the front seat.

"My dude, she's having a really bad day. She got fired and is fighting with her boyfriend." Vivian looks back at me. "What do you say we let this nice man go on with his day?"

"When you put it like that," I mutter. Making sure I'm not about to open the car door and clothesline some biker or hit another car, I carefully check the road before climbing out. The door is barely closed before the driver takes off.

When I look back, my friends are all standing in a line, watching me. But it's when they all step to the side, revealing a dark figure standing just past them, that my heart stops.

Josh is standing there looking more rumpled than I've ever seen him. His shirt is untucked, his tie is loose, and his hair looks battered from how many times he's no doubt run his hands through it.

"Taryn," Josh says, his voice anguished. "I'm not even sure there are words I can use to convey how sorry I am for not being there for you this morning."

"Josh," I start, but he holds up his hand to stop me.

"Please, I need to say this. It was never my intention to hurt you. I know that nothing I can say is going to make up for me not being there for you when you needed me. But I want you to know that I quit. I can't work somewhere that is going to try to sweep what happened under the rug, and after you've gotten your settlement money paid, I plan to salt and burn that company."

I open my mouth to say something, but he shakes his head and hands me a single flower.

"I don't deserve your forgiveness yet, but I'm going to earn it by proving that I'll show up for you every day. When that flower wilts, bring it back to me, and I'll give you a new one, and I will do that every day until you're ready. But I want that flower to remind you that I'm not giving up on us."

"Why did you quit?" I ask, taking the offered flower, a callback to *La Traviata*. This one is a red gerbera daisy.

Josh takes a step toward me, and when I don't step back, he takes another step forward. I tilt my head up to him as the tears start to well in my eyes. Gently, he cups my cheeks and strokes his thumbs across my face, wiping away the tears that have fallen.

"Because I'm not going to continue to earn money for a company that is going to disrespect the love of my life. I made sure my clients knew why I was leaving."

"What about Quincey?"

"God, when I thought I couldn't love you anymore, treasure. She's alright, I promise. I wasn't going to leave her high and dry any more than I'm going to leave you wanting."

I press my lips closed as I look up at him, unsure of what to say. I want a future with him. I want the comfort he's offering, but the hurt is still there. I needed him, and he wasn't there, and maybe I'll be able to reconcile that soon, but for now... for now, I'm hurt, and I need the time to lick my wounds, even if the place I want to do that most is in his arms.

Emotions are so fucking complicated.

Josh leans forward and presses a chaste kiss to my forehead. "When you're ready, we can talk about what happened today, but only when you're ready. I'm more sorry than you know that I left you to deal with this on your own."

Still unsure of what to say, I just nod. I'm not ready to give up on what Josh and I have.

"I love you, treasure."

It looks like it takes him a considerable amount of effort to take a step away from me. I have to choke down the urge to go to him. Before he walks away from me, he lifts my hand holding the flower.

"Remember: when it wilts, come back to me."

I look down at the flower, but I can barely see it through the haze of my tears. It won't be long before I'm going to have to return the flower to him. When I look back up, all I can see is the slumped shoulders of Josh's retreating back.

My friends don't give me a chance to fall into the pity that threatens to swallow me whole. They're right there to wrap their arms around me, to hold me up when I can't handle the task of keeping myself upright.

As much as I love them for being there for me, there's only one person I want to comfort me, and I just let him walk away.

Twenty-Five

WHEN I WAKE up the next morning, more than a little hungover after double-digit margaritas, it takes a second for my reality to crash back in. Ainsley was less than thrilled to have to play sober sitter as she corralled us into cabs to take us home.

I'm surprised to feel the weight of another body in the bed, so I slowly turn my head to see Vivian passed out with her arm over her eyes and her mouth open. I wince because even that movement is difficult. Set on the nightstand is a half-finished glass of water that I must have had, along with a torn open packet of Advil.

When I check my phone, I curse the five a.m. time on the clock. God, I hate waking up early after drinking. I take my time waking up and trying to feel normal, even as my body is still trying to reject the amount of alcohol I consumed.

Slowly, I'm able to emerge. I find Charlie standing in his kitchen, shirtless, while he wipes the sweat off his face.

"Still doing your daily workout?" I ask, sliding onto one of the stools at the island.

"Every day. Well, when I can. Not every hotel we stay at when we travel can accommodate my request for a rowing machine."

"Goodness, then what is the point of being a billionaire?" I tease.

He scoffs and turns to grab me a water, sliding it across the table to me.

"We can be good at helping friends in bad financial situations." Charlie leans on the counter, mimicking my position, and my stomach sours further. "Why didn't you talk to me?"

I let out a long breath. "Because it's not your problem to solve. Because you're my friend and not an ATM. Because I think mixing friendship with money is a recipe for disaster. Take your pick."

Charlie drums his fingers on the island before standing up. "I can respect your choice, but I hope you know that you're one of *my* best friends, regardless of your relationship with Elia. I care about you too, and I don't want you to ever be in a position where you're suffering. That extends to hiring you at my firm if you need."

"I appreciate it, but I'm going to take a breath until the settlement paperwork is signed and before deciding on the next step. I'm honestly too afraid to show my face in an office setting right now. Our industry is huge and small at the same time."

"I hear you, but just remember you have a safe haven here whenever you want."

"Thanks, Chucky," I say, squeezing his wrist.

"I really wish you and Ainsley would retire that nickname," he grumbles before giving me a platonic kiss on the top of my head.

"Never," I tell him with a laugh, but it makes my head hurt, so I keep it short as he disappears into his bedroom.

I sit in silence until Vivian emerges an hour later, dressed. I'm working on another water, still not ready to stomach anything else.

"What are you doing today?" she asks, sidling up beside me. She looks remarkably put-together on the heels of our binge drinking the night before.

"I don't know," I admit, spinning the water between my hands.

"I need to get to work, but know I love you." She gives me a kiss in basically the same place Charlie did, but before she goes, she places the flower Josh gave me the night before on the counter in front of me.

I don't actually need to think about what I'm going to do with my day. It was always going to happen this way.

I'm afraid it's too early as I walk up the steps.

I tried to be patient as Charlie and Elia got ready and settled in for work, but it only reminded me how I would not be going to work. Since graduating college, I have always had *something:* school, a job, an internship. It feels strange to not have a reason to get out and get going with my day.

So, I did the only other thing I could do at seven a.m.

I went to Josh.

It was never going to be a question of if I was going to return the flower to him; it was just a question of when. The flower that Josh gave me was in remarkable shape after being manhandled during dinner. But popping it in the microwave for five seconds at a time certainly did the trick of wilting it.

Josh's same neighbor is sitting on the stoop, this time with a cigarette and a mug, which she holds out to me in a toast.

Choosing Josh is never going to be the wrong answer. I just hope he's awake.

Raising my hand to knock on the door, I stumble back a step when it opens before I can make contact. Josh is standing there in all his shirtless glory, looking at me. He's still a little sleep-rumpled with his hair stuck up and creases on his face from where he slept a little too hard.

"You wanted this back?" I ask, holding out the very cooked flower. He swallows thickly before taking it from me.

"I did." He looks away from me to place the flower on a side console, but he comes back with another gerbera daisy, this one orange.

"You know Ainsley looked up the flower's significance," I tell him, tilting my head up.

"I was hoping someone would."

"Red means you're fully immersed in love."

"And orange means you're the sunshine of my life. I promise you, treasure, you mean everything to me."

I'm silent while I try to gather my thoughts. "Yesterday really, really sucked." When Josh stays quiet, I glance toward where his neighbor clearly has her ear turned toward us. "Aren't you going to invite me inside?"

Josh leans his head out the door. "Good morning, Mrs. Bristol," he calls before stepping back and inside. "I wasn't sure if you wanted to come in."

"Always, Josh."

We make our way in toward the kitchen, where Josh works on preparing coffee for both of us. As he slides the full mug into my hand, I can't help but smile over how our whole relationship started over coffee.

"It is by no means an excuse, but I got a call early that morning after getting to the office that the client I had been trying to court, the one I was trying to sway when I ran into you in Union Square, finally agreed to hear me out. So I jumped on the chance to meet with him. I didn't want any risk of distractions, so I turned my phone off. I never would have done that if I even thought–"

"No, obviously you wouldn't have. I don't think either of us had 'sex tape' on our relationship bingo card."

Josh chuckles softly. "No. No, I certainly didn't." He looks into the depths of his coffee like it might have some answers for him. "I turned my phone back on while I was already on my way back to the office. There was nothing that I could have done to get back to you faster."

"I know."

"I'm so sorry, Taryn. If I could have been there, I would have. I would have razed the building to the ground."

I reach my hand across the counter to take his hand in mine. "I'm glad you didn't. The last thing we both needed was to have to deal with a criminal trial in addition to both being unemployed. Seriously, Josh, I get it. I'm just..." I'm stuck again, trying to find the words. "I was alone, you know? I was about to give a presentation in front of my clients with my team, and then there it was, with full audio. And I had to hear the comments and see the reactions of people as they watched us."

"I still don't get how," Josh snaps, straightening up and running a hand through his hair. "I'm sorry. I'm not angry with you. I'm just so confused and angry about you being in this situation. I never saw the video, but Quincey told me that I was obscured and only you were exposed, and..." I can see him getting worked up again over what happened yesterday, and it's a reminder that while my situation and outcome were worse, I wasn't the only one affected.

"It's really kind of horrible, but we're going to get through this together. One day at a time."

The look he gives me nearly breaks my heart. There's hurt mingled with hope. "Together?" he asks, coming around the island to me.

"Of course. There is no other way forward except with you."

I grip his cheeks and slide off the stool so I can kiss him. I put everything I have into that kiss, desperate for him to know that there was never a question about *us*. He lifts me like the treasure he calls me, allowing me to wrap my legs around his waist.

He carries me off to the couch. We still have a lot of questions that we have to address, such as what we're going to do now that we're both unemployed and how I'm going deal with the financial fallout if Knox doesn't pull off this settlement.

They're all problems that we can deal with later. For now, I need to connect with Josh and reclaim the intimacy that should only belong to us.

Twenty-Six

I TRY to look at our sudden joblessness as funemployment instead of staring down the face of destitution. Josh assures me that it's not all that bad, but when we sit down and actually look at the numbers, he's slightly less optimistic, if only because I still refuse help.

We manage to survive the week in his house, job hunting and fucking while sitting in the small backyard he failed to show me during the first tour.

Han and Bex come by on Friday night after Josh offers to cook.

"This I had to see: my cousin, home before midnight on a weekend, wearing Bermuda shorts and cooking. What happened to you? Have you been exchanged for a changeling?"

Josh points his spatula at his cousin, who sits on the outdoor couch with Han and me. The two of them are holding hands, both with a cocktail I made for them resting on the small glass table. "That is enough out of the peanut gallery," Josh says.

We spent the day cleaning the backyard space and trying to get things more manageable for entertaining. It's only been four days, but sitting outside with a mug of coffee in the mornings has brought me just a little bit of peace.

I miss the gym and all the classes I took at my office, but I'm taking classes and doing yoga in the mornings before the day gets too hot.

"This is what unemployment looks like on both of us," I say, my smile wavering a little.

"Wait, what?" Han demands, sitting up.

Josh glances my way, letting me go forward. We talked about what details we were willing to share and with whom. The details of the severance are still being worked out, but Knox has assured me that if they keep jerking him off like this, he plans to file the wrongful termination suit against them. For my mental health, I told him to just keep me posted.

"Someone shared a very intimate video of Josh and me with the entire office, and now I'm fired, and he's quit." I take a very long sip of my cocktail.

"That's fucking bullshit!" Bex shouts.

"So, neither of you has a job?" Han asks, tilting her head to the side.

"Thanks for rubbing that in, Han," Josh pouts. "Just for that, your filet mignon is going to be well done."

"That is a *crime*," Han, who already requested it be just this side of dead, scolds.

"Mess with the bull," Josh warns, again wielding the spatula. Domestic Josh might be my favorite Josh.

"Back to you being unemployed," Bex scolds.

"We're using the term 'funemployed' so it doesn't feel like I'm rubbing dirt in the wound every time I have to say it," I interject.

"Whatever the fuck you're saying, you should come work for me, Taryn," Han says with a manic gleam in her eyes.

I laugh into my drink before taking another sip. When I look back at her, I lower my beverage. "Wait, you're serious?"

"As serious as I am about wanting my steak very rare." She cuts a glare at Josh, who whistles, ignoring her. "Listen, it's the worst secret in the family that I'm trying to get pregnant, and even if that doesn't succeed right away, if we adopt, I want to be able to take time off to bond with my family. It's a privilege that not all companies even offer, but knowing that I have a competent person to man the ship will make all the difference. I've hesitated taking on new clients, not because I can't handle it time wise, but because I can't have so many companies that I'm beholden to. So, think about it. Come work with me. Salary is competitive because my overhead is so low. I'd be paying myself and paying you, and with two Ivy League degrees, I can up my daily fee to six, maybe even seven, thousand a day. Vacation time will suck, but we will make it work."

When I look away from Han, I glance at Josh, who isn't looking at me but his cousin. The look they're sharing tells me this was all coordinated to make it seem like our idea.

"I think that sounds awesome, and if you're sure I'm not a waste of money..." I say.

Bex, Han, and Josh all scoff.

"Shut the fuck up," Han tells me with a shake of her head. "You are an absolute boss, and I don't care what a bunch of crusty old men have to say about it. A degree from Dartmouth, a degree from Columbia, and you worked through school to pay for it. That doesn't scream lazy and entitled to me, like some other people. You're a hard worker, and I don't even have to have known you for long to know that."

"Obviously, you don't have to give Han an answer right now," Bex hedges, giving her wife a look.

"Right, no. Of course, you should talk it over with Josh and take some time to be funemployed. Take a vacation or something. I mean, you'll have like nine months' notice for when I'm going to have a baby, so no rush," Han laughs nervously, then sips her mojito.

"She's not pregnant. She just means to actually put no pressure on you to make your decision. You do what feels right," Bex tells her.

"Now that the business talk is over, dinner is ready."

We settle at the table on the porch when we hear the doorbell ring. Josh gives a long-suffering sigh, but I put my hand on his shoulder. "I'll get it."

I take a glance at the monitor in the kitchen to see who is there, and when I see it's Knox, my eyebrows raise.

"How did you know where to find me?" I ask him by way of greeting.

He gives a sardonic smile. "Vivian. I told her I wanted to come by and tell you in person. There should be a nice sum of money working its way into your account by next week. I also wanted to give you this." He reaches into his back pocket and pulls out a folded piece of paper. It's an arrest record for Darren Williams. "I'm not supposed to have that or show you, but he's being charged for corporate espionage and some insider trading. It seems he may have actually caught some information on that recording that he stupidly used to make a deal on."

"You're shitting me," I say, still reading over the list of charges.

"Everything okay?" Josh asks, coming up behind me and placing a hand on my shoulder.

"Knox Benedict," he says, offering his hand.

"I remember," Josh says, reaching out and taking it. "Josh Bartlett. Thank you for taking care of my girl."

"I'm sorry that I had to be in a position to have to come in like that, but like I said, fat check hitting your account. They've been working on getting the baby NDAs signed, and I even managed to get it so they didn't get one from you."

"How?" I ask, leaning into Josh's side.

"I told them fat fucking chance they're getting you to sign one."

Josh laughs.

"Thank you again," I say, not sure what to do here. A handshake feels too informal for a guy who did so much for me without getting a dime.

"Not a big deal. I went to NYU with Jeremiah, so I sure as fuck preyed on that kinship to do what I could. Like I said, just grateful I got to come in and help. Usually, my skills aren't as in demand."

"What law do you practice?" Josh asks, hugging me close.

"Mostly real estate, but it looks like you have company, so I'll let you go. Have a good weekend, guys. Sorry again for everything that happened." He turns and leaves.

Josh motions at the paper in my hand. "What's this?"

"Looks like Darren was much scummier than we thought, and he's going to the big house for insider trading based on your calls. I think I'll frame this."

I fold it back up and put it in my pocket, heading back into our dinner with a big grin on my face.

As I'm getting ready for bed that night, Josh comes up behind me, wrapping his arms around me. I look at him in the mirror as I spread lotion on my arms. We both felt hot and sticky after eating outside, so once Bex and Han left, we took an inappropriately long shower, one that got us hot and sticky all over again.

"What are you going to do with the money?"

"I'm going to pay half my parents' mortgage to get them out of hot water and half my student loans. I should probably put some in savings, but I'm moving in with my rich boyfriend, and I think I'll do the sugar baby thing for a few months until I find steady work."

Josh's eyebrow quirks. "You're not going to take the job Han offered?"

"You think I should?"

"Yes, I do, but I also understand if you don't want to."

I spin in his embrace to face him. "I'm going to take it. I think it's going to be a lot of work, but I'm not afraid of getting my hands dirty. I want to help grow her company from the ground up. I have a lot of faith in it."

"I have a lot of faith in you," he says before giving me a long kiss. I lean into it, following his mouth as he tries to break free of the kiss. I refuse, walking him back and pushing him down onto the bed so I can straddle his waist.

For the amount of sex we've been having for the last week, I'm impressed I can feel his erection pressing against my thong-clad pussy, but I grind down onto him, loving how he feels between my legs.

His hands comes up to my face, and he holds me while I grind down harder, until I'm chasing a baby orgasm from the friction alone.

Once the aftershocks have cleared, he's careful about rolling me over and pulling his boxers down just enough to free his cock. With one hand, he moves my thong to the side so he can look down at my sex.

"You're nice and soaked for me, aren't you, treasure?" He drags the head of his dick through my folds, and I arch.

"Yes. Yes, I am. Only for you," I whine, wishing I could get him to push inside me.

"That's right."

Then Josh is sliding in, and our frantic movements have us chasing the high of each other. When I feel my orgasm hit me, I grab Josh's ass, holding him inside me until his own orgasm hits, and he's filling me until we're both spent. He's kissing my neck and chest before he rolls off me.

"Does this mean you're moving in?" he asks, following me as I go to the bathroom to clean up.

"That's what you caught on to?" I ask with a laugh.

Once cleaned up, he presses me into the bathroom counter.

"You just want me for my soaker tub," he growls into my neck while holding my hips.

"You've got me there."

"Well, now that you're accepting a job, I guess I can finally accept the one that Charlie has been up my ass to take."

"Seriously?" I pull away from him and swat at his bicep.

"What?"

"How long have you had this offer?"

"Since it happened, but I wasn't going to go back to work when you weren't. We're a team. Besides, it's been great being funemployed with you. Everything is better when you're by my side."

"Isn't that the truth?"

When we settle into bed, I snuggle close to him. Life might not be perfect, but it is pretty damn close.

Epilogue

SIX MONTHS LATER

"YOUR BOYFRIEND LOOKS SO DREAMY," Ainsley sighs, looking at where Josh has a sleeping Ayala on his chest. He's lying back in the recliner with a baby hand wrapped around his finger.

"He does, doesn't he?" I ask, smiling at where he's starting to doze himself, but he keeps waking himself up and patting the baby on her diapered bottom.

We put off a New Year's celebration until Ainsley felt up to getting together. She did manage to force a human out of her body a month ago, so it was only fair that we wait.

"Are your ovaries ready to explode?" Ken asks me, walking into the room with a tray of drinks. While Josh and I offered to host at our house only a few blocks away, Ken and Ainsley insisted that they wanted to stay home because it would be easier for them.

Vivian comes in the front door, loaded down with bags. "Sorry, sorry I'm late. I know I'm late, but I wanted to get a few things."

Ken looks up at her. "That doesn't look like a few things. That looks like you bought out a restaurant and a baby store."

"Excuse me for loving babies. I actually think just looking at that is making me ovulate," Vivian says, gesturing to Josh and Ayala.

"Funny you should mention ovaries. We were just asking if this was inspiring babies in Taryn," Ainsley says, leaning into her partner's side.

"Can we...maybe not talk about ovaries?" Charlie asks, grabbing a mimosa. "Nothing against them, but maybe we can talk about something else?"

"How about my cracking nipples, Chuck? Would you like to talk about my bleeding nipples?" Ainsley says, looking at her ex-fiancé.

"Wow, really selling the motherhood thing," I tease, trying to lighten the mood somewhat. "No, I mean, I'm not ready to have a baby right now, but I'm also not sure I want one. I'm enjoying being the auntie. Not to mention Han and Bex just announced they're clear of their first trimester! So, this means lots of babies."

"They're having twins," Josh mumbles, less from trying to keep the baby asleep and more from, I think, his own lack of sleep. I might have been feeling a little frisky.

It's hard to deny the biological imperative to make a baby. Looking at the paternal way that Josh is caring for Ayala, sure, it does make me a little hot and bothered, but I like my career. Working with Han at My Way Consulting has brought me so much joy, so much more than I expected.

I actually *love* my job. I love getting up and doing something that doesn't make me feel dirty and depressed.

Instead, I feel a different kind of dirty for another reason entirely.

Now that Josh and I can work from home, it means we can have sex during the workday whenever we want. I like that freedom. For now, I have my IUD, and if we feel ready or want to, we can talk about what a decision to have kids could look like.

"Twins," Elia says from Charlie's lap. "You are going to be a busy aunt and uncle."

"Does that mean you're at least giving me a wedding to look forward to?" Ainsley asks hopefully.

When Ayala starts to fuss, Ken gets up to take her from Josh and hand her off to Ainsley, who barely gives enough warning before popping out her boob to feed her baby.

"Are *you* giving us a wedding to look forward to?" I counter.

"Nope, I'm too busy popping out the only baby in this group."

"Hopefully there will be a nice little brood," Ken says, smoothing his hand over the baby's head.

"I'll see if I can convince Taryn to marry me, but it was hard enough talking her into moving in with me."

"Listen, maybe I enjoyed the secondhand high from Zelda. But also, it took you like two weeks to convince me. You haven't even proposed," I point out.

"I guess you'll just have to wait and see when I pop the question."

"Good, leave me to be nice and single. And the fun auntie," Vivian says with a relaxed smile. I think about how Knox talked about my friend and wonder if she has any idea.

"Do you want to get married?" I ask that night as we settle in the bubble bath built for two.

"Are you proposing to me?" Josh asks with mock surprise.

"No, but do you want to get married ever? Like to me or anyone else?"

Josh kisses my cheek and holds me to his chest. "There is only ever you. If you want to get married, we can get married, but the idea of a wedding has never really excited me."

"It's almost like we're meant to be together or something," I say, willing my butt against his cock. "I don't know, maybe it's because I'm not a billionaire and money has always been tight, but I never wanted a floufy dress nonsense thing. I'd rather use that money on a bomb-ass vacation."

"Then, let's say we travel to wherever you want while I convince you that I'm the man you need."

Josh's finger presses against my ass before sliding in. His other hand moves around to the front of me, and he starts to circle my clit. I'm trying to roll my hips when I press up a little so I can shift my body onto Josh's cock. It's awkward at first, but he fills me up, adding a second finger to my ass until my body is clenching around him, and he's moaning his release after.

Relaxing into Josh's arms, I turn my head to look up at him.

"I've always wanted to go to Australia," I tell him, enjoying the post-orgasm bliss.

"Then I think I need to get planning."

With Josh in my life, I'm happy to always make plans.

****

Thank you so much for reading Josh and Taryn's story. If you enjoyed their tale, please be sure to leave a review!

****

Interested in another slice of life featuring Josh and Taryn, sign up for my newsletter here to read the bonus epilogue!

****

Want more from the *Love in the Big Apple* crew? Vivian's story is coming 2025! Join my Facebook Group, Nicole Sanchez's Reader Grove!

Acknowledgments

I want to thank my readers who have been clamoring for Taryn's book, I hope it was everything you wanted and more.

For Tracy and Katie for keeping me sane during the crazier moments of this job.

To Murphy, Alexia, and Nyddi, your support means so much to me. Thank you for always being there when the going gets tough.

Harper and Brea for going with the flow even when it means putting on a sheet mask while getting destroyed in Uno.

To my editors, Amanda and Taylor for bringing this home, your feedback and reactions helped shape this story and give me the boost to keep going.

Mom and Dad for always supporting me through everything, from sports to pageants to writing smutty books.

Mike, my favorite human in the whole world, I can't say thank you enough for holding the massage gun to my shoulder or making sure I stayed hydrated (with water or wine).

My cats Chip and Harvey for being goofy and the perfect distraction when I need it.

Lastly, you, my dear reader for making it this far in my journey and for picking up one of my books to take a chance on.

Interested in Romantasy?

Check out the Game of God's series - a Hades and Persephone re-imagining. Start Daphne Hale's story with The King's Game - available now!

About the Author

Nicole Sanchez has been writing stories on any scrap of paper she could get her hands since before middle school. She lives in New Jersey with her high school sweetheart and love of her life along with their two quirky cats, Chip and Harvey. When she isn't writing or wielding the Force, she can be found traveling the world with her husband or training for her next RunDisney Event.

For more books and updates:

Newsletter

Website

Facebook Reader Group

Also by Nicole Sanchez

Love in the Big Apple Series:

Central Park Collision

Las Vegas Luck

Madison Avenue Mediator

Financial District Fantasy

Game of Gods Series:

The King's Game

The Queen's Gamble

The Royal Gauntlet

Standalone Novels:

Desirable (Steamy Contemporary)

Made in the USA
Monee, IL
16 May 2024